Mysterious Death at the Mall

Mysterious Death at the Mall

PEGGY REID RHODES

Copyright © 2004 by Peggy Reid Rhodes.

Author photograph by Jean Beam Sketch by Sarah Reynolds Dixon
Novels also by Peggy Reid Rhodes

Rosemary for Remembrance: An Historical Fiction
Charlotte Greystone
The Property of Joseph McBaden Attorney-At-Law

Library of Congress Number:		2004093027
ISBN:	Hardcover	1-4134-5602-2
	Softcover	1-4134-5601-4

All rights reserved. No part of this book may be reproduced or transmitted in any form or by any means, electronic or mechanical, including photocopying, recording, or by any information storage and retrieval system, without permission in writing from the copyright owner.

This is a work of fiction. Names, characters, places, and incidents are the product of the author's imagination or are used fictitiously.

This book was printed in the United States of America.

To order additional copies of this book, contact:
Xlibris Corporation
1-888-795-4274
www.Xlibris.com
Orders@Xlibris.com

Dedicated to

My friend Judy Vassar
And
my brother Carl T. Reid

Chapter 1

I was only a volunteer seeking to do a bit of good as I stood checking people in who had preregistered for the seminar. The simple task required scanning skills of forty to fifty names and rudimentary traits of politeness while informing nonlisted inquirers that their names would be added to the waiting list.

The overall friendly tones in the room were interspersed with negativity as a few men and women asserted that they had telephoned and been assured they were preregistered. Fifteen minutes before the start of the program called for crowd control measures. Folks in line pressed closer, conveying they were not disposed to relinquish their places or their reserved seats. While the disgruntled persons reluctantly stepped aside, I focused on the lengthening queue – some with confident expressions of being admitted, others with frowns of doubt.

I was careful to check names with the pencil attached to the clipboard and that all without reservations were listed according to the order they had arrived. A simple act of placing the clipboard on a nearby table to assist briefly with another task turned into an opportunity for malevolence that I was unaware of for some days. Nor were any of the professionals on duty any the wiser.

This seminar topic, "Healthy Heart Habits," was to be led by Jonathan Belding, imminent professor and cardiologist with Central University Medical Center. He could be seen through the closed, glass-paned double doors that separated the small auditorium and the multipurpose reception room. The doctor watched the center's computer technician adjusting the slide projector and testing the microphone; and when images were sharp and sound level appropriate, he signaled all okay.

People bunched near the door commented quietly: What a large man for a doctor! Kind eyes. He shows patience with getting the microphone right. A minor matter to be sure. Reading his profile in the newsletter, one man spoke and pointed to some lines in a glossy publication in his hand.

"Here comes Amy," a gray-headed man of ruddy complexion said in a low voice and turned slightly toward the other fifty-plus-year-old men and women huddled behind him. In unspoken accord, their feet retreated a couple of steps. They had previously attended seminars at this Healthy Living Center in the largest shopping mall in Windermere.

Amy Umstead, having welcomed the speaker and observed that all was in order with equipment and seating, walked with purpose toward the door. The people on the other side of the door were her purpose – her reason for being where she was now. Instinctively, she touched her nametag above the top pocket of her navy jacket: it felt straight. She squelched the urge to finger the words AMY UMSTEAD, DIRECTOR. Nevertheless, her heart-shaped face radiated with confidence and happiness. This recently created job had appealed to her so intensely that she had given hours researching various aspects of the university and medical center. Upon being called for an interview, she displayed not only interest in the new program but also an abundance of energy and enthusiasm, both natural traits. The committee was favorably impressed with her knowledge of the history, the ongoing programs, and the philosophy of the educational aspects of both the university and the medical center.

She survived three rounds of interviews. Following the offer for the position via a telephone call, she cried in her husband's arms. "You really wanted this, didn't you, honey?"

All she could do was nod and spill more tears on his shirt. "I'm making a mess, Lou."

"Not to worry," he assured her and kissed the top of her curly, black hair. "I'm very proud of you. Should we go out to dinner and celebrate?" He looked down and sought her wishes in her dark brown eyes; he made no comment about the rare tears or swollen eyelids.

She had given a closed-mouth smile and tilted her head. "Thank you. For caring and . . . and your support," she said between moments of swallowing tears in the back of her throat.

"Hey, love. You did the same for me while I was fighting for my place in the big world out there. Welcome to the realm of increased responsibility, not to mention the extra hours and irregular schedules."

"Oh, Lou. We will have time for each other, won't we?" she uttered in desperate tones.

"We will make time. Count on it. And I'll be freer to help you around the house." He held her at arm's length, contorting his face into a mock seriousness. "I'll be turning out the cleanest, neatest laundry on the block. And I'll dial up the maid service to scoot over here every week or two and do all those cleaning chores you're so expert at."

"And we'll do a lot of take-out meals. Will you hate that?" she asked.

"Nah. I'll get used to it." He hugged her and she sighed within his embrace.

That episode flashed through her mind in an instant. He had been faithful to his promises, and her job had been demanding. With support from Lou and the industrious, committed staff of Healthy Living, she felt a thrill each time she greeted the members and introduced the seminar speaker. Thus, today as all days the past months since initiating the program, Amy moved rapidly, her eyes sweeping left to right and across again taking note that papers and pencils were in all the chairs, the floor was litter-free.

Her posture was erect, her gait steady; being short, she chose clothing with continuous lines – suits with jacket and pants the same shades or solid-color dresses. Her jewelry was unusual, attractive, and eye-catching, never flashy, and close around her neck. If she could alter any aspect of her natural "gifts," it would be her curly hair. It had a mind of its own and refused to stay flat and straight around her face. She wished for that! To her way of thinking, straight and shoulder length would be the more businesslike style. She'd been called cute and curly top forever! Certainly all through school. Before she applied for this position, she had consulted the most acclaimed hair stylist in Windermere to work some magic. No one had alerted her that her choice was also the most expensive man with a pair of scissors and a comb. However, blessed be, he had created an acceptable style for a director who had to meet not only members the age of her father but also highly placed individuals of the university and medical center.

Catching a glimpse of herself in a pane of glass behind which a man in a dark sweater stood, she noticed that her hair needed a trim. Mentally, she stored in her short-term memory to make an appointment at his first opening and her first unscheduled hour.

Director Amy Umstead unlatched and opened the left door, greeting the familiar faces with first names, and spoke a cheerful hello to the others and a sincere smile to all as she opened outward the right door. Now, the ingress was easier for the determined older attendees, who were intent on claiming a preferred space.

Right up front? No. Chairs were placed along the length of the room facing a large overhead screen. An aisle was in the center. People in the first row had to crane their necks backward to see listings and diagrams high above them. Preferred seats were third and fourth row back.

Prior to the seminar, Amy and a center receptionist or a volunteer set up the number of chairs to correspond with registrations, plus one for Amy and one for the volunteer who greeted members. A full house of fifty was expected for this event.

Today, I filled the greeter role. A badge clipped to the collar of my blouse stated my name Nola Gilbert and position as volunteer of Central University Medical Center. I was required to wear it when volunteering. And I held my clipboard just below the badge, for I had learned that some evidence of your right to authority could be achieved with a display of badge, pencil, and paper.

I made it a point to check the number preregistered and counted the chairs as soon as I arrived. After I had done so, my statement was honest to the unregistered: We'll see if there are any vacant chairs. Members, who had previously attended, kindly remembered to alert greeters if a spouse or friend were on the way, but may be a tad late. Thus, an asterisk beside the name and the words "may be T" were duly made. And a chair was reserved, so to speak, with a sweater across the back or a parcel in the seat. When the tardy person checked in, the greeter pointed out the saved chair.

After all, this was a friendly organization, formed to educate people about health matters with its chief aim to provide resources to improve their knowledge of health and provide materials and professional services toward attaining and maintaining good health. Pragmatic people in medical fields realized ever-increasing medical advances were unknown by a large number of the general populace; so, the concept of taking medical knowledge to the public materialized.

Windermere was the largest city in the foothills of North Carolina and home of one of the state's most prestigious universities, medical schools, and hospitals. This new service program was placed in a showplace mall located only a few miles to an exit off the interstate highway from the hospital and a similar distance by a parkway from the university. Driving time was about ten minutes. The university and medical center, along with their satellite facilities, could stay in touch instantly by clicking onto their education electronic network.

For this seminar, I spotted three vacant seats and connected visually with Amy. I held up three fingers and pointed to the clipboard: she nodded affirmative. I glanced toward a couple patiently waiting by the reception desk. They came forward and spoke a thank you as I stood aside for them to enter.

I checked their names, read the next on the list, and sought the man among the few people left in the room. He immediately dashed forward, a slight fellow, pale, medium brown hair, with obvious, jerky movements. He blurted, "I'm next." I nodded, made a check mark.

At the doorway, he surveyed the room, sighted the vacant chair on the fifth row, and noiselessly slid in, picking up a sheath of papers from the seat. He grimaced and shifted the chair, trying to get a better view of the screen and speaker. Then his expression switched into a satisfied look.

I was vaguely aware of the man because of his movement; however, I was alert for a signal from Amy. As soon as she nodded toward me, I put the clipboard on a table then pulled the doors together, lowered, and closed the blinds to eliminate distractions. While Amy welcomed the group and introduced the speaker, I sat on the back row in my reserved chair, second from the aisle and the projector.

Having spoken with or recognizing many of the people in the auditorium, I knew the topic to be of personal interest either because they or a family member had some heart condition. They were interested in being educated, updated, about habits that increased the chances of a healthy heart. The majority of the audience sat up straight, ready to listen and learn, but not anxious: they were mature in years and demeanor. Their pencils and handouts lay in their laps, convenient for making notes.

Except for a few restless individuals, I noticed. A wry older gentleman who couldn't seem to get comfortable and continuously moved his feet and legs and shifted his weight from left to right hip on the plastic chair seat. A woman with thin, white hair combed to appear as thick as possible had a nervous tic, evident with constant head movements. She had taken a chair in the third row near the wall; I thought that a kindness. Sometimes, I wish I were not so observant, but what can we do to change our natural inclinations as we near the half-century mark? I must have sighed, for a lady across the aisle looked at me. Quickly, I smiled and turned my attention to the speaker.

Everyone else did likewise as he began to talk. Soon though, my eye caught the man in front of me, the nervous latecomer, alas the not-preregistered fellow. His movement was barely noticeable. It was a pivot of his shoulders to the left, his head jerked forward then he was still. The lights dimmed and the overhead slide changed to a diagram of the heart. My attention returned to the speaker's voice and the giant screen.

He used a laser to point toward material overhead. The audience was attentive, appearing to be absorbing the material. Many were taking notes. The slight fellow in front of me fidgeted with his jacket then dropped his pencil. It must have rolled beneath the chair in front of him. He was very quiet and didn't disturb the concentration of the woman sitting in the chair even though it took him several minutes to retrieve the pencil.

Finally, grasping it, he slowly raised his body and pushed himself upright with his back against his chair. His arm moved as if he was writing on his handout sheet. I tried to recall his name and fussed silently to myself at the quick loss of memory: after all, his was the last name I had checked off. Memory had been a strong suit for me during a quarter century of teaching.

The speaker was nearing the end of the information projected on the screen, and I was attempting to catch up to his point as I had lagged behind while watching the man in front of me. Once again, I was distracted as he rose from his seat, hunched as he eased past two people before he stepped into the aisle. He drew himself in and kept his head ducked to minimize interrupting the screen projection. I glanced toward the door briefly to see if he needed any assistance. He opened the door and left the room, closing the door after him.

Several minutes later, the projector was turned off and the lights brought back up. My wristwatch showed ten minutes left in the program time. Dr. Belding opened the session for questions. He politely answered in an unhurried manner, yet he spoke directly to the question without elaboration. Most people limited inquiries to the one question.

Then I heard a familiar voice and had to restrain myself from wagging my head. Mrs. Bessie Kester, who perpetually waited until several questions had been asked, launched her first inquiry. If anyone had ever been in a seminar with her, they could expect after it was responded to, she would then go into personal lamentations. She would rattle on with statements that she evidently assumed were understood to be questions although she scarcely halted for breath or for the speaker to answer. After he said a few words, she'd resume her personal difficulties with an ill husband, which made her seem dense or merely demanding attention. Obviously, from her verbiage, her husband never conversed with her, and he was confined for some unstated reason to the house.

Poor man, I thought. She was enough to drive a body ill or daft. If I were a betting woman, I would wager that the man thanked Healthy Living for offering frequent seminars so she had somewhere to go. He probably didn't waste any of his freedom concerned about what she was saying, because she wasn't haranguing him at home.

I didn't look at Amy for we would never display any exchange that would show disrespect of a member or guest.

Some of the men and women who had turned toward Bessie first puzzled by her prolonged questioning, then frowned, finally grimaced and faced front rather than be any ruder. When she paused for breath or effect, the learned doctor pointed to a lady in a red dress and said, "You had a question?"

After she asked a short simple question and was satisfied with the equally short answer, he announced that his allotted time was up. Amy immediately stood, walked to the podium, and thanked him for the fine seminar.

The thank-you was my cue to open the doors and stand nearby to collect pencils and evaluation forms. Some people had questions that I answered if I could. If not, I referred them to the nurse Joyce or receptionist Phyllis at the desk. Occasionally, in the group were friends of mine eager to exchange a few words. If they had time, they waited until the crowd thinned and we could talk.

Today, I lingered to speak to a friend who thanked me for recommending Healthy Living and looked forward to other seminars and activities. "It's so comfortable in here. I know the older people really enjoy the air-conditioning and dread going back into the heat. With temperature forecast of one hundred degrees, the cars will be even hotter." As she talked, I spotted Bessie at the refreshment area. After closing a large handbag, she gulped a cup of water and tilted her head backward. She poured more water from the clear plastic pitcher, drank that, and then tossed the cup in the trash container. She left by herself.

I said goodbye to my friend with a promise to get together for lunch one day soon. As I generally did, I returned to the auditorium, collected left-behind items, added them to ones I had taken at the doorway, along with the clipboard of names in attendance, and took all to the reception desk.

Once or twice I had tarried to ask a question of the speaker. Tonight I had no problems that needed clarification of a heart specialist. Neither of a physical nor emotional condition. My recent annual checkup gave me an okay on the first, and my calendar showed no dates to confound the latter. I was pleased with the first but was beginning to wonder about the second. Was this a problem for the half-century aged female?

Darn, here I was again using the century word. Was I that old? Where was a mirror to check my image?

I pivoted, surveyed the auditorium, and then the reception area. No mirror! Nor clock, I further realized. Was there a reason for the omissions? I must ask Amy. Was time too important to the over... whoops! To the elderly? Did they need a release from checking the hours and the minutes? And did they not want to see their reflections?

Well, my dear Nola Gilbert, put those questions in your memory bank and pull them out some other day to debate. After all, you chose this particular program to volunteer in even before you're old enough to be a member. Chew on that fact for a while. Perhaps you're the one rushing time! But do keep the perplexities to yourself or you'll be classed right along with old Bessie Kester: a shrewish, bitter, unattractive woman who annoys the life out of everyone. What was that rumor I heard? Yes, that she used to be a bothersome woman who volunteered until her husband became ill and demanded constant care. The day she turned in her volunteer badge, a huge sigh of relief rose from those to whom she was assigned. A rare occurrence! Ninety-nine percent of the volunteers were deemed as gifts and treasured as such.

None of us present today realized how much of a bother Bessie had been to someone or if she had been too overwhelmed with problems. The next day, we knew that she wouldn't ask any more questions. She was dead.

Chapter 2

Amy Umstead pushed two numbers on speed dial then hugged the receiver between her right shoulder and ear. Her hands stacked extra printouts, the evaluations, the name list, and her notes from the seminar, then pulled from a stack on the shelf over her desk, a new file folder. Across the tab, she wrote Heart Seminar August year 1.

"Hi, Lou. I'm leaving here in a few minutes. How about my stopping by Italian Pizza and bringing home supper?"

"Sounds great. How did the day go?" Lou asked with interest.

"Super. Dr. Belding is such a good speaker. A full house." She added Heart Healthy Habits to the tab. "Lasagna and salad okay?"

"Um. With lots of cheese. A loaf of bread?"

"After the health guidelines from today, what about low-fat cheese?"

"What about one order of each?"

Amy grinned as she inserted the papers and closed the folder. "And we'll share?"

"Well, half a calorie is better than . . . Sure. If it were not for your judiciousness, I'd push those scales up daily. Oh, your dad called. He'll be in town tomorrow."

"Great, maybe he'll stay for dinner. Listen, I'll hang up and phone in the order. See you in about half an hour." Turning around, she affirmed no one was in the room – often staff or visitors entered quietly and waited until she was free before getting her attention – and said softly, "I love you."

"I love you, too."

Amy filed the folder in her cabinet in the front of events for the month. Her neatness was apparent in her filing system and throughout the small office. There were stacks of magazines, papers, stationery, books, and other paraphernalia, but it was organized. She was a much focused person who knew what she had to do: keep an eye on the whole picture. It included long-range plans, next month's agenda, printing of calendars, updating numerous lists in the computer, reviewing tomorrow's schedule, adding to her calendar numbers to call, people to see, details and more details. Concentration was another of her natural gifts. She gave to the task at hand, let it go at the appropriate moment, and never carried baggage. She packed and took through life what was needed for each adventure.

So far in this first year, she had handled the new position with praise from the committee that had hired her. She had a predilection with its growing popularity that Healthy Living could mushroom into a service beyond what the university and medical center had projected and perhaps beyond her own abilities and knowledge. She had a college degree, ten years' solid work experience in public relations, an inquiring mind, and smart friends and colleagues who constantly added facts of their lives and occupations along with great fellowship. However, with the assurance and comfort of all that, she knew this job could require more personnel than it was set up to employ. This was not baggage; this was sensible reasoning.

Amy put her trust in the institutions that had conceived this enormous outreach program and expected they could take care of its future. Her part of it – well, she'd do her best and that was all she could do.

She phoned in the dinner order, went to the employee's restroom, and tidied herself. After a final check of all rooms, she touched base with the evening staff, Jill and Celeste; both stayed until the mall closed; she walked out into the still-hot evening. She wished they could leave early, too, but knew that the purpose of the center's being open whenever shoppers were in the mall was being fulfilled. Jill was a competent administrative assistant, and Celeste was equally qualified as a nurse. Amy imagined that both of them preferred to be at home with their young children. The photographs they had mounted on the office bulletin board showed happy, smiling faces. The pictures brightened the spirit of everyone on the staff. Well, Amy thought Jill and Celeste didn't come in until late afternoon, thus they had much of the day with their preschoolers. And their husbands relieved the sitters after work.

Once Amy and Lou agreed to wait until their careers were established to have a family, she didn't allow regrets to enter her mind or conversation. The couple recognized that they had abundance of energy and eagerness of spirit to tackle the world of business and the public for which they had spent intense years of preparation.

Reaching her car, she noticed that there were many others parked in the lot and considered it must be a good night for shopping. Sliding onto the hot seat and buckling up, she lowered two windows, switched on the engine, and air-conditioning. She noticed doors opening on a van beside her and idled the engine, as a man got out on the driver's side, slamming that door and sliding the passenger door wide open. Youthful voices were audible in rebellion of some instructions. The man ordered them to stop picking at each other and get out right now. Two elementary-age boys, seemingly all arms and legs emerging at awkward angles, took their time getting out.

In her rear mirror, Amy saw a woman cautiously approaching from the rear of the van, holding firmly the hand of a younger girl, probably a kindergartner. She frowned at the man and the boys and shouted, "Come on, you guys. We shouldn't dawdle in this parking lot. You know all the bad things that you read in the paper that happen out here."

She turned her head and surveyed the parking lot as if she expected someone was lurking behind every car ready to grab them. "Get a move on," she hissed. The little girl clung to her mother's slacks and impeded forward movement of both.

"Let me carry her or the stores will be closed before we get inside." The man reached down and lifted the child who was still holding her mother's slacks.

"Whoa!" the woman said sharply. She uncurled the girl's fingers. "Go on, but wait for me," she ordered.

The boys darted across the driving lane. The man shouted for them to hold up.

Now that the commotion was over, Amy put the car in drive. Before she could move forward, she had to wait for a car to exit across from her. It was not out of sight before several people approached. A family of two adults and five straggling children, each laden with one or more packages, searched for their van. Nobody could remember where the van was parked. The children laughed and walked in zigzag lines while the parents stopped in the center of the driving lane and peered right, left, back, and forward. They declared it wasn't this row; maybe it was two over. The seven people slowly moved like lost souls in a strange city out of Amy's sight. The woman called out, "Don't drag your feet. Keep up. If you get lost, we'll never find you."

She realized parents and children were already hitting sales before schools started. The driving lane clear, she eased her car forward and toward the restaurant.

Across town, Nola Gilbert completed dressing for the concert at the downtown theater center. She'd had a message on the answering machine that her friend couldn't go with her and would relate the full story tomorrow. In spite of the disappointment, Nola decided to use her season ticket for this final summer event. First though, she would treat herself to dinner at a restaurant near the theater. There would be an empty seat across the dinner table as well as one beside her in the theater. She shook her head to dislodge any sighing. It simply was not her style to feel lonely even if she were alone. She innately sensed that to project loneliness was a sure way to reach that state. Retiring early was partly to see what else life had to offer.

She added a bright red and blue swirl-designed scarf to the neck of her white summer sweater, clipped on small gold earrings centered with rubies, and lifted the corners of her mouth with a grin.

In another part of Windermere, Dr. Belding drove along the parkway toward his home, enjoying a musical number on a CD. He anticipated going with his wife Alice tonight to the summer series of light music with memorable Broadway show melodies: they were more to his taste than many of the regular-season heavier selections. Once, he had overheard Alice tell a friend of hers that she thought he liked the happier music because his work was so filled with patients' serious physical problems. He saw death one minute, then without visibly carrying the loss, proceeded to the live people. He hadn't said that, but he didn't correct her. Who knows, perhaps her perception was accurate. He moved on to the next task, or the next patient, as he assumed everyone did with his work, whatever that might be.

Yes, after this full day, he looked forward to the concert. He had enjoyed speaking to the group at Healthy Living Center. The people had made an effort to register and attend a seminar to learn about habits to keep them in good health. He liked that. He had not quite known what to expect even though he had heard positive comments about this latest university and medical school – sponsored program. It seemed to be working. The membership was growing daily.

When Amy asked him to speak, he wasn't certain he could fit a time in his schedule. He called his secretary on the intercom and asked if he had a free hour or two. She leafed through the appointment book and told him that he had this midafternoon open. After he and Amy batted around a few topics, they agreed on emphasizing good habits for health of the heart rather than a specific disease. It had been a good choice and quite a change of pace from lecturing to students.

At nine o'clock, the humid summer air closed around the emerging shoppers. Having been chilled with turned-down low air-conditioning inside the mall, many people complained about the lingering heat. Mothers hurried the kids, saying that the sooner they got in the car, the cooler they'd be. Dads walked fast and the kids kept pace, not feeling so secure with the darkness that lay just beyond the area lit by the lights on the tall standards.

Couples strolled more leisurely, hand in hand.

Inside, mall security adjusted door locks so that customers could leave but no one could enter. Security personnel waited until clerks and other store employees left. The frequent turnover and the irregular schedules of workers made it difficult to keep up with when everybody had left. Usually, there was one supervisor or another person responsible for each business that would say upon his leaving that everyone was out of his place.

On nights that a store requested a security guard to walk one or more women to their cars, a guard would be standing ready. During the busiest seasons and on weekends, employees were asked to park in spaces furthermost from the complex.

Tonight most of the guards were on duty, because of the large number of children expected. Two patrol cars circled the mall and drove up and down the parking lanes, as much to dissuade lurkers as to assist drivers if needed. Occasionally, someone would lock keys in the car and need to call a friend or family member to bring an extra key, or call a locksmith. Few people preferred to leave a car overnight in the parking lot even though it was well lighted. Security could help with the phoning.

Guards were trained to pay attention to persons walking around the parking lots who appeared to have no purpose, especially men who gave no indication they were searching for their own cars or who acted suspicious or uncomfortable when patrols passed by.

Guards kept in mind cars that had been parked a very long time. Occasionally, they knew that a mall employee might take in the nine o'clock movie after work. Long-time workers often halted the patrol car and informed the guard that they would be there until the movie let out. The message was passed on to other security on duty.

About 9:45 p.m., Hector Turner, age twenty-three and recently hired by the security department, was cruising the lot between the mall and the cinema building. In an end space under an elm tree, he spotted a Chevrolet sedan that had been there since he came on duty at four o'clock.

He passed it very slowly. It appeared empty. He stopped the car, read the license plate, and decided to call the security office. When he got a contact, he asked if the Chevrolet's owner had alerted anyone that he would be leaving the car until later. He read the license number and waited a few seconds until he heard there had been no report on that vehicle.

Hector, being a real eager beaver for some action, asked with tension in his voice. "Want me to investigate?"

He was instructed to take another swing around the complex; if on the return drive-by the vehicle was still parked that he could go up and take a look. And call in if he was getting out of the car and doing so.

"Gotcha!" Hector replied and pulled off more quickly than usual. He was itching for some real action and so far this first month of work, there had been only some false alarms about shoplifters and a fire started in the trash barrel in a restroom. The latter was assumed to be from teens smoking on the sly.

During high school, Hector had ridden with a deputy sheriff some weekends. And he had one year of law enforcement class at the community college in a nearby county. He had worked with an independent security company for three years, but he had aspirations to be a policeman in a big city. He didn't know why he hadn't been accepted for the police academy; but now he was at least working in the city. All he needed was to do something spectacular and get noticed by the local force. Attention was the key. And he was anxious to make an impression.

The few cars parked in the largest lot, the one located east of the mall, were already familiar to Hector. Those belonged to the men who generally were last to leave their stores. He didn't know why the men stayed so late. Maybe they loved their work as he did his, or maybe they had wives that made staying away more fun than going home. Man, was he glad he was never tempted into tying any knots. No sirree! Excitement pursing the troublemakers was what he had always wanted.

He hoisted his shoulders and stretched his neck trying to appear tall as he gripped the steering wheel. Then lifting his left hand, he felt the distance between his hat and the inside roof of the car. The weather was so hot most guards didn't wear the hat, but Hector desired the image of authority to be complete. Satisfied, he lowered his hand to the steering wheel and kept his upper arm close to the window, letting his security emblem be clearly seen.

Of course, the white car and the dark lettering of Saunders Mall Security were hard to miss.

Curving around to the north lot and finding it empty, he turned the car toward the west parking area and decided to survey the fully occupied section surrounding the movie complex. He drove slowly, scanning the interiors, all of which were empty, peered between the vehicles for any lurkers. He told himself he would not get out and look under the cars – that nonsense story about men hiding underneath then grabbing drivers' legs as they unlocked a door, well, he wasn't falling for that. On a really dull night, he had driven around a second time checking out inspection stickers and another time, license tag dates.

The clock showed a few minutes till ten. It would be an hour before most of the films ended for the last run. So Hector swerved toward the mall. There were half dozen cars scattered over the large lot.

At one of the mall entrances, several people were walking out. They stayed in a group as they crossed the asphalt. Hector partly opened his side window. He could hear their voices, agreeable even with complaints about the heat and the long day. As each one reached his car, he put a hand up in a wave. This continued until all the drivers started their cars and shined their headlights. Hector watched the cars approach one of the many exits to the crosswise main traffic lanes. As drivers hit the brakes briefly, taillights glowed like twin lumps of burning charcoal.

Having watched them disappear down the roads, Hector shifted from park to drive intending to move on. He noticed one car remained; he figured he'd missed spotting it while he watched the group getting into their cars and driving off. Now, he recalled that this was the vehicle he had been curious about on an earlier drive-by.

Slowly, he cruised by the vehicle. The license tag sticker was not expired. Circling, he glanced at the state inspection sticker on the front windshield; it too was up to date. He stopped the car, flipped on the parking lights, and reached for his flashlight.

He got out of the car and slowly walked toward the driver's side of the Chevrolet. The elm tree that provided shade during the day now played a similar role for the light on the overhead pole. Hector had been cautioned during training to approach any vehicle slowly, alert, but with no show of timidness. Having been spooked once by friends sneaking up on him when he first learned to drive, he wasn't going to surprise anyone who might have a gun in hand or some object that could be used as a weapon. For sure, he would have hurled something that night if he had had it to hand.

Both windows on the side he approached were closed to the top. A dark shape angled toward the steering wheel, which he guessed was the car back tilted to keep the sun off the steering wheel. That's a silly thing for a driver to do if he isn't going to leave until after dark, he scowled.

Staring at the driver's window while still several feet away, Hector saw the mass was too big to be only the seatback and reckoned there was also a package in the front seat. He turned sideways and looked right, left, then behind him. No one was in sight. Once more he stared at the car before stepping closer.

With a bit of bravado he brought his flashlight up, switched it on, and shined the beam on the car door. It hadn't been tampered with, that he could see. He moved the beam of light directly up the window. He froze. He wanted to back off. His feet did not heed. He willed the flashlight switch off. No response. His eyes could neither blink nor shut. His throat tightened, his mouth gaped.

The seat appeared tilted forward. No, it was a tall backrest and a person, a woman. She was still. As the flashlight shone directly on her, her face had an ashen hue, more than just from the overhead fixtures.

No previous rides with the sheriffs, no experiences in security training, nothing in his life had prepared him for what he saw on the other side of this window. The closest he had ever been to a dead person was during a visitation at a funeral home. Down in the pit of his stomach, he knew that death was in this driver's seat.

Chapter 3

Ralph Pierce, head of Saunders Mall Security, stood between the bright headlights of his patrol car and the Chevrolet. Hector Turner paced forward then retreated while Pierce talked on his cell phone. When his boss signed off, Hector halted.

"We'll see who's the first response. Police or rescue squad. Hector, you say you called in earlier about the car?" Pierce clipped the phone on his belt. He wrapped a handkerchief around his right hand and approached the Chevrolet. Peering through the windows, he saw all lock projections pressed down; however, he attempted to open the driver side door. It didn't move.

"Yes, sir. No one had contacted security about taking in the late film. It was here when I came on duty around four this afternoon. Being so far from the entrance, it could belong to a helper in a store." Hector fidgeted as he talked, stepping to the left then to the right. "Maybe somebody wanted to come back to a cool car. Parked under the tree." He pointed up to the dense elm foliage.

Pierce continued around the car and tried all the door handles. "Did you call in again before you approached the car?"

Hector gritted his teeth and swore under his breath. "No, sir. Nothing looked suspicious until I got closer."

"Oh, but you got out of the cruiser and checked the car?" While removing the handkerchief and pocketing it, he looked at Hector. The young man was nervous, fact almost spastic, and Pierce chose an even-toned manner to question him. He had learned from years with a wide variety of new men under his supervision that the eager but nervous type like Hector could forget proper procedure and get confused in relating what they had done or seen.

If that happened and the young fellow became embarrassed, he would go over and over the details trying to reword what he'd said. Such a waste of time and energy, Pierce knew. Thus he tried to clarify a report on the spot. Pierce noticed Hector fingering his pepper spray and was relieved that he didn't have a gun. Placing Hector on late duty primarily to patrol the lots had been a good choice.

Hector blurted. "The door was locked. I could see that," and nodded toward the driver's door. He pulled off his hat and wiped his forearm across his head. Damp.

"It's hot for a hat. Toss it in your car," Pierce said.

Hector did as he was told. His reflection on the car window reinforced what he knew – he didn't look official without the hat. Its dark brim with its rigid form and large size somewhat camouflaged the paleness of his buzz-cut light hair and pale skin, and he was reluctant to doff it. But the breeze was welcomed as it cooled his head to counter the loss, he jerked his shoulders up and back.

The men heard sirens blaring and looked toward the circling drive. The white vehicle with horizontal orange stripe identified it as the Emergency Medical Services. It cut across the empty upper parking lot and stopped close to the security cars. Pierce waved an okay. The sirens ceased, the headlights darkened, the doors opened.

The emergency medical technicians got out. The driver was a calm, focused man in his midthirties who appeared in a physically fit condition. He asked Pierce if the car had been unlocked. The security chief answered no; he and the driver walked toward the sedan. The second EMT moved toward the opposite side of the car. He appeared to be a few years younger and of heavier weight. As the three approached the sedan, the hush of the night air was again pierced with the shrill sirens. A police car sped along the main drive and headed into the parking lot – stopping on a dime.

Hector shouted to the group. "Police!"

The EMTs knew the police could open the car doors. After a reassuring glance that the vehicle was a police car, the emergency crew peered into the sedan.

The front door on the police car flung open and a patrol officer emerged. Pierce called out that the doors were locked. The officer held a center punch tool for breaking glass in one hand, in the other a ring of keys. He quickly moved to the driver's door. He inspected the key lock. It showed no scratches or attempted break-in. He selected a key from the ring and inserted it in the lock. As the EMT had done, the officer surveyed the car interior, but with a flashlight. The driver's door unlocked easily. The officer slightly opened it. Hot air escaped. It was odorless.

The front seat was flipped forward; an older woman was pressed against the steering wheel. He put his hand on her wrist. There was no pulse. He checked her neck also for pulse. From the limited close-up inspection, he saw no signs of violence or struggle. No blood. No weapon. No disarray of her clothing. He stepped aside and an EMT checked pulse points and the face and eyes for discoloration.

Again, sirens broke the stillness of the night air. All eyes turned in the direction of the sound as a police car sped toward them.

The patrol officer unlocked the passenger side door. Pierce strode around the car to check the woman from that side. The EMTs stood near the open left side door. They waited for a signal.

The second police car stopped, and two detectives exited and approached the Chevrolet.

The patrolman told them there was no pulse, no sign of foul play; then he stood aside for them to view the car and the body.

The detectives identified themselves: the older one Detective Smith and the younger as Detective Efrid. They scrutinized the body and the car interior.

Smith stood, pivoted and said, "Okay, you may get on with checking the individual. Watch where you step. ID unit may want to put down commassie blue on the pavement. And luminal in the passenger area. Remove her as easily as you can without disturbing any more than need be. Keep your gloves on."

Efrid watched the proceedings. He expected the EMTs knew those precautions, but they looked young and if they were miffed so what.

One technician eased the car seat back; the other placed a hand on the woman's head. She did not move. He felt her carotid artery for a pulse, then her wrist. He glanced back at the officer opposite him. "No pulse."

Carefully and efficiently, EMTs removed the body and placed it on the stretcher. After officers surveyed the body, the EMTs began a check for any unusual signs: cuts, bruises, foul play, or fluids.

"Check under the front seat," Smith directed the patrolman. "There's no pocketbook on the seat. Maybe she had shoved it back on the floor."

After pulling on vinyl gloves, the technician reached around the driver's seat and pulled the rear door lock up.

Smith asked Hector, "You were the first to notice the car. Did you see anything unusual? Any objects lying about the car? Any suspicious people in vehicles or on foot?"

"No, sir. Nothing. The car had been here several hours that's why I checked. I called Officer Pierce as soon as I saw a passenger inside. She looked dead."

Smith nodded his head. "Good call. Next time, alert Pierce sooner."

Efrid persisted. "No one was in the car when you first spotted it?"

"I don't look in every car I drive by," Hector defended himself.

"How'd you remember when you first saw it?" Efrid continued.

With an edge to his voice, Hector answered. "I had to wait for a long line to pass on the through road. It was hot as . . . As each car drove by, I looked right at the car," he pointed to the Chevrolet. "The tree shaded it. But the tree and car partly blocked the view of oncoming cars. Lucky parking spot I said to myself."

"Yeah," Efrid tilted his head toward the stretcher, "only not for her."

Pierce's cell phone beeped and he flipped the switch. "Pierce, here." He listened, his eyebrows drawing together, then said, "Hold on!" Pierce strode toward the Chevrolet. "Have you found any identification of the body? There's a message that a man called in a few minutes ago saying his wife had been shopping today and hasn't returned. His name is Kester."

"Not yet."

"Give me his phone number." Pierce fished in his pocket for his notebook and pencil and jotted the name and number. At times like this, he appreciated an answering service, especially this one whose owner was reliable and accurate with messages, including spelling of callers' names. "Thanks. Hope you get time for a nap. Oh, you slept this afternoon. Well, lucky for you. Can't say the same."

"When security goes cruising outside the mall and doctors leave the office, someone must hang about the office phones."

Pierce felt a smile tug at the corners of his mouth. She was linguistically clear and correct while giving clients a message, but if there was a moment for a personal exchange, her voice had a melodious and feminine quality. As he pressed end, he noticed Hector was moving close to the sedan and following the investigation of the car interior.

Pierce understood the desire to learn but knew that young fellows crowded folks; he'd sized up Hector as having few friends. Often the recruits' buddies would hang out at the mall and follow them around. He hadn't seen that happen with Hector. But again, assigning him mainly to parking lot patrol, he couldn't be sure. No reports had come his way of Hector loitering about from mall customers or from other security personnel.

Across town, Jonathan Belding unlocked the door to his house located in an upscale neighborhood and entered the spacious foyer. His wife, Alice, had insisted that their home have a large area for the coming and going of groups of people she knew they would be expected to entertain. It was carefully designed to allow for close and distance viewing of the many original paintings that they had collected. Not having been pressed for paying tuition during their years of schooling, the couple had purchased art, often from young painters, prior to their time of public recognition.

A long, narrow table with wrought iron base centered the foyer. The Beldings or their guests could place beverages or plates on the glass top during their viewing of the artworks, and the family could leave messages on the table for each other, especially notes that were important or timely.

Belding spotted a white paper anchored with the only ornament on the table, a bronze horse its head uplifted and turned toward the door as if it sensed a presence. The doctor smiled, walked over, and rubbed the horse's nose. "What do you have for me?" With a slight lift of the statue, he pulled the paper free.

He read the words silently. Doctor, Mrs. Belding called. She will not return until late tomorrow. She stayed over to go with Marilyn to take the children to get school shoes. Plate of cold cuts in refrigerator. Concert tickets in right hand desk drawer. Mercy

He folded the note and slipped it into his pocket. He thought how like Alice that was to offer to help their daughter with the children. A good mother, a good grandmother. He felt a thought scudding through his mind – one he chose not to verbalize. It nagged at him as he walked to the kitchen and opened the refrigerator. Drawing out the saran-covered plate, he compared it to the prepared salads displayed at the hospital cafeteria. T'would be filling to the stomach, but cold just like it looked.

As he began to slide it back onto the refrigerator shelf, the thought he wouldn't give words to a moment ago suddenly overlaid the supper: another night alone. He shook his head and shoved the plate forward and closed the door.

Walking upstairs to the bedroom, he allowed himself to wonder if the sequence would someday revert to good wife, good mother, and good grandmother. He glanced at the bedside clock and decided he had time for a shower before getting a bite to eat somewhere near the concert hall.

However, after showering he uncharacteristically lay down on the bed and fell asleep for three-quarters of an hour. Waking quickly from the sound sleep, he sat up and saw he would have time only for dressing and getting to the concert on time. Debating whether to call the answering service to say he would be staying in or to go on as planned, he chose the latter. After all, he would have his cell phone, no one else would be disturbed for he would only feel its vibrator.

The lights were dimming as he entered the auditorium. He knew where his seats were but noticed they were both filled as he approached. Realizing the disturbance that would ensue if the people occupying them had to move, he looked around for an empty seat. There was one on the aisle two rows up from his regular place. He asked the person seated just to the left if the empty seat were taken.

"No. The person will not be coming."

"May I sit here?"

"Yes."

Nola Gilbert looked at the man who sat beside her. She recognized him from the afternoon lecture. He opened his program and skimmed a few pages as the house lights dimmed and the curtain opened upon the orchestra seated on platforms graduated in heights similar to bandstands. Out of the corner of her eye, she caught the doctor's expression softened from the specialist who oversaw the condition of patients' hearts into the listener who anticipated another kind of beat. The sight caused her to feel joyful in her own heart.

At the intermission, both rose. He moved into the aisle to let her pass.

"Thank you, but I'll stay here. Just standing for a change of position," she said.

He moved back in front of his seat. "Likewise." He looked at her as if attempting to place her.

"You're Dr. Belding, aren't you? I was at the seminar this afternoon. I enjoyed your presentation."

"Yes. That's where I have seen you. It was a good group." As she turned and surveyed the audience, he appraised her: nice-looking woman, late forties, healthy complexion. He wondered if her husband was to occupy this seat.

She faced front again and pulled her shoulders up and stretched without raising her arms and hands overhead, but stretching she was. Um, nice shape the lady has, nicely fitted dress he noticed. She sat down and smoothed her skirt and opened her program.

He asked after sitting. "Do you regularly come to the concerts?"

"Yes. This summer I've had this seat." She looked at him and smiled pleasantly.

He pointed forward. "And I've had those two seats. Thank you for letting me sit here. I'll stay unless you're expecting your friend to come late?"

"No. She had a last-minute change of plans."

"Well, then I will not have the couple move."

Nola and Jonathan enjoyed the musical selections and could sense that the other one had a fondness for the show tunes. After two encores, the house lights came up and the curtain closed.

Because of the flow of the crowd, they walked together up the aisle and through the foyer. He held the door for her to exit. On the sidewalk, both headed right. At the corner, he paused and noticed the café was open. On impulse, he asked Nola if she had had dinner. When she said "yes at this café," he asked if she'd like to come in and have a cup of coffee.

"I haven't eaten and I'm hungry," he stated.

She looked at the café, then at him. "Yes, I would like coffee. If you can take time in your day for educating the public about Healthy Heart Habits, I will be happy to help keep you honest."

He laughed and held another door open for her.

Chapter 4

The back door slammed shut as Amy scooted across the threshold of the kitchen.

"Hi," she called.

"That you, Amy?" a pleasant male voice responded from another part of the house. His approaching footsteps were audible upon the carpeted hallway. As he entered the kitchen, his face spread in a welcoming smile. "Need any help?"

"This is all, but thanks." Carefully, she leaned over the kitchen counter and set two large stacked dinner containers down carefully so as not to tilt tall beverage cups balanced on top. "There're still warm. Dinners that is. And the Cokes are cold," she added while moving the cups onto the counter.

Lou Umstead waited until Amy had finished the task, then he walked easily forward, stopped and circled his arms around her. Tall, he stooped and brought his face beside hers and rubbed it gently. "And so are you. Warm, that is."

She smiled and turned her head, welcoming the kiss that she counted on at the end of each day. When she pivoted toward the counter, he pressed against her. She stopped and let herself be hugged a moment longer.

"As appetizing as you are, how about some edible sustenance now?" Amy leaned to uncover the dinner containers and remove the beverage tops.

After a brief squeeze, he sighed, exaggerated. "Okay. That first." His eyes twinkled and sought a similar response. It was half-hearted.

For the past six months, that had been the most often answer. He forced an agreeable expression. As if trying to keep the door open, he craned his neck and visually searched the counter. "No sweets from the restaurant? Um. I do like the alternative for dessert."

He lifted a dinner and Coke and sat in his usual place at the table in the dining section of the large kitchen. This was one room that he had particularly wanted in this first house they had purchased. Even though Amy was full-time, and often overtime, director of the health program, he knew she had a love of and knack for cooking and someday would be spending many hours in here. There was a large area for dining and another for lounging with a comfortable couch, chair, and a combination table ottoman: a place to put their feet up, relax, read, talk, nibble – whatever they wanted. And a fireplace where they looked forward to kindling a blazing fire as soon as the weather turned cool enough. They'd been in the house about as long as the health program had been open to the public. Neither had experienced a full year's cycle to date.

Lou was normally patient. Like his kindly face, both were welcomed in a big bear of a fellow. He had an open expression usually spread in a grin with large full cheeks, a flushed outdoors tone, bright blue eyes that seemed smaller as they wrinkled at the corners, and short-cropped sandy brownish blond hair. Amy often said as she touched his ears in tender moments, the same words that she had murmured when first she stroked them: they're as soft as down.

As they ate the lasagna and sipped the drinks, he told her about his day. He was well established in his chosen field. Early on he had pegged himself a salesman: he didn't say company representative. He chose the old-fashioned term for he liked to make sales. To him that's how companies stayed in operation – exchanging their products for money. It was the same for businesses or stores, too. Nonetheless, he had spiraled upward into a supervisory position because the company he represented was impressed with not only his selling techniques but also his ability to communicate his skills to the other representatives. Lou worked closely with new employees, especially salespeople, explaining the catalogue items. When new products hit the production line, Lou was called on to help come up with some selling ideas and to explain the unique features to the men who would in turn do so to the buyers. Lou's success was highly regarded by his bosses. They measured by the current very low number of reps leaving the company and the few negative comments from the buyers. Recently, he was promoted to East Coast sales manager.

Amy had been a brick in Lou's eyes to delay a family and accept his long hours with few complaints. Now they had a house they had dreamed of owning, and his work was usually finished during regular office hours while her job started at eight thirty and often went to nine or ten at night. Her horrendous schedule that they had expected to be a few months was about to hit a full-year mark. She had been asked to apply for the position. Her qualifications in public relations were highly regarded by the many organizations she had had contact with in her previous job. Both she and Lou had seen this offer as an honor for two reasons. First, she was quite young for this level of leadership and had been the youngest applicant. Second, the program was new and innovative, and if successful, it could be a long-term position, if not, certainly a super mention on future résumés. And the connection with a medical center and a university offered numerous benefits now.

The health program was up and running with membership and registrations for classes and seminars well above their projected numbers. The few times he had dropped into the center there was a bunch of folks milling about. Some were chatting, others were helping themselves to hot coffee or iced water, and several were perusing the library shelves. Phones were ringing; individuals were asking the receptionist to explain what the Healthy Living program involved. Somewhere in the midst of a small crowd, Lou usually spied his short, vivacious wife. She naturally drew people toward her. And those men and women respectfully circled her leaving a comfortable space.

Lou flipped the television remote to the continuous news station, the volume low, and propped his feet on the ottoman.

After tossing her disposable dinnerware into the trash container, Amy left the room. Lou could hear the water running in the powder room, a term Amy liked to use; he called it the lavatory; the builder had termed it a half-bath.

Returning, she paused by the chair and shook off her shoes then walked to the couch and sank wearily, wiggling her back against the cushions. She let out a deep breath. "May my feet join yours?"

"They may."

Her short legs struggled against the expanse, and she had to flex her feet for her toes to touch.

"Whoops," he said and leaned forward and pulled the ottoman closer.

"Thanks," she said, turned her head and smiled.

"Anytime." He leaned and kissed her. "That was only a sample of dessert."

She gazed contently at him a moment before closing her eyes.

"Rest a bit. I'll keep the volume on low." He punched the remote then placed it on the couch. He reached over and covered her hand with his. Her lips curled and he thought he detected a slight purr. After a few minutes, she drew her legs beside her and dropped her head on his shoulder.

By nature she could drop off to sleep quickly almost anywhere. Lou didn't mind nor was he insulted. He knew a quarter-hour nap would refresh her.

Ironically, he used to be the one who came in very tired. Though he didn't nap, he would relax on a chair or a couch for a short time, ostensibly to view the news or flip through the TV guide.

Feeling her easy, quiet breathing against him, he allowed his mind to review a disturbing bit of news he'd heard today. The information itself had jolted him. The manner in which he had been made aware of it was very unsettling.

Midmorning he had gone to the snack area. Pouring a cup of coffee with his back to the table where employees sat, he heard a few deep laughs. Before turning to ask "What's up?" he spooned sugar and creamer and stirred the coffee.

"Some statistics, eh?" "Good for you starting earlier, young man." "Wait till Mary hears this." "Are you going to tell her?" a deep voice inquired. "Well, now we know why some over-thirty guys . . .," the medium-pitched voice didn't complete the sentence.

Lou took a sip of the hot coffee. It was mixed to his liking, and he tossed the plastic spoon away. Turning to the table, he noticed the three salesmen hastily draining their cups. One folded the newspaper and pushed it center table.

"What do you know about over-thirty guys?" Lou asked as he leaned back against the counter.

The three cast sideways glances among themselves. Two stood and angled their chairs toward the table. The third wiped up a few spills, crumpled his napkin. Arising, he said with a typical good-fellow voice, "They've reached a new age of maturity."

Briefly, he looked at Lou, nodded then joined the other two in the hallway.

"You owe me one, both of you," was all that Lou heard before they rounded a corner.

Curious, Lou approached the table and reached for the newspaper. Surely, he had heard a hasty putting it back together. He spread it out and scanned the front page. Nothing caught his eye that seemed relevant to their dialogue. Several pages over, his attention was arrested with a small headline under the medical news. Study shows male ability to impregnate women lessens after age twenty-four. Quickly, he read the article. Then he reread it.

What in the Sam Hill is that all about? he wondered. He knew plenty of married men way into their thirties whose wives were still bringing babies into the world. Some even after both were forty. The study, he noticed, had a small number of participants. With stats like these, one would be led to believe men had only a few years to add their genes to the population, Lou muttered abashed and shoved the paper aside.

He turned and stared at the doorway and hall. Were they talking about me before I came in or some other guy who had no children? Could be that and they were embarrassed when they realized I was standing there. Why hadn't I ever considered that they might be thinking I was sterile or Amy infertile? Or, God forbid, that we weren't . . . No, they couldn't think that!

But they could have thoughts that ran the gambit of all the talk he had heard over the years. He'd probably made a few wisecracks himself about impotent men. Never had he projected any such delusions about himself. *Whoa, there, man!* Now he'd made himself immobile. Plum shocked his ego. Did his head drop? Was his mouth agape? Had his color drained? Or more embarrassing, had he flushed red as a beet?

He opened his mouth and gulped air deeply, licked his lips, and shook his head. Rousing himself, he stood up, poured a half-cup of coffee, and added more sugar and creamer. He felt his energy level had dropped, so he reached into the candy box for a chocolate bar then put in some change.

Returning to his office, he hadn't had any more time to mull over the article and its implications. Now that Amy was snuggled up beside him, he reviewed his approach of their childless state in conversations with his coworkers and his and Amy's friends. He never brought up the topic. When anyone fished for reasons, he had merely offered "someday." Lou considered his and Amy's sex life a private matter and didn't put forth the subject of children for conversational fodder. Of course, there had been one or two best friends the past few years when the topic of having a family had surfaced and each had been honest about some aspects such as "sure, we want kids" or "not for a while."

To be honest with himself, he had to acknowledge that many nights he returned home as tired as she was now. Perhaps she had desired closeness, but his energy had been lacking. Not because of the newspaper article was he anxious about a relaxed evening with Amy. No, he had been tracking her monthly schedule and deemed this was a favorable time for conception. Hopefully, she was ready, too. After all, nine months was a long time away. She'd still have time to finish incubating Healthy Living through more than a full year; then she could have a few months to slow down and prepare a nursery.

What had that article said? It was a study of a limited number of men. The bottom line was that it was more difficult for a man as he aged to get a woman pregnant. And the slowdown started after age twenty-four. For the love of God that read more like a Ripley's Believe It or Not. Well, I choose not to set any stock on that small research conclusion.

He lifted his arm around Amy's shoulder and drew her closer. She roused and drew her shoulders up a bit then yawned.

"Golly, have I've been sleeping?" she murmured.

"You have. Feel better?"

"I do. I didn't mean to drop off, but thanks for being a comfortable pillow." She looked up at him. "Do you think we could have an early-to-bed night?"

"I vote for that." He bent his head and kissed her. "Are you up to dessert?"

"Give me time for a shower?"

"Off with you now! I'll do the closing up." He checked the doors and shut the blinds and was undressing when she emerged from the shower.

He enfolded her in his arms enjoying the warmth and fresh scent of her skin and the loving look in her eyes.

Chapter 5

The voice that came blaring through the telephone connection was so irritating that Security Chief Pierce held the handset several inches away from his ear.

"Mr. Kester, could you describe your wife, please, sir?" Pierce asked calmly as soon as there was a pause.

"Yes, for the second time. She's sixty-five years old. Gray-headed as a used mop. About five feet seven. A hundred forty pounds. What was she wearing? What she always wears – a blouse, white or blue – a khaki skirt."

"Would she have any identification with her, like in a wallet or a . . ."

"Confound man, don't you know women always carry one of those big handbags. Pocketbooks they used to called them. Why they don't have clothes with pockets like men, I don't know." The ill-tempered caller sounded to Pierce as someone who was more intent on sharing his negative opinion of his wife than being helpful in describing her.

"Mr. Kester, can you come down to the mall now?" Pierce asked.

"Now? Why, is she there? Can't she drive on home?" he shouted crabbily.

"Do you have transportation, sir?"

"No. She has the car. What for?"

"Can you tell us the make of the car, the license plate number that she was driving?"

"Was driving? Is she there? Is the car at the mall? Was it abandoned?"

"It would be helpful, Mr. Kester, if you could tell us the car color and make and the license . . ."

Abruptly, he said, "It's a Chevrolet. Dark maroon. About six years old. I don't know the license number. I haven't driven for several years. It starts with a *K* for Kester. Has about four numbers."

Pierce glanced at his notes. "Mr. Kester, hold on a second." Pierce put his hands over the mouthpiece and spoke to the patrol officer. "The license number starts with a *K* followed by four numerals."

The officer verified the information. Pierce asked if he could send someone to pick up Mr. Kester at his home. Receiving a "yes," Pierce spoke again into the phone.

"Mr. Kester, a police officer will be at your home in a few minutes and drive you to the mall to identify the car. Please bring a key to the car also. Thank you." Pierce hung up as quickly as possible.

The patrol officer got an okay from the detectives to go for Mr. Kester.

The emergency squad hung around for identification of the body. They leaned against the vehicle. The driver said quietly to his partner, "Maybe it was the heat. It was a scorcher today. Up to one hundred degrees."

"Think she could have panicked when she couldn't find a key?"

"Maybe. Could have been dehydrated. Did you see a water bottle in the car?"

"No. Did you hear the ball scores tonight?" And the conversation turned toward sports.

The detectives continued searching the car interior and shining flashlights underneath.

Baffled, Efrid commented, "Where is the key? She'd need one to get in?"

"Not if she'd left the door unlocked," returned Smith.

"Nobody leaves a car unlocked out here."

"Happens all the time. Drivers are in a hurry and forget. Some lock their keys in the car," Pierce overheard and commented.

"That's what puzzles me," added Smith. "There's no key in the ignition. Or anywhere in the car."

"No wallet, no handbag. That's strange, isn't it?" Efrid glanced at the other men.

They nodded. Pierce asked Smith, "No sign of foul play?"

"Not that we can see. The car is neat. No packages. No personal belongings."

"What do you make of it?" Pierce asked.

"The woman came out of the mall, opened an unlocked door, and passed out. Maybe heart attack."

The younger detective projected his doubts. "But wouldn't she have a key on her, in a pocket or a purse?" He paused, thought then continued. "If she'd lost her key, why would she be back in the car?"

"Could she have died somewhere else? Then be put in the car?" Smith asked.

Efrid sputtered. "But this is her car. You think someone knew who she was and set her inside and left her?"

"If he carried her any distance in this parking lot, he could have been noticed," Pierce interjected.

"That would be chancy!" Efrid added.

Smith wiped his hand over his damp hair. "We do have questions about this woman. But there's no sign of physical abuse on her or obvious tampering with the car. And we won't get into medical speculations."

All the while, Hector Turner had been eagerly darting from the rescue squad, his boss, and the policemen. He'd asked questions, which had been answered with an "uh," "oh," or "maybe." Several times, he started to repeat how he'd found the body, a note of importance creeping into the tone, but he'd been pretty much ignored.

Exasperated, Hector rubbed his crew cut. Knowing he appeared a raw recruit, he retrieved his cap from his vehicle and slammed it on his head. Working his shoulders to loosen mounting tension and clasping his hands behind his back, he walked toward the mall and scrutinized the tarmac as if a clue lay waiting discovery.

Retracing his steps, he spotted a police car entering the drive then headed toward this lot. He quickened his steps and reached the area of the Chevrolet shortly after the car stopped. The patrolman opened the driver's door, exited, then opened the rear door.

An elderly man emerged. He took hold of a walker that the police officer had taken from the car, and he bumped it over the smooth pavement.

The man appeared to be about seventy or so years of age. Slender, probably once measured above average height but now stooped, he shuffled the few yards toward the Chevrolet. He halted a few feet from the car, scrutinized it.

Smith strode toward the man. "I'm Detective Smith. Mr. Kester, thank you for coming. Do you recognize this as your car?"

"I do. It is. Where is Bessie? Or the woman? A policeman you sent told me there was a woman in it."

"Over here," Smith answered and reached his hand to indicate the way.

Mr. Kester irritably motioned him out of the way. "I don't need your help."

Smith stood aside but stayed nearby. As they approached the stretcher, the EMT driver moved forward and pulled the sheet away from the woman's head and upper body. He stepped back.

Mr. Kester stooped, leaned forward, and looked at the face. "She's eerie looking in this light. That's Bessie. My wife." He jerked the walker three-quarters around and stared at the officer who had spoken to him. "What happened?"

"She was discovered inside the car. We unlocked the door, and the medical technicians confirmed that she was dead. The cause we don't know. There is no sign of attack or struggle. Has she been ill, sir?"

"Ill? No. Not sick. Always ill-natured. The car was locked, you say?"

"Yes, sir. And there was no key in the lock and no handbag."

Mr. Kester pointed a slender, bony finger at the officer. "There's a mystery here, Officer. She'd never let go that handbag without a struggle unless she was dead."

All the officers absorbed the irony of his statement.

After shifting his walker and taking a step toward the patrol car he had come in, he halted, thought a second, then swung the walker around to face the men again. His head projected forward. "Did you see a tissue box in the car?"

The group reacted as one; all eyes stared at him as if attempting to garner some reason for the question. Pierce was the first to react. He turned toward the officers. "Did you?"

The officers looked at each other. The patrolman nodded then turned and answered. "There is something wedged tight up under the front seat."

"Well, get it out!" The tones were gruff.

The patrolman opened the passenger door, wrapped his hand with a handkerchief, and withdrew the box.

"There was a key taped in the bottom." The old man edged his walker a few steps closer, eyeing the search.

His hand still wrapped, the officer moved the tissues aside and fingered the cardboard bottom. Slowly, he removed the short stack of tissues and peered inside.

"There's a key all right." He held the box at an angle for the light to show the key clearly. "Looks like a car ignition key."

Smith took the box and walked to Mr. Kester. "Do you recognize this key?"

"Car keys look alike. But, since it's in my car, and I put one in a box, I'd reckon that it starts that car." Mr. Kester spoke in a voice as tight as his grip on his walker.

"Did your wife know the key was in the car?" the officer asked.

"Confound. Yes, she knew. There's still a mystery here. Why didn't she use it!" The outburst left the old man weak. His strength was gone. His body slumped forward, his elbows angled, and his voice became almost inaudible. "Take me home."

Quickly, both detectives rushed to assist Mr. Kester to the patrol car. The EMTs hurried to his side. Mr. Kester waved them away. "Don't touch me!"

Smith said, "The patrol officer will take you home. If you need medical help, he'll call your doctor. Or an ambulance." He told the patrol officer, "See that he gets in. If he appears evenly slightly to need a doctor, get his own doctor's number and call him. Oh, tell Mr. Kester as soon as the identification unit checks the car, it will be returned to his house. Maybe tonight."

After Mr. Kester was in the backseat of the car, he pulled the sleeve of Smith's shirt. He whispered. "The funeral home – Howard's on Center Street. Take the body there."

The officer walked back to the EMTs and relayed the message. The driver nodded. "We'll take the body to the hospital ED – the Emergency Dead – not the ER. We'll tell them the funeral home of choice."

The ID unit vehicle arrived. The police officer pointed to the Chevrolet. He handed a plastic bag with the key inside that had been retrieved from the tissue box. "Try this ignition key."

The following morning as Amy was changing a few items in her purse, Lou walked into the bedroom. "Honey, I forgot to tell you last night that when your dad called, he said he'll be in town tonight. He has an afternoon meeting in Groton and will have lunch with Rob. He'll drive over after the meeting."

"Great. Did you ask him to stay with us?"

"I did. I said we'd fire up the grill."

"Thanks. Can you get some steaks or do you want me to?" She closed the purse and picked up her keys.

"I'll do that." He reached for his keys and wallet. "What time do you think you'll be home?" he asked and walked over and hugged her.

She lifted her face, stood on tiptoe, and gave him a kiss. "Five or five thirty. It would be nice for Dad to have someone to share dinner with. Besides us, I mean."

"I agree."

She scrunched her face thoughtfully then grinned. "I know someone to invite over. Nola Gilbert. I've told you about her. A very nice woman."

"Ah ha! Amy the matchmaker." He smiled.

"She's single. Never been married. She's a good conversationalist. I'll call her as soon as I get to the center."

"Let me know. I'll be in office most of the morning. Otherwise, try the car phone. And honey, have a good day."

Amy wiggled her nose and left the house with a happy face.

She arrived at the mall before it was open to the public, so she let herself in a service entry right angled in a recessed delivery area and closed the door behind her. The long, windowless hallway all painted battleship gray intimidated her daily. Her inch-and-a-half-heeled dress shoes clicked on the cement floor then resounded from the interior cinderblock walls. Every week, she determined to buy some pumps with soft soles and rubber heels, believing that would prevent her being spooked by her own steps.

The hallway was L-shaped with the short end leading to the Healthy Living Center. The inside hall had protected equipment and supplies during the remodeling for the center. Many sections of the mall had open dock areas for receiving merchandise. Amy instinctively held her breath until she rounded the corner, and the heavy metal door stood before her. After she unlocked it with another key and entered the health center storage corridor, she could relax and breathe normally.

She was the first to arrive. She went straight to her small office and checked the posting of volunteers scheduled for today. Nola's name was not on the list. She clicked on the computer. While it was doing its setup, she changed to her office sneakers and shoved the others under her desk. Her purse went into a file cabinet drawer.

She pulled up the phone list of volunteers and dialed Nola's number.

While waiting, she brought up today's calendar. When Nola answered her phone, Amy cheerfully said, "Good morning. I hope I'm not calling too early."

"Hello. No. I've been up awhile. It's a lovely morning."

"It is. Nola, if you don't have plans for tonight, could you come have dinner at my home? I know, it's a bit late to ask you, but we'd love to have you."

"Why, Amy, that sounds very inviting," Nola spoke with pleasure.

"It'll be very informal. Lou, my husband, will grill steaks on the deck."

"I'll be glad to come. What time?"

"Will six thirty be all right with you?"

"It will. What may I bring?"

"Nothing. And Nola, my dad is having lunch in Groton with my brother Robert. Then he has a meeting over there this afternoon. Since we're only thirty minutes away, he's going to drive over. He'll be here for dinner, too." Amy held her breath. She had never invited a woman over when her dad visited, and she hoped the invitation sounded appropriate.

"Amy, you've spoken highly of him, and I look forward to meeting both your father and your husband. And what's the address?" Nola pulled a pencil and pad forward.

"It's a new section, Cambridge. We're at 164 Hunt Road. Have you heard of it?"

"Yes, I have. In fact, I've driven in the area." As Nola wrote the address, she asked, "May I have your phone number just in case there is some delay or I make a wrong turn?"

"Sure. Oh, did I say my dad's name is Bruce Braddock?"

After the call, Nola added Bruce Braddock under the phone number. Bruce Braddock, a nice name, she mused after spelling and pronouncing it. If he's anything like his daughter, he has to be a special person. Amy is so agreeable, friendly, and generous. The old saying – the apple doesn't fall far from the tree – came to mind. Another thought popped up. Amy's my boss. I'll have to take care not to be too informal even though that's how she described the dinner.

Later that morning as she undertook cleaning the oven, a long-delayed and never a favored chore, she considered baking a pie or a batch of brownies. Not an apple pie for it was the most likely to run over. A lemon meringue was always a treat in hot weather and could be refrigerated if not needed tonight. Yes, she'd be up to that and would phone Amy's house and leave a message if the pie turned out well. No reason to have the busy Healthy Living director prepare dessert upon her return home.

Nola wondered if Bruce Braddock was short or did Amy's statue genes come from her mother. Her step became quicker with a different sort of evening to anticipate. Two nights in a row, she would have the opportunity of conversing with new male acquaintances. Last night, she had enjoyed the company at the concert with Jonathan Belding, but he was a married man who, obviously from his comments, enjoyed cultural events with his wife.

Once, Nola had foreseen her future as a happily married woman. The disappointment had left her distraught for a year. Then a stage came of avoidance, as much as possible, of all men except those in her family, who were few. Next, she accepted some invitations to dinner or a lecture, a few to fill in at bridge foursomes, and occasionally to meet some girlfriend's highly touted male friend – nothing long lasting came of the "dates."

She had trusted a man with her heart once and had been so certain she had his love that when the later belief was shattered, she promised herself next time . . . well, that time or rather that man had not come into her life. Thus, she merged her time, energy, and talents into her teaching. The role was demanding and draining with the number of students, the long hours during and after classes, and the continuous updating her teacher's certificate and knowledge base. The job could be a handy excuse for rejecting invitations, and she freely employed it when the event or the guy-to-be-met didn't interest her.

Many she did accept. Many she enjoyed for an evening or two. Keeping up to date with the fashions of hairstyle, clothing, and entertainment, she had frequent invitations. She considered she'd become somewhat shy, spoken more formally with the strangers than did women who had frequent and casual contacts with men. After a few years of teaching junior high, she could talk to her teenage, hyperactive male students easily. Over the long run though in her free hours, she had been a loner, but a cheerful, contented one.

The invitation from Amy appealed to her and she played upbeat CDs and searched her closet for a colorful blouse and stylish slacks.

At Healthy Living, the reception room was abuzz with little groups talking about the woman found in the car. The staff whispered together so as not to alarm the people, who were reading, getting blood pressure measured, or cooling off with water following a brisk walk around the mall corridors. Two or three walkers huddled and exchanged facts they had heard on the morning television news. Men volunteers, who were setting up the auditorium for a noon program, were surprised that the car was at the end of the parking lot near where the volunteers and staff often parked. On hot days, shoppers chose it for its location near two large department stores and the shade trees.

When Amy interrupted Joyce and Phyllis to ask for the signup lists for the noon event, they asked if she knew anything about the woman. They whispered as if reluctant to speak her name.

"Which woman?"

When they told her about the woman who died, and her name, Amy gasped. "No. Not Bessie Kester. She was here yesterday."

Quickly, Phyllis, who was nearer Amy, hopped up and urged her to sit down.

Joyce said in hushed tones, "We remember her being here."

Weakly, Amy asked, "What happened?"

"The news report only gave her name and the fact that she was discovered about ten last night. Slumped over the steering wheel. A security guard on routine surveillance discovered her. There weren't many details."

"Had she been," Amy searched for a word, "attacked?"

"No. No evidence of attack or a car break-in." Joyce added, "My husband called and told me to be careful and not to walk out alone."

"My mom and my sisters called me that if it happens again that I should quit!" Phyllis said emphatically.

Two women came up to inquire about registering for a seminar.

Quietly, Amy said to Phyllis, "If you hear anything else, please, let me know." She reached for the desktop and pulled herself up and slowly went back to her office.

She sank into her chair letting the news run through her mind. She was here late yesterday afternoon. And such unpleasantness Bessie always projected. Often, I had to steel myself not to enter into anyone's negative conversation about the overbearing woman. My responses were the same as those of the others in the audience, but I had to be above the consensus. She bowed her head in prayer. "Please, let Bessie's death have been of natural causes. And may her invalid husband be consoled."

Chapter 6

The dark blue Mercedes-Benz convertible nosed into the driveway at 164 Hunt Road in the Cambridge section of Windermere and slowly rolled right toward the widest area of the pavement. It came to a stop immediately back of a deep green Jeep. Behind the Mercedes steering wheel was a driver with black hair, slightly graying, who sat tall in the bucket seat.

He opened the door and easily emerged, long limbs and all. Turning to close the door, he inspected the interior briefly then the exterior and heard his name called.

"Bruce?" Louis Umstead stood on the rear deck, leaning outward to identify the driver.

"Lou, yes, it's me." Bruce smiled. He waved, walked to the rear, and lifted the trunk lid to pull out an overnight bag of sturdy nylon and a laptop case. He heard footsteps on the wooden stairs.

"Well, I be! You're driving in class, sir!" Lou put forth a hand and the men shook amicably. "Did you make a killing in the market? Gain a high-bracket new client? Or lots of buys and sells with good commissions?"

Bruce grinned. "Just time for a trade. A car trade. A bit of a change. How do you like it?"

Already with arms akimbo, Lou answered. "Swell. Is it yours? A rental?"

"Mine." Bruce watched Lou's appraising the new-model sports car, walking in front to view the grill and moving to the passenger side. He stopped and admired the light beige leather upholstery and pile carpet.

Looking at the console, he pronounced, "All the latest features. This will blow all the other cars off the road."

"With you driving maybe, but not me."

"But it has the power to, right?"

"So the salesman told me." Bruce gestured to the door. "Open and get in, if you'd like to."

Lou heeded the invitation. "Don't you want to pull it around me," he pointed to the Jeep, "and park under the trees? This leather is hot!"

"Well, later." Bruce scanned the sky. "The birds will be sighting their nest soon. Better they lighten their bodies of the last meal over your grass."

Laughing, Lou nodded. "That's why I have a hard top. It was a nice afternoon for you with the top down, right?"

"It was. Is. This light-colored leather won't be as hot as something dark." Bruce leaned his lanky body against the driver's side door. "How've you been? And Amy? Is she working sixty hours a week?"

"We're both fine. Amy's a bit tired in the evening, but she's got lots of stamina. And not quite sixty hours a week."

"Any letup in sight?"

Craning his head and squinting at the numerous gauges, he replied, "She says in a few weeks she will have a day or two off each week. Some evenings free."

"That's good to hear. She's always had energy for whatever she was into. Does she cook anymore?" he asked with interest and focused on his son-in-law, much as would a bird cock its head, alert for a sign of some change of features.

He uttered deep in his throat. "It's mostly take-out."

"Well, in a few weeks that up-to-date kitchen may get some testing," Bruce said with a mix of positiveness and lightheartedness.

"Yeah. Tonight, I'm firing up the grill. Shall we go in and stash your luggage?" Eyeing the laptop case, Lou commented, "You're bringing the office along?"

"Always." Bruce picked up both pieces. "The market was active up to closing."

"You know where everything is." Lou took a few steps toward the deck, spotted a flock of birds flying over, turned, and asked, "Sure you don't want to put the top up?" He pointed toward the sky.

"I thought I'd leave it down until Amy returned. Did she say when she'd be home?"

"Early." He peered at his watch. "About half an hour."

"It'll be okay until then. What I need is one of those scarecrows from the farm," Bruce commented catching up with Lou.

"Yeah, let it sit in the back. How're things back home? And on the farm?" Lou called over his shoulder as he climbed the stairs to the rear deck.

"I'll bring you up on the news when Amy arrives. She always asks, too."

Lou held the storm door open and stood aside until his father-in-law entered. He stopped beside the refrigerator. "I'll get some things out. Make yourself at home."

"Right," said Bruce and moved down the hall.

The men were a contrast in build and coloring. Lou at thirty-two, was thicker in girth, shorter in height by a few inches, and tended to be more flushed of face. Bruce had an abundance of black hair albeit streaked with some gray, intense dark brown eyes, and a thickness of dark eyebrows that gave his rectangular face a photographic quality. His nose was straight and well portioned to the others features and his mouth was generous. His naturally fair skin was darkened during the warm weather months, for he spent much of his spare time out of doors playing golf, puttering in a small garden at his city apartment, or walking the fields of the farm.

At the moment, his face was relaxed in its customary, genial demeanor. He paused at the guest bedroom that Amy had labeled: for dad anytime he can come. Seeing no indication of its being used otherwise, he tossed the laptop on the desk and his bag on the luggage rack and began to unpack.

The door to a bathroom placed between two guestrooms was open; the one opposite it was closed. He went in and ran the water warm for a quick wash-up before dinner. After inspecting his beard, he decided a shave was in order. No need to scratch his daughter's face during a hello kiss. He thought that's the trouble of dark hair – it has to be shorn often. He brought his toilet bag in, opened it on the counter, and took out his shaving supplies. After removing his shirt, he shaved then tidied the countertop.

He partially folded his white shirt and shoved it into a plastic laundry bag that he placed in a dresser drawer. He pulled a blue, knit sport shirt over his head and straightened the collar. Last, the gray trousers were exchanged for tan khakis. As he brushed his hair away from his face, he heard Lou call out. "Amy's here."

"Good," he exclaimed and headed toward the kitchen. Lou was chopping some vegetables, so Bruce walked to the storm door and opened it.

Amy burst in. "Dad! Hello. So good to see you." She hugged him then leaned back and asked, "Where is your car?" She looped her heavy shoulder bag on a wall peg.

"It's outside. Didn't you see one parked behind the Jeep?"

Her eyes expressed puzzlement, as did her voice. "Just the Mercedes. Dad, that's not yours, is it?"

"It is."

"But it's a convertible! Dad, it's indescribable!" She turned and looked out the door. "I can't see it from here, but . . ."

"Well, shall we go out and get a better look. Lou has already fully inspected it. Lou, can you spare us a minute?"

Amy crossed to the maple block counter that centered the kitchen where he was preparing the salad ingredients. She flung her arms around his neck and kissed him as he turned his head.

Briefly, Bruce watched them and smiled approvingly. Then he turned toward the outside door. A barely perceptible sigh escaped his lips before they lifted in smile of having reassurance that all was well between his only daughter and her mate.

"Let's have a look-see. Lou is finishing the salad and wants to wrap the potatoes." As she joined her father, he opened and held the door for her. "Did your car conk out?"

"No, but it needed some work. Ten years old – so the time was ripe to consider repair or trade-in. I'd seen some ads for this model and it caught my eye."

"Dad, it'd catch anybody's eye. What a great color! Such a classy model! How does it drive?"

Her continuous questions in short bursts of exclamations showed enthusiasm, but Bruce regarded her and considered she was running on high similar to someone near exhaustion.

Putting his arm around her shoulder, he directed, "Hop in. We can go around the block." He opened the passenger door and she scooted in.

"Whoops, kind of warm. Have you thought of carrying some towels?"

"For the seats? I'm thinking of it now. Thanks. Is it too much of a hot seat for a short drive?" He waited beside the open door for her answer.

"I'm tough. Let's go for it."

He laughed genially. "I'll make it a fast one. Stir up a breeze."

"Will it reach so low?" She jested and slid her hands between the seat and her slacks.

He backed the car, then pulled around the Jeep, made a wide turn at the end of the drive, and headed toward the road. Amy leaned against the warm seat.

"I think this will be a wonderfully comfortable ride when the day is not so hot," she pronounced. "But I'm okay. The car rides so smoothly." He turned and smiled at her, seeming pleased she liked the car. "This is a new you, Dad. Anything to tell me?"

"No. Do you have anything new to tell me?"

"No. And I'm not pregnant. Nothing new." She surveyed the neighbors' yards as they drove a few blocks. "Are you certain you're not seeing someone special? Someone to impress?" She spoke as one who is comfortable exchanging personal matters with her father.

"It's for myself, dear. A sports car is in every young man's dreams. Some of us put off making it a reality."

"I'm happy you're rewarding yourself. Nevertheless, a handsome man like you in a car like this will surely be turning the ladies' heads."

"Keeping an eye on the road is a driver's first priority," he grinned.

"Oh, Dad, did Lou tell you that we've invited a woman for dinner tonight?"

Bruce looked quickly to see if she were serious. "No. Someone I know?"

She shook her head. He slowed and stopped at an intersection. "Maybe we should head back. I need to freshen up, change clothes before she arrives. Her name is Nola Gilbert. She volunteers with me at the health center. She's a super nice person. A retired schoolteacher."

Again, he glanced at Amy. "Retired? Like sixty-five?"

"Not sixty-five. She taught for many years then just decided to leave and be more in touch with Windermere in a different role."

"As in volunteering?" His voice sounded doubtful.

"And other things. Dad, she's really nice and been a great help to me. Like a right hand. She's had lots of experience and is really good with the members at the seminars. We just clicked immediately."

"Well, Amy, I trust your judgment of people. And since you've never set me up with a – what did you say, a woman – I'm sure you have a good reason. Not returning a favor or anything?"

"Hush. I'll let her make her own impressions and you draw your own conclusions. And I didn't tell her that you were a wealthy stockbroker either. I decided on the spur to ask her only because it felt a good thing to do. Thanks for the ride. It was heavenly." She opened her door as soon as car was in park and dashed down the drive.

Bruce stayed behind to raise and secure the top. He thought about how proud Amy's mother would have been of her being selected to direct the health program and having made a good, solid marriage. She had lived long enough to see Amy educated and on the way to doing what she wanted, and to know that she and Lou were engaged. She had been a beautiful person, kind, and steady, hospitable until her last few months when cancer wasted her. Being thankful she had not had years of suffering, he and their children Amy and Robert picked up their lives after a few months of grieving. Bruce often said to close friends that blessings still existed and pointed out that both of their children were happily married and settled in North Carolina within easy driving distance.

During the past few years, friends of his took turns encouraging him to start dating. Occasionally, they boldly invited single women, or others who were separated or in the process of divorce, for dinner or a hand of bridge. Some were interesting, some dull, but no one had held an attraction for more than a few weeks. Now, he wondered about this woman that Amy had asked to join them. How old is she? Is she prim and neat? What age did she teach? To his limited knowledge, college professors didn't retire early. Is she short like Amy, as most of her friends seemed to be? With such scant information he let the questions be. This was beginning as an evening of surprises.

As he strolled toward the house, he reminded himself that Lou had been a good provider, not only in managing his career and income that had allowed them to buy and furnish this house and drive new cars but also in enfolding her with love and attention. Amy, having grown up knowing both a city where she attended high school and living on a farm a few miles east, seemed to need both environments for a fulfilled life. Windermere offered her the twain. Her work was city based, while Cambridge residential area with its large lots had been developed from dairy farmland where a section was still fenced in for cattle and a large barn amid acres of pasture.

Bruce, relaxed in a spirit of gratitude, entered the kitchen. Television was on. Both, Lou and Amy, were paused in a still frame similar to pedestrians who had witnessed a hit-and-run accident. Bruce joined them.

The announcer reported that at this time there was no indication of foul play. "Well, that's good news," commented Lou. As he turned to mix a dressing, he saw Amy was quite pale. "Honey?"

She swallowed and drew a long breath. "The center was buzzing about this early today. It really hit me. I'm embarrassed to say I was so shocked that I had to sit down. Go to my office." She dropped her head and breathed deeply again. She fingered the silver necklace, an action both men watching her knew to be a sign she was centering herself, resolving a matter of a personal nature.

Lou said, "Sudden death is always a shock. Especially when it happens near where you work."

"But, Lou, it is not only at the mall, but in the parking lot nearest our entrance. And I know her!" Amy looked up with a stricken expression.

"How? Where?" Lou asked

"She's a member of Healthy Living! I saw her yesterday afternoon. She was at the seminar."

MYSTERIOUS DEATH AT THE MALL | 57

Bruce stepped to the television and turned the volume low. Turning to Amy, he asked, "She wasn't ill when she left?"

"No. Not physically ill." She swiftly looked at the men. "Oh, I was so unkind to her. In my thoughts, that is. I didn't say anything. I just bear with any of her pushy comments, her monopolizing the question-and-answer time." Her face showed self-chastisement.

Bruce put his arm around her shoulders. "You're the soul of discretion. Do you want to talk about what happened?"

Mixing the oil and vinegar, Lou suggested, "Probably, she had a sudden heart attack. Wasn't the seminar about how to keep good habits for a healthy heart?"

"Heart Healthy Habits was the topic. It could have been a heart attack. But the staff thought she was coming to so many heart seminars because her husband had a heart condition. He's an invalid." She stopped but her expression was taut and she appeared as if she wanted to say something else. She picked a celery stalk from the salad mix, started to munch but lowered her hand. "She'd begin asking questions about her husband's medications but pressed on with laments about how hard this was on her and da . . . da . . . da."

"Oh, that woman! I recall your talking about her. She was a regular pain in the . . ." Lou picked up a bottle of mixed dried spices and scooped a spoonful that he dropped into the oil and vinegar cruet. As he shook the mixture, he said, "How about filling us in on what you know while I do this. Bruce, would you roll silverware in napkins on the edge of the counter and I'll get the bread. And, honey, you want to fill the pickle dish?" He pointed toward the ceramic dish also on the counter. He opened the refrigerator and took out a bottle of pickles and a stick of butter.

She lifted pickles with a fork, suspended them over the jar to drain before placing them in the dish. "There were mall security personnel up and down the halls inquiring if anyone had seen or talked with Bessie. Since the health center is the first place inside the entrance nearest where Bessie was found, they lucked up with us. Phyllis, the receptionist, knew her. She referred to seminar attendance lists for yesterday and showed the officer that Bessie's name was checked. She thought the seminar concluded about ten minutes late and everyone was out of the auditorium by five o'clock. About that time, several people came in for blood pressure checks. The evening shift took over."

She finished the pickles and capped the bottle. "I need to change. Can you get along without me?"

"We can manage," Lou replied. "Oh, did the police come in, too?"

Already on her way, she paused in the family area. "They did. I was in a meeting, so they said they'd be back tomorrow."

"They may have some more information then," Bruce commented. "Go on. I'll be a second hand in here."

"I'll check on the grill. Will you stash the salad bowl in fridge? Thanks." Lou went on the deck, and Bruce transferred the salad then checked there were tongs and glasses on the drink tray. He knew Amy always had coffee ready to perk after the meal, so he poured the water and filled the basket with a paper filter and regular coffee. He poured half-and-half into a ceramic pitcher and returned the carton and pitcher to the fridge. The sugar bowl was full, so he set it and spoons on a small tray near the coffeemaker.

"Bruce, I heard a car drive up," said Lou coming in. "Check the front door, please. She may come in that direction. I haven't met her, so I can't give you any clues." He chortled. "All I know is that Amy says she's very helpful with the older members."

Bruce grimaced and slightly drew his shoulders upward then proceeded on his mission.

Chapter 7

Bruce Braddock made his way from the kitchen through the dining room into the living room. He stopped midroom and looked toward the large picture window that gave a view of green lawn. A hedge of neatly pruned four-foot-high evergreens edged the right away from the street, and, perpendicularly, softer-shaped azaleas extended several feet this side of the driveway, stopping at the cement walkway. Along this came a tall woman, erect, fashionably slender, and likewise stylish in well-fitted slacks that he knew women called dressy with a long-sleeved apricot shade blouse that reflected the late rays of sunshine, a soft, appealing shimmer.

Bruce did a double take, stepped back a pace, a questioning look on his face. With no one nearby to ask, he mentally wondered, "Can this be the retired schoolteacher?" She differed from teachers he had known. Approaching the house, she moved with grace, head high, and carried a covered pie container. He'd seen enough of those round containers to recognize one anywhere.

Her complexion was fair, and her hair, combed back from her forehead, was full and fell to her shoulders where its ends flipped up. How casual, how well put together, this woman appeared. Bruce expected to answer the doorbell as she rang it only to hear her say she was a neighbor just running over an extra pie.

The last few feet of the walkway and the steps to the recessed front door, Nola was doing some thinking herself. She had looked in the driveway and didn't see Amy's car, which she knew to be a small four-door sedan. The classy Mercedes-Benz caused her to think that there must be other company or that she had the wrong house. Well, she decided I'm this far up the path, I may as well ring the bell; and if this is the wrong address, someone will surely set me right.

When the bell chimed, Bruce moved into the foyer and opened wide the wooden door. He paused before taking the latch off the storm door and stared at the visitor. Head still high, eyes alert, and a smile on her apricot-tinted lips, she stepped back holding the pie waist high.

God, she's lovely, he appraised her silently, but he felt his eyes engage hers and his cheeks fill out and his jaws lift. He returned her smile. Then he opened the storm door. "Good evening."

"Thank you. Is this the Umsteads' home?"

"It is. And you're Amy's friend Nola?"

"Yes. Nola Gilbert." She smiled with such a pleasurable expression that he pulled his shoulders up and back. As he stepped sideways, he said, "Do come in."

While she passed closely, the top of her head just below his nose, he detected the fragrance of roses. "Um," he intended an inaudible pleasantness; however, she cast a sideways, slightly backward glance.

"Yes?" She waited for him to close the door and step beside her. Being a first visit, she refrained from leading the way.

"This way. Lou is in the kitchen. Amy's changing." The hall being wide, they walked side by side. "I'm Bruce Braddock, Amy's dad."

"Hello, Bruce. You have a very special and very capable daughter." Her voice rang with sincerity.

Where is the sternness, the stress of authority that rules the classroom, he wondered? She had a well-modulated voice with warmth that emerged from a deep center. He felt the need to respond with a genuine compliment.

"She appreciates your assistance at the health center functions."

Lou halted in filling a glass with ice from the automatic dispenser on the fridge door to greet them. "Hi, there. I'm Lou Umstead, Amy's husband."

"It's such a pleasure to meet you, Lou. Your wife makes volunteering a great adventure. I left a message on the answering machine that I would bring a lemon pie."

"You did. I checked the calls earlier and really appreciate that. Lemon. One of my favorites."

While Lou talked, Bruce reached over to take the pie. Customarily, plates could be passed from one person to another without hands touching – one attempted to do so with strangers as with collection plates in church. Whether with intention or from a primitive desire for contact, she extended the container with both hands and in reaching out his overlapped hers. He could have expected her hands to be warm from a freshly baked pie or cool from one previous frozen; however, first, his touch registered her firmness of grasp, long fingers, polished and manicured nails, and soft, smooth skin. Afterwards, his senses recalled the warmth. For a long moment, neither of them moved their hands.

Glancing up from the pie, their eyes asked who would release this container first. But the question melted into a gradual exchange of interest in the other person, followed by a mutual let's see how this goes.

Nola spoke. "If you have a good hold, I'll slide my fingers out. Okay?" There was lightness in her tone.

"Got it." Bruce placed the pie on the center counter. "Does it need refrigerating?"

"I think not, but I usually remove the cover so the meringue won't weep." She turned, unlocked the lid, then looked for a place to lay it. Bruce had not moved away, and she was aware of his nearness, of her sleeve against his arm. Watching her visual search, he put his hand on the lid, once more covering her hand.

Lou finished filling the ice bucket and the clatter of the dispensing ceased. He turned to speak, caught the action of their hands on the container and the look in their eyes. Oh, ho, he chuckled quietly. "Bruce, over here. Stand it up on the back of this counter. It won't get lost in the clutter later on." Watching the always-under-control Bruce, he was itching to tell Amy about this main attraction he had seen – course, she may see it before he has a chance to share the glee with her.

"What'll you have to drink, Nola? There's an assortment there." He waved to the counter near the door to the deck. "And you, Bruce, can you tend to the drinks?" A smirk slunk into his last question.

"I'll take a look at the stock," he answered as he joined Nola at the counter.

Amy entered the room. She wore a long light green jumper with a bold design of a single iris blossom topping a curved stem and a couple of blades from the bodice to the knee area. The sides were slit and her bare legs were not tanned. Her green sandals clicked on the kitchen floor tile and announced her arrival.

"Hi, everybody. Nola, did you have any trouble finding the house? It's so good to see you."

"Not at all. Your directions were clear, as always. Did your seminar today go well?" Nola said as she walked toward Amy.

"Yes, I did the greeting and only three people didn't show, so the waiting list was accommodated. I hope you enjoyed your day at home. And thanks for the pie. It is one of our favorites." She moved to the counter. "The meringue is so high and fluffy. A miracle in this heat."

"I'm ready to take orders for the steaks. Nola, how do you like yours? Well done, medium, or on the rare side?" Lou asked.

"Medium is fine, thank you."

"Bruce, you're medium, too, aren't you." Bruce gave a nod. "Amy, well done, is it?"

"Sure. Is there anything left for me to do?" She surveyed the counters.

"All is ready except waiting for the steaks. The potatoes need a bit more time in the oven. Then I'll put the bread in." Lou took the plastic container with the steaks from the refrigerator. "You all can take your glasses out to the deck if you like. The sun should be off it now."

Bruce held the door open as everyone exited, then joined the women at the table.

Nola spoke. "Amy, I heard on the car radio driving over that Bessie Kester was found in the mall parking lot late last night."

"I know. I heard about it when I got to the center this morning. Wasn't that awful?"

"The news report was so brief. Did you learn any details? She was at the seminar yesterday afternoon. She sat two rows in front of us," Nola commented.

"I remember. No, there were no details. I was in a meeting when the police came by. They said they'd come back." Amy sighed.

"It is distressing. Even though she was a very annoying person, I'm sorry she had to die alone in a hot car."

"I know." Amy took a long swallow from her glass then slowly wiped the condensation from around the sides.

Meanwhile, Nola sensed that Amy might not want to talk about the death. She glanced at both the men. They gave barely perceptible nods so she changed the topic.

"Bruce, I recall Amy saying you lived in the eastern part of the state."

"I do. Raleigh." He gave her his attention.

"Would it be presumptive to ask if you're involved in government?"

"Not at all. Not presumptive and not with the government," Bruce answered genially.

While arranging the steaks on the grill, Lou said, "Bruce still claims to be from Acorn, where Amy grew up. A gentleman farmer, he is." Lou paused in arranging the steaks, waiting a reaction.

Nola's eyes widened a bit and there was a lilt of surprise in her uptake of this news. "Why, that should offer a diversity in lifestyles."

Bruce replied, "It does. I'm not sure what that nomenclature stands for these days. My father had a farm, and he was a farmer all his life. I am the eldest son, and the farm was passed on to me. I have a brother, and he went north and has made a career in the automobile business. My sister married and moved to a town further east. Her husband has a farm, but like me, he doesn't live on it. He rents the house and land."

Lou closed the heavy black top on the gas grill, hung the turning fork by a leather loop on a side hook, then pulled out a chair and joined them.

"We've got a real family saga. My parents have a place twenty miles east. They're still farming some. But it's not as profitable these days. Times past, raising tobacco was a natural way to go, or it was an accepted crop by just about everybody. But it's not always viewed favorably now. Fortunately, Dad has always had other business interests." Lou tilted his head and drained his glass.

Amy smiled at him then turned to Nola. "Now, you know where our roots are. Would you like to tell us about yours?" The question was simply stated without pressure of an answer.

"I'm not farm rooted, but I am from a small town southeast of Windermere. Grayson. My family was in textiles."

"Oh," said Lou. "I know Grayson has some mills, but tell me, is it mostly dependent on industry?"

"There are no textile or industrial giants there as in Windermere. However, I think it's still safe to say that the town's numerous mills, many quite small operations, provide its economic stability." She focused her attention on Lou then Bruce. "But the town is surrounded by farms. Drive beyond the city limits and you'll see fenced-in homeplaces, many of which are still actively farmed."

Bruce joined the conversation. "And they wish to stay outside the city limits?"

"Right," she agreed. "A matter of taxes. Amy, the county does have a first-rate hospital now. I saw a couple of ads on television last week about some of their outstanding departments."

Amy asked, "Are you thinking about going back to Grayson now that you're retired?" When Nola didn't immediately reply, Amy quickly spoke. "Of course, I hope you'll stay here. But at least there would be a good place for you to volunteer."

"I've been in Windermere half my life and it feels like home. Amy, one advantage of being retired is the options one has about the future. There are so many paths and multiple destinations."

"Why, Nola, what interesting and comforting thoughts. I'll keep options, paths, and destinations in mind when I plan seminars for the center. Thanks." Amy's face glowed. "So Dad, what brought you to Groton and Windermere?"

Bruce leaned back in his chair. "The farm. I had a meeting set up in Groton for the afternoon and decided to go earlier and have lunch with Robert. Nola, that's my son. Since he was available, I called here to find out if I could come over. The point of talking to you both is that I have an offer for the farm and the house."

With a slight gasp, Amy said, "No? Did you have it on the market?"

"I didn't. Even though neither of you had indicated any interest in going back there, I would have talked it over with you first. No. I had a phone call from Larry Becker. You remember him. He married Tamara Spruil from over by Running Brook community."

"I do. Lou knows them well, too. They've been down on the coast, haven't they?" Amy replied.

"They planned a weekend scouting around Raleigh and stopped in Acorn for gas. Larry struck up a conversation with Billy at the station about property. Billy told them he should drive down our road. That there was some prime property along it. He didn't know if any was for sale, but one could get a feel for what good farmland was in the area. So Larry, taking Billy's advice, drove past our farm and saw the For Rent sign, stopped, backed up and he and the family got out to look the place over."

"Dad, I didn't know the Stubbs were leaving. What's happened?"

"They have a few years on them and wanted to make a change while they were still able to learn new skills. They vacated the premises about three weeks ago after they had harvested the crops."

Lou said. "The Beckers put in a bid to buy?"

"Yes. It's a good offer, so I believe they're serious about returning to the area. His dad still works his farm. From what Larry says, he's healthy and hearty and strong as many men younger than he. But Larry wants some land of his own to farm now. His wife wants to be closer to her family. They're expecting again." Bruce stopped and looked at Amy.

Amy didn't blink. "They had two kids the last I heard."

"Soon there'll be three," Bruce added. He saw Lou stare at Amy, who didn't give him a glance.

"What did you want to ask us? Robert and me."

"Do either of you want the house or the farm?"

She thought a minute with her head bowed, her hands clasped together. Nola made a move to rise. Amy put out a hand, so Nola remained.

"Lou and I have discussed staying here or returning to Acorn or moving to Raleigh. We decided to stay in Windermere. We like it here. It doesn't mean we will ever stop loving the east and the farms where we grew up, but being we're from 'settling people' we decided to transplant some roots in the Piedmont." She leaned forward, extended her left hand as far as possible, crossing over Nola. Bruce sat up and clasped her hand. Nola held her breath as if the familial bond touched her. "Dad, so much of our heart will always be in Acorn and wherever you are, for you're home to me, to us."

Bruce's eyes became moist, his lips pressed together, and he squeezed Amy's hand. As he released his daughter's hand, Nola experienced the warmth of his arm and hand as he slowly leaned back, careful that not a bronzed hair of his arm grazed hers. Nevertheless, the sensation of the gesture burned into her soul.

Lou watched the scene with vibrant emotions of his own. He controlled his reactions and his countenance. From the first few days of knowing Amy in school, he was aware of the love her family had for one another. Amy's love and respect for Bruce had developed her capacity for devotion and love that a husband so desired. The ten years of marriage had been happy and agreeable, but seeing this closeness, this father-child bonding sent a shock to his gut. Envy! He'd never felt such a yearning. A sin, he knew. But he couldn't squelch the words from his cognition: God, I want a child with Amy. I want an heir . . . someone who will look at me like Amy looks at him. Someone that no other man will come between.

Pushing himself out of the chair, Lou went to the table and refilled his glass. "Anybody else still thirsty?" The others shook their heads. "So what did Robert say?"

"The same as Amy. He and Susan have made their home in Groton."

"Well, I agree with Amy. We're too far away to try to take on overseeing the farm in any dependable manner. It surely is a good piece of this earth though," Lou declared.

"So, you're going to sell it to Larry?" Amy asked.

"As neither of you want it, I think this is a good offer and timely."

Everyone was quiet. A last call of the birds resounded. Faint whispers rasped from dried tulip poplars. Locus fiddled in giant oaks.

"I'll miss knowing I can go back and run barefooted over the fine loamy soil between crop rows or sit on the old rope swing out in the backyard. Or pluck apples from the tree, grapes from the arbor, or gather pecans in the grove. It won't be long until they fall, will it." Amy spoke wistfully, somewhat collapsed against the cushions.

Bruce tightened all his muscles then dropped his jaw as if to speak.

"Dad, I have good memories. If I indulge myself once in a while, promise you'll never flog yourself. Never regret you didn't hang onto it for us to take rare sentimental journeys." She brought herself upright. "I'll be fine. It's just that the news of parting with the farm is such a surprise."

She stood up and walked behind Lou's chair. She leaned over and put her arms around his neck. "Now, I have my – our – place where we're making lots of good memories, too. Like the pleasant one tonight." She kissed the top of Lou's head. "Thanks, honey."

He turned his head and kissed her arm, his eyes accepting the appreciation. "The steaks should be ready. Everybody hungry?"

While Lou tended to the meat, the others brought the remaining foods from the kitchen to the deck. They ate and chatted and finished with leisurely cups of coffee.

"I thank you all for inviting me to share this evening. Now, I shall be going to my own little house," Nola said. "And I will look anew at it, taking memories of this pleasant evening." She rose and being that Bruce did likewise, she could say directly toward him as he stood only a foot away. "I enjoyed meeting you, too, Bruce."

"Likewise." He extended his hand. She put hers forward. As they shook hands, he asked, "May I see you to the car?"

"Thank you, yes. Lou, the steak was delicious. It was perfectly grilled. May I help you clean up?" He answered no, so she said, "Amy, I'll see you at ten tomorrow morning at the center."

Amy walked over and gave her an affectionate hug. "Thanks again for the pie."

She and Lou followed Nola and Bruce through the house where Nola picked up the pie container and her handbag. They stayed in the house while Bruce walked out the front door with Nola.

"What do you think? Did your dad and your friend get along?"

"They seemed to. Look, they're admiring Dad's car." Amy pointed toward the picture window.

He started to say something but she spoke first. "He's opening the door for her. Gosh, Lou, she has a car. Surely she drove here!"

Hearing her surprise that the two may want to continue the evening, he refrained from the jesting he had planned about the looks between them. He knew Amy was considerably more alert about nuances than most people thought she was. Perhaps tonight, her interests were captured with talk of selling the farm or even the death of the Kester woman she knew. Whatever, his plans did not include riling her. If it weren't for Bruce's overnight with them, he'd be carrying Amy straightaway down the hall, having been stirred by her tender comments and affection on the deck and being she was very relaxed. How grateful he was for the private bedroom arrangements and soundproof building materials.

They worked together in companionable quietness clearing up the dishes.

Outside, while Nola sat in the passenger seat, Bruce leaned inward and pointed some of the features of the console as he had done earlier with Amy. Nola spoke enthusiastically of the innovations.

"Would you like to take a quick ride? I know you said you had to be on your way." He waited expectantly.

"Yes, I'd like that," she smiled at him. He closed the door and hastened around the car and into the driver's seat.

As they made their way down the road, she commented, "Smooth ride. Cambridge is an attractive development. The architecture is varied, but the houses complement each other."

"They do. Amy and Lou selected the lot then the house plans. Overall, they were pleased with the builder. They had the opportunity to check on the progress every few days."

"Amy spoke nostalgically about the farm. I'm glad she has so much undeveloped land behind their house. When the center's been open a year, she'll have more time to putter around outside. Plant a flower bed, stake a few tomatoes."

"She really likes the challenge of the center."

"She does and she's up to the task. Very creative. Quick to realize a topic that is suitable for the membership. And she works very hard."

He glanced at her. "Nola, you don't have to sell me. But I do appreciate hearing someone else's praise of my girl."

"I did go on a bit. She such a nice person that I expected her husband to be nice also. And I feel good that my assumption was correct. Am I sounding too much like a schoolteacher?" Now she turned toward him.

"I couldn't say. I've been away from the classroom so long. Expectations, assumptions, maybe; but the word *correct* rings like a school bell. Many connotations, Miss Nola," he joked.

"Well, thanks be, I left before I was called that!"

Realizing he may have treaded on a sore spot, he tried to make amends. "I would conclude that you took early retirement."

She was thoughtful for a few moments. "Actually, I spent twenty-five years in the school system here. I came right after college. I liked teaching very much." She paused and turned toward him again. "I gave myself a year."

He waited, glancing toward her. When the traffic permitted, he pulled over to the side of the road and stopped, engine idling. "And?"

"That's all." She stared at him then asked, "Are you recalling the paths and destinations from the talk on the deck?"

He nodded. She continued. "It has been months used to be lazy, to set few time schedules, to explore the city and its cultural offerings. To unwind. To walk and think or not think. The freedom has been marvelous."

"No path taken, no destinations immediately in sight?" he asked and she smiled without commitment. "How about a drive in the mountains tomorrow? The forecast is for sun and mideighties. We could put the top down."

"I have to help Amy tomorrow at ten." Thoughtfully, she scrunched her face. "The seminar will end at eleven, and I could be out by eleven thirty."

"What time may I pick you up?"

Her eyes brightened and her voice was lush. "Twelve thirty. I'll run by the deli and have them pack a picnic. There are a couple of state parks off the expressway."

"Sounds great. There's a city map in the door beside you. And a light overhead. Locate your street. Draw a circle around where you live. There's a pad and pencil in the glove compartment. Would you write the street and number? And your telephone in case I make a wrong turn."

She searched the map, circled and jotted his requests; she deduced that he never made a wrong turn. Finished, she put the pencil and map away. He headed the car back to Amy's street.

After he parked and walked her to her car, she reached in her handbag for her keys. He moved very close as if to know how far he could enter her space. She showed no apprehension or sign of alarm; she felt the keys, searching for the right one by touch. Only her fingers moved. The high-security lights reflected the glossiness of her blouse, the apricot lipglaze, and the sheen of her long hair. He felt the heat of night between them and knew his own rising temperature was adding to the torpid waves. She breathed easily, quietly, but slow and deep. When she found the key she wanted, she began to lower her empty hand. He reached and clasped it, held it in the narrow space between them.

"I'm glad you came tonight. I look forward to the drive tomorrow." He squeezed and released her hand and stepped back.

She turned to unlock and open the door. Before seating herself, she spoke softly as befitted the night. "I'm glad you came and are staying over."

He watched her pull out into the street and waved as she disappeared in the night. Stepping up the drive and front walkway, he considered the good fortune at having an offer for the farm and affirmation that his son and daughter were in agreement. But he attributed elevation in his heartbeat to anticipation of tomorrow and pure excitement to a retired schoolteacher – lovely and available. Thank you, God, for early retirement!

Chapter 8

Bruce Braddock checked the circled block on the Windermere map before folding and placing it in the door pocket on his side of the car. The even house numbers were on the right on Glamis Drive. He proceeded slowly toward Nola's house number 1800.

The residential section was one of the finer older areas. Homes ranged from half-million dollars to around one hundred ninety thousand in current valuation. Glamis Drive displayed a variety of architectural styles and prices. Tall, well-crowned maples and oaks stood right-away distance from the street, deep green giants giving shade to the tarmac and the grassy front lawns. Beyond their circumference, smaller trees including the native dogwood and imported red maples afforded the fronts of the houses relief from the sun and a mode of privacy from passing on-lookers.

Bruce was impressed with the view. The neighborhood indicated a level of prosperity, regular maintenance to the grounds and the houses, and individuality. Altogether, the appearance was one of a comfortable haven. He had to admire a single woman who chose this section. His curiosity heightened about this retired schoolteacher, Nola Gilbert. He knew the range of state teachers' pay, and this place would take some stretch.

He pulled into the driveway. Her car was not in sight. Getting out, he looked to the front of the house and the door was opened. A full-plated glass door stood guard. He advanced up the curved flagstone walkway along which the grass was neatly cut and edged. Three steps with wrought iron railings rose to a flagged porch where iron-legged-

and-armed benches were placed either side of the door. Iron tables topped with geraniums, an umbrella stand, and a large mailbox completed the tableau.

He rang the doorbell and stood back. The brass numerals 1800 shone on the lintel. Suddenly, a thought hit him: did she live alone? He hadn't asked and Amy hadn't said. This was obviously a house built for more than one person. Two-story, brick, shutters that closed, large chimney with two smoke stacks, shake roof – the architect intended a long existence for his handiwork.

Nola entered the long hall from the right. A rear door opposite the front was open and through a full-length glass door, he caught a glimpse of potted red blossoms on a patio or terrace and large trees. Again, he admired her graceful walk as she came forward.

Smiling, she opened the door. "Hello, Bruce. Come in, please."

He entered and closed the door behind him. "Hello. You're looking ready for a drive in the country. I hope you weren't too rushed?" He noticed she had on a white shirtwaist dress with a collar and three-quarter-length sleeves and flat-heel shoes. The sun wouldn't burn her neck or arms and she could maneuver gravel in parking areas.

"And you, too." She scanned his neat tan, twill slacks and blue-and-white-striped shirt. "You're right on time, so the directions were clear?"

"Yes. I haven't driven in this section before. I'm quite impressed. It's one of the older areas that didn't get demolished as the city grew outward."

"True. Much as we're not overjoyed with the mushrooming of shopping centers on the fringes of town, they perhaps spared some of the older developments. Of course, we generally don't describe the older sections as developments, but most likely there were several lots sold from big estates at some point. The day is nice for a drive."

"The forecasters called it correctly."

"The picnic basket is in the kitchen," she said and started to turn. "May I help you with it?" he asked. "Thank you." She retraced her steps down the hall.

A long Persian runner covered the center of the highly polished oak floor. Their footfalls were muffled. He recognized this was a house designed for the southern climate, opposing doors and windows to allow for breezes to blow through, and updated most assuredly with air-conditioning and double-paned windows for summer and winter climate insulation.

He caught only glimpses of the large living room to his left and considered it a blend of formal and comfortable in off-white, deep blue, and bit of rose. A carpet matched the one he was treading. The dining room to the right was centered with a rectangular table featuring rounded corners with high-backed chairs all about, buffets and hunt tables to the sides.

"Your home is lovely. Well planned for the weather and seasons." He slowed and paused at the rear door. "Quite a view you have. Peaceful. Shady, but still open."

She stepped to his side and looked out. "I keep shrubbery to the property line. And trees pruned so there's sun to help grass grow," she stated. "The view is not as expansive or pastoral as Amy's."

Quickly, he interjected. "But the effect is private and pleasant and also open."

"Thank you. Those are the adjectives I strive for." She took a step toward the kitchen and added, "I'd like more flower beds, a herb garden. Perhaps next year."

She went into the kitchen and stopped at the table in the center where a hamper stood open. "This year has been a gift to myself. Mostly relaxing. I think the order is complete." Her hands moved a few of the containers aside as if she were tallying the items. "If you'd like to take this, I can manage the thermos of iced tea and water and the ice bucket."

"Why don't I take the hamper first and come back for the beverages?"

"Great. I'll get a scarf."

She made her way down a shorter hall to the right of the kitchen while he continued down the hall and through the front door. He placed the hamper on the backseat of the car. Looking toward the house, he reckoned that the wing on the left could be a bedroom or den. It would be the way she had turned. How convenient, he thought. The bedrooms upstairs would be quite large unless there were four instead of the usual three.

Back inside, he walked to the kitchen and picked up the thermoses and the ice bucket. "Anything else?" he asked as she emerged from the hallway.

"That should do it." She closed the back door and clicked the deadbolt. Over an arm, she carried a tote bag and a chiffon scarf of varying shades of blue.

He opened the glass door and held it while she pulled the other one shut, locked it and dropped the key into the bag.

"How do you feel about the top down?" he asked.

Enthusiastically, she replied. "I'd like that."

He released the latches and eased the top back and down. Finished, he said with humor, "Amy scolded me yesterday for a hot seat. She suggested I have towels or some seat protection. My compromise was to keep the top on during the morning." Opening the door for her, he said, "Let me know if the leather gets too warm."

"I will. This is lovely. The car and the day." She leaned over and said conspiratorially, "The neighbors will be wondering about the handsome stranger and the luxury convertible."

"You don't mind, do you?"

"No. It's fun to surprise them." They rode a few blocks as if happy in the sunshine and the expectation of a delicious lunch and an enjoyable afternoon. "My neighbors are really nice people, Bruce. I wouldn't trade for any others. And I am willing to give them a few hours of gossip and guessing who you are. I trust you accept that is said in good spirit."

"I do. But I venture to say this is not the first gentleman caller to drive up to 1800." He turned to her.

"No."

"A beautiful woman like you . . ."

Her expression turned serious, her voice deepened. "Please, no accounting of friends we may have had, loves, and losses." She raised her chin and sideways looked over her shoulder. "This will be a fun day. It's glorious. The sun and the air feel so divine." She touched his arm gently. He tightened his hand on the steering wheel. "Later, we can share histories, if it comes to that?"

He nodded. As she slowly withdrew her hand, he took one hand from the wheel and clasped hers. Still focused on the road, he pulled her hand to his lips and kissed it. Lowering his hand and before releasing hers, he said, "You are wise. Not just as a teacher, but as woman. This is a day for living, not reliving."

She leaned back on the warming leather, breathed as if relieved. Her face began to glow, her lips to gloss, and her expression to soften. She sensed he was staring at her.

"Is my cavalier watching the road?" Her voice was melodious.

"Only when I have to." He laughed.

She smiled. "And to think I am trusting my life to you at this moment. Be a good, forward-looking scout."

Reluctantly, he kept his eyes on the highway while he pulled into the moving traffic. In his mind's eye, he rewound the expression of her face, labeling it the most desirable he had seen. He felt inflated that he had helped it come to be.

Three-quarters of an hour later, they entered a state park and stopped near the picnic tables. He placed the hamper atop one, and she withdrew two cups and filled them with tea. They leisurely consumed the chicken salad, sandwiches, potato salad, fruit cup, and chess tarts. After dumping the containers, paper ware, and utensils into the park trash barrel, they strolled along one of the nature trails.

Though one side of the path was cleared with a low stout rail to keep viewers from crouching too near the edge of the cliff, the other was bordered with volunteer seedlings from nearby trees growing on the banks. The clearings opened to views of the land they had just traveled over. The lush summer greenery spread to the horizon, creating a fresh, calming effect. In unspoken agreement, they continued up the path. The hard-packed earth had a film of granite dust that barely showed the imprint of their shoes. The incline being easy to walk – not breath robbing – and wide enough for three people to negotiate side by side; they conversed easily about the views, the trees, and the birds sighted.

The walk back to the car was more rapid. He spread the map on the trunk. "There's an interesting river here," he pointed and she bent to see. "There are two state bridges several miles apart, but almost in the middle here's a mark with a notation. Low-water bridge is one that can be traveled when the water level is low. However, after a heavy rain, the bridge may be underwater." He turned toward her and his shoulder grazed hers.

Her head eased around so that she looked directly at him scarcely a hand away. "It should be dry today. There's been no rain for several days."

"Shall we give it a try?"

"As the young say, let's go for it."

He deemed her smile genuine, but beguiling. "So we shall."

Along the secondary roads, she continued to take in the scenery and admitted these byways were new to her. He asked if she wanted the top up being that they had been in full sun for most of the drive. She shook her head and her hair tossed side to side.

Before they reached the river, she asked, "Could we stop at a fast-food place in the next town? I'm not hungry, but before crossing the river, a restroom break would be nice."

"There should be one a mile or two up the road. Economic conditions must be stable in this county. The farms are well tended. Fences upright, houses painted. This particular section's main use of land appears to be for dairies," he commented.

"And the cattle are unusual. I've never noticed tan-colored cows before. Quite a variety in that field over there, to the right. And they are bunched together and peering this way." She spoke, surprise mixed with humor. "They could be seeing a Mercedes-Benz convertible for the first time."

He laughed. "Or standing for a turn at the water trough."

As they rounded a curve, he saw an increase in the number of houses and a quarter of a mile further he spotted small golden arches on a tall standard near the road.

"There's a place just ahead. Would you like a Coke or water here?" He drove into the parking lot and stopped near the door.

"A Coke to go sounds great."

He ordered while she went into the ladies room. The clerk was handing him two tall cups, as she returned. She took both cups then walked to the self-service counter and picked up paper napkins and straws. Waiting for him, she looked out the front window. She saw a highway sign and realized a highway intersected the secondary road they were following. Golden Arches and the other fast-food places had really reached out to serve travelers coming and going. And she had asked for a fast-food place, hadn't she? Years ago on a meandering trip or even on a busy road, one was more apt to see a mom-and-pop grocery store or a service station with a gas pump, or at most two, at the side of the road. And one hoped there'd be a clean bathroom. Such an old place would seem more appropriate in this lovely, rural setting. Surely, there had to be some remnant of the past tucked in these hills. While they were in the mountains, this route they had chosen must be near the top. They were driving up and down, circling age-rounded peaks.

Softly, behind her, Bruce said, "What do you think of the countryside?"

"Serene. Home of people who love their land and privacy. And neighbors a short hike away." She turned as he came beside her. "Or if they're very modern, a quick acceleration around the curve."

"Well, shall we see what waits beyond the next hill?" He opened the door and they returned to the car. "Let me know if you want the top raised."

"I will. After the river maybe. Up this high, we might hear its rippling or the rushing sounds." She handed him a cup and straw. Poking her straw through the lid, she sipped the Coke.

After he drank several swallows, he inserted the cup in the nearest holder. She placed hers next to it.

Winding down the narrow road, she pointed to a herd of cattle catching late-afternoon sun on the side of a steep hillside. "Ah! A magnificent still-life picture." She corrected her analogy. "I know it's of something alive, but they are like statues. I doubt that a painter could pose anything so breathtakingly real!"

Curious, he glanced at her and slowed as much as he felt safe for the car was approaching a sharp curve. "Are you sure you didn't grow up in the country?"

"If I had, I may not be quite so ecstatic." After some minutes of quietness, she spoke. "Tell me about your farm."

"It's unlike this area. Our land east is mostly flat. One commonality is the varying soils. I see clay and rich dirt here. We have that, too. We have a river not too far away and a good rainfall most years. There are barns for livestock which we don't have much of now. Years ago, we kept cows and Amy and Robert had horses. Our chief crop has been tobacco. We raise corn and other marketable vegetables. My wife liked flowers and supplied a few shops with cut flowers from spring to late fall. I would till gardens and prepare the beds. My own preference was roses. She said they were too much trouble and she left those to me. In the evening, I would inspect the beds, deadhead the spent flowers snapping off the hips, spray, or pick the bugs and beetles off."

"Did you leave them all in the garden?"

"I cut roses as long as they bloomed, stuck them in whatever vase was handy, and set them on any vacant tabletop." He stopped then asked, "Are you allergic to roses?"

"No. I like their fragrance. Someday I hope to have roses near the patio so I can enjoy the scents. Perhaps I may ask this for it doesn't delve into the past, but are you ready to give up the farm?"

"I think it's time. The children don't want it. There are no grandchildren to leave it to. I stay busy in the city. Since I had the same good manager for so many years, he will be hard to replace. I'd have to do all the telling of how I like the place run."

"Will you miss a home to return to?"

"I think not. I have many old friends in Acorn. If I get a hankering to see the place, I can visit up and down the road." He smiled at her. "I've lived in Raleigh for nine years. I have an apartment there that is quite comfortable. I bought it while Amy was in college. Before I had a manager, I'd stay on the farm a few days, then in the city. But after I had someone reliable and worked with him a few months, I let him and his family live in the house, and I came out once or twice a week and we'd exchange ideas and decide priorities."

"Sounds very businesslike and congenial."

"It was." He slowed the car and pulled to the far side of the road onto a narrow, sandy strip in front of an old, weathered gray building with a front porch protected by a slanted, tin roof. He leaned right; Nola pressed her back tightly against the seat. "Shelton's Store. The sign is barely readable. Does it give any hours?"

She sat forward to turn and squint at the lettering. "Saturday 8 to

8, Sunday 1 to 6. Isn't that strange for opening?" Turning again, she was a mere few inches from his face.

So close they could feel each other's breath, see curiosity in their eyes. As he said, "Yes," and she repeated, "strange," an agreeable tension was evident.

Suddenly, but quietly, he directed, "Listen."

She sat very still, at first straining, then detecting a sound, she whispered. "The river. Do you hear it?"

"I do. And the trees."

"They're rustling. Can we drive on? The water can't be running so rapidly it'll cover the bridge." Her tones were eager. She leaned forward forgetting he was so close. Her breast pressed against his arm. Instantly, she angled away.

Bruce moved in the driver's position and released the handbrake. Checking the rearview mirror and seeing no traffic, he lifted his foot from the brake and allowed the car to slowly roll forward down the deep slope, flanked on either side by tall trees from which spidery Spanish moss hung, dangling, blown by gusts of wind, as if in search of tangible forms to grasp. Lower branches, broken from trunks and lying askew among the dried weeds, were unreachable. The car crept downhill. Through openness between the mossy curtains, the river moved into view.

Twenty yards ahead, they glimpsed the water splashing over and around rocks rising high in the riverbed. Not gigantic rocks, but large and numerous, a few feet higher than the rushing water. The sound increased as if nature had turned the volume high in speakers right, front, and left.

Nola inhaled and brought her right hand up and clenched her fist against her shirtwaist bodice. "How marvelous! What a sight!" She stretched her left hand toward Bruce. He clasped it and held it tightly.

He was silent, physically expanding. "A natural wonder. Why has no one publicized this river? And the bridge? It is low. The bed and the guards along the side. Hardly a foot and a half."

"Would the people using this route be marooned if the water covered the bridge?"

"If the river flows over a few inches, probably the cars could still drive across," he surmised.

Skeptically, Nola scrutinized the wide river racing from a source she didn't know to a destination she could not see. Not impeded by the multitude of rocks darkened from years of battering nor the bridge stretched a few scant feet above, the river stayed its course.

Unless he was to back up and turn around in the driveway of an abandoned house on the left bank, Bruce knew that he had to move forward.

"Are we satiated? Ready to go on?"

"Cross the bridge? Look, there's a truck coming down the hill!" she pointed. "What if he drives on the bridge while we're on it?"

With a small laugh, he replied. "He won't."

"How can you know?"

"There's a pull-off just before the bridge. He'll let us go on." Bruce put the gear in low and aimed for the center of the bridge. "Are you game?"

"What if he does come on the bridge?"

"It's only wide enough for one car at a time." He heard her gasp. "See, he's pulling off the road. He's probably local and done this more times than he can recall."

Reluctantly, Bruce released her hand to have both of his on the wheel. He kept his sight on the road ahead. Nola pivoted and watched the water. Then she turned in the seat and looked back as they exited the bridge. Bruce returned the hand wave of the older driver with weathered skin and a ruddiness of an outdoor worker. The man had grinned as if this was a maiden crossing of Low Water Bridge for the couple.

Nola settled again in a forward position. "Wasn't that a beautiful sight? And the air smells so fresh, so full of evergreens. Pines, cedar, boxwood. So sensuous. What a find you made on that map."

He glanced at her. "I'm glad you liked it. As you said, an unpublicized state treasure."

"Do you think the people want to keep it a secret? Unspoiled with heavy traffic?"

"Yes. That would require a new bridge, and Low Water Bridge and its challenges would be demolished."

She lifted her chin and slightly pursed her lips. "Yes, a challenge when two vehicles meet. Do you think the teens dare each other to drive across when the river overflows the bridge?"

"Probably a traditional rite of passage up here. For the males," he offered.

"Excitement for the date beside him and commendations following a safe crossing."

With exaggerated scrutiny, he looked at her. "And?"

"Oh, yes sir, thank you for navigating Low Bridge today."

They laughed in harmony. The landscape took on a more level view as the secondary road joined another state road. Several miles further, a left turn led them down an access ramp to the expressway. Traffic was heavy with people running late errands and returning home from work.

With Windermere's tall buildings peaking on the skyline, Bruce asked, "Would you like to have dinner with me?"

Surprised, she turned to him. "Are you staying over?"

"I'd like to. I didn't hear of any other reservations for Dad's room."

"Yes. I'd like that. What time did you have in mind?"

"How about seven?" She nodded. He added, "Good. I'll check in at Amy's and pick you up then."

Nola's mouth had an upward turn that reminded Bruce of someone who had just bitten into a piece of chocolate and found it filled with her favorite flavor. Once more, he harbored the feeling he had a part in bringing the pleased expression.

Enjoying her thoughts privately, she replayed scenes of the day beginning with his appearance at her door. Tall, attractive, well dressed, alertness in his eyes, cordial, polite, mannerly – so much favorable before he even spoke. Then she permitted, to glide through her inner ear, echoes of his eastern tones in well-cultured words that would find favor anywhere. The day had been continuous harmony. Talk came easy and silence was comfortable. What had he said as we started this adventure? Let it be for living. She had to control a desire to purr for the fulfilled request.

Chapter 9

Amy finished her lunch at the sandwich shop and glanced at her ticket. She swallowed the last of the iced tea then delved into her wallet for bills and change. Usually, someone from the center, volunteer or a friend, joined her when she ate in the mall, but today Nola had left early to pick up a picnic basket for the mountain trip and the staff was tied up otherwise.

After paying the cashier, Amy walked back to the center. Phyllis was talking with a man at the desk. As she spotted Amy approaching, Phyllis motioned to her.

Amy stopped at the end of the counter.

Phyllis said, "Amy, this is Detective Smith. He wants to speak with you."

"Hello. I'm Amy Umstead, director of Healthy Living."

He extended his right hand. "Hello. I'm Jim Smith. May I have a few words with you?"

Amy appreciated his firm, brief handshake and direct eye contact. Neither made her feel threatened. However, having exchanged introductions with so many men in her jobs, she realized he was aware of her physically – posture, gestures, voice, and signs of emotions – and sizing her up. She, too, took in his neat appearance. He was alert, not wary while absorbing first impressions, with an openness that she would not have expected in a detective.

"Yes. Shall we go into my office?" She turned and he followed her. She swiveled her desk chair to face the open area and indicated a seat nearby. "Will you sit down, sir?"

"Thank you. I understand Bessie Kester attended a lecture here yesterday afternoon."

"Yes, she did."

"Has she been here before? For programs?"

"She has been to several."

"She was someone you recognized then?"

"Yes." Amy did not comment further.

"Did you notice anything unusual about her? Her behavior, was it different from what you'd previously noticed?" Smith asked his questions in an even tone, being professional in manner, straightforward without implications or leading to a viewpoint. He was a well-built man, in his late forties, projecting an image of self-control. His blue jacket and twill trousers, as well as his white shirt, appeared to be freshly pressed in spite of the early-afternoon high temperature.

"Mrs. Kester tended to be consistent in her manner and her appearance," Amy noted.

"Could you describe what they were?" Smith opened his notebook and clicked his ballpoint pen.

"Yes. She wore a white blouse and a skirt. She sat in the third row from the front on the left side. From there, she could read the overhead screen and see the presenter easily." She paused as he wrote a few words. "After the lecture, during the question-and-answer time, she often asked a number of questions. She did so yesterday."

"Did she seem upset by the answers?"

"No. But she tends to ask several follow-up questions."

Smith looked at her keenly. "Did she ask so many that the audience became annoyed with her?"

Hesitant but relenting, she answered. "Yes. She would monopolize the session."

"Any particular person so annoyed that he would want to 'tell her off' or waylay her after she left?"

Shocked, Amy replied, "Oh no. Our members, especially those who attend seminars, are the nicest people. They are very respectful in their manner. Some give her quick glances, maybe a few frowns, but they don't continue to stare or make unkind remarks."

Smith continued. "Did she come by herself or with a friend?"

"Always by herself."

"What topics did she come to hear?"

"Heart seminars."

Smith wrote a few more lines. "Did she have heart trouble?"

"Not that we know of. She gave the impression that her husband had problems. Often, she spoke of him as an invalid and that caring for him confined her to the home. She indicated that coming here was a break for her."

"Could I take a look at the room where the lecture was held yesterday?"

Amy stood. "I'll show you now. There's nothing scheduled for the auditorium."

He stood and walked behind her to the auditorium. Amy stopped at the row and pointed to the chair Bessie had occupied. She indicated the overhead screen and the podium where the presenter had stood. Smith looked around.

"Were you in the room the entire lecture?"

"I was. I introduced Dr. Belding, a cardiologist, then I sat two rows behind on the end seat."

He turned and looked. "And you noticed nothing unusual?"

"No. A volunteer sat beside me. I could ask her if she noticed anything."

"Thank you. Let me know if she says she did. A couple more questions. Did she leave alone or did you see her at any time after she left the center?"

"I was up at the podium talking with Dr. Belding immediately after the program, but I have no recollection of her leaving with anyone, and I did not see her later."

"Thank you for your time. If anything comes to mind that seemed different about Mrs. Kester yesterday, you can call me at this number." He wrote a phone number, tore the page from his notebook, and handed it to her.

"Has the cause of death been determined, sir?"

"Not yet." He expected the report to be on his desk this afternoon. He refrained from sharing mere expectations.

"The newspaper stated there was no evidence of foul play. I hope it will be from natural causes." Amy spoke with concern and sincerity.

"We all do. Good afternoon," he said and walked from the auditorium through the reception room and into the mall corridor, surveying the surroundings right, left, and ahead.

Amy walked to the reception desk to check if Detective Smith had questioned the women. Phyllis said he had, but she really didn't have much to comment about. Joyce said, "I didn't see him. I was out for lunch. All I could have told him was that I saw her get some water from the pitcher and take a pill."

Amy said, "I wonder if that's important. But we wouldn't know what she took."

Joyce replied, "Not me. She never discussed her medications with me. Maybe something for high blood pressure."

"I didn't know she had that," commented Amy.

"Well, she often had it monitored when she came in. But it was never alarmingly high. She didn't even record the reading. More or less shrugged and got up. Never said 'thank you' like most do who come in and have it checked."

Amy thought a few seconds. "Well, I'm sure the doctor or medics who saw her will follow up about any health problems or conditions."

She returned to her office and Phyllis answered the ringing phone and Joyce stood up to take a blood pressure reading for a couple, a man and woman, who had walked in. They were regular drop-ins and she cheerfully called them by name.

Amy pulled into the driveway and was surprised that Lou's car was not there. Neither was her father's. As she lifted her briefcase and handbag from the front seat and closed the sedan door, she surmised that Bruce had mostly likely gone back to Raleigh after the mountain trip.

Unlocking the front door, she called out, "Anybody here?" No answer.

She went to the family area and dropped her case on the table and walked onto her bedroom and put her handbag on the dresser. After kicking off her shoes and removing her earrings and necklace, she crossed the hall and looked into her father's room. His bag and laptop were still there.

Back in her room, she changed into shorts and a tee shirt then stretched out on the bed. She lifted her arms high overhead and fully extended her legs and feet before curling on her side and closing her eyes.

Ten minutes later, the back door opened and closed. She recognized Lou's footsteps. Lazily, she waited, knowing he would come down the hall having seen her car.

His steady tread, muffled by the carpet, ceased at the doorway.

"I'm awake," she spoke quietly and opened her eyes.

"Hi. Have a busy day?" She watched him loosen his tie as he approached the bed.

"Yes. And you? You're later than usual."

He sat down beside her. "A screw-up with an order, but it's settled now. Is your dad gone?"

"No. I thought he was when I didn't see his car. Golly, I hope he didn't have any trouble with the car. You know how new cars have their quirks."

"He'd call us if there was a major problem."

"But I thought they'd be back by now."

Lou tossed his tie aside and unbuttoned his shirt then lay down beside her. "Is that why I see the worry furrow?" he asked as he traced a finger up the crease between her brows.

"I'm sorry it shows. The worry. It isn't Dad. It's Mrs. Kester's death. The police were in the center today. They aren't saying exactly what caused her death. An officer asked me some questions. But I really couldn't give him any information other than what the staff had told him yesterday."

He continued to rub the furrow gently. "Well, let's not borrow trouble. It was probably a routine visit. I know you're concerned, because she was one of your members. And you had seen her only a few hours earlier, but let the medical people and security shoulder the concern and find the cause."

He moved his hand, kissed her forehead, and placed his arm around her. She snuggled against him.

"Thanks for listening. I feel so safe when you hold me." She stroked his chest.

Tightening his arm against her back, he held her close knowing what she needed now was comfort. "I love you."

"I know. I love you, too," she said very softly and kissed his chin before moving her head back. She closed her eyes and slowly her muscles began to relax.

Twenty minutes later, the back door opened and closed. A cupboard was opened, followed by water running from a faucet.

Lou said, "Bruce must be home." He rose from the bed and walked down the hall, closing the bedroom door. Amy rose and went in the bathroom to freshen up.

"Hi, Bruce, how was the drive?" Lou asked as he entered the family area.

"Very nice. We had a picnic up at a state park off the expressway and took some secondary roads in the mountains." He set the empty glass on the counter. "If you have no reservations for my bedroom, I'd like to stay another night."

Lou's eyes glinted. "No one has dibs on it."

Lou did not ask why; however, Bruce knew his son-in-law well enough to know he'd be curious. "Nola and I are going out for dinner." No shirker, Bruce met his gaze.

"Sounds great." He waited for more information.

"Is there a new place you'd recommend? If not, we'll go into the Plaza."

"There are a couple of new places that we've tried and liked. One is downtown in the Historic West area. Another is off the expressway and in a shopping center. It's a classy place for dinner." Lou offered the choices easily and leaned back on the counter.

"Thanks. I'll mention the Plaza and the downtown restaurant to her. See if she has a preference. Amy's home?"

"She is. And a bit uptight. The police had been in about the woman found dead in the parking lot. So Amy had a short nap."

"Good that she could relax. I'll go check my e-mail if I may use the telephone line for fifteen minutes or so. Then I'll shower."

"No problem."

Bruce said thanks and went to his room. He closed the door, opened his laptop case, and set the computer on the desk. He unplugged the telephone and connected the laptop, thinking how considerate Amy and Lou were to have put in a phone jack in "Dad's room," allowing him to bring his work along.

Coming into the hall, Amy saw the closed door and went on to the kitchen. Lou was pouring a drink and upon hearing her approach, looked up and asked if she wanted anything.

"Iced tea, thanks. I saw Dad's door closed." She said as she took the glass handed her.

"He's checking his mail." His face had a knowing expression. "Then he'll shower."

Surprised, she darted a questioning glance. "Shower? Is he staying tonight?"

"He is. Planning a dinner out." Bruce teased.

"Oh, where are we going?"

"We? Nowhere." Obviously, he was enjoying the tease.

"But you said . . ."

"What did I say? Oh yes. I said 'he's planning a dinner out.'"

"Come on. What is he planning?" He waited for her to sort it out. Her puzzled expression changed. "We're not invited . . . going with him?"

He shook his head, still tantalizing. "But he's not going alone."

"Is he taking Nola to dinner?" Her eyebrows rose, her eyes brightened. He nodded. She grinned. "They must have had a nice day. He rarely changes his plans. He hadn't said anything to me about staying two days. But it's grand to have him."

They laughed together and launched into a discussion about their own dinner.

Meanwhile, Bruce checked the stock market closings and companies he followed regularly. He opened e-mail messages and answered those that required follow-up. He reconnected the telephone, then shaved, showered, and dressed in khakis and a fresh polo shirt. He checked his appearance in the large mirror over the dresser. Always neat and well groomed, he was aware he was inspecting the closeness of his shave, the comb of his hair. Making a good impression tonight was important to him as much so as for any business appointment. He couldn't remember when he had dressed for a date with such high expectations of a good time in such agreeable company. And with such a lovely woman. He thought of his dread earlier yesterday when Amy first told him of the retired woman. That image vanished quickly for him on his first sight of her. She was full of life, carefully adventurous, graceful, and beautiful. By Jove, he realized she was beautiful. And – he reasoned – a challenge. If no other man had captured her, what were his chances? He stared at his image in the mirror. Serious, he spoke to the reflection. "Be yourself. You're too old to play a false game. And you do believe she's a genuine woman, not leading you on falsely? Yes. Okay. Enjoy the evening. This is man's prime of life, they say."

He pocketed his keys and wallet and a fresh handkerchief.

After the waiter cleared the dishes from the table, Nola and Bruce ordered coffee. Nola commented, "Excellent meal and service as always."

"Yes," Bruce agreed and settled back against the tall booth. "Is this a time we can share the past?"

She looked at him intently as if giving the question serious consideration. He returned the gaze in like manner, strengthened with openness. The mental and emotional atmosphere between them heightened, but the tension was without hostility. He waited.

She blotted the corners of her mouth with her napkin then slowly spread the cloth over her lap; her hands remained beneath the table. Her shoulders raised, her breathing steady and deep, and her eyes narrowed – all revealed an inner struggle.

The waiter returned with a tray of two cups and saucers, a small metal coffeepot, and a pitcher of cream. He opened his mouth as if to speak when he recognized the intense silence between them and quietly filled the cups before placing them on the table.

With slightest turn of his head, Bruce said thank you to the waiter who responded with you're welcome and departed. Bruce never broke eye exchange with Nola.

Decisively, she spoke. "Yes. Perhaps I should begin. You've shared some of your past: your happy marriage, your life in Acorn, spoken of Robert and the apartment in Raleigh. And I know you, too, from my work with Amy. I consider Amy a friend. She's a good person, happy and well adjusted. That speaks well of you and your wife. You keep in touch with your children. I admire that.

"I had a good life growing up. I have wonderful parents and a brother, who is married and has a dear wife and two very normal children about to be teenagers. He took over one of Dad's textile mills when Dad retired a few years ago. Mom and Dad made a difficult decision to move to a retirement village at an age earlier than many people. It's a lovely place. They've made many friends. And they are free to travel which they enjoy very much. Their health is very good.

"Dad always treats Jack and me equally in financial matters. He sold one mill and split the profits: a second for himself and Mom and their retirement home, and to buy a house for me. Jack is the president of a third mill and runs it. All of us have stock in that mill. And wisely, in my opinion, Dad and Mom are on the board."

Bruce relaxed and followed her story with interest. He poured cream in his coffee and held the pitcher toward her and she paused. She reached for the pitcher, poured, then stirred the coffee. He said, "If it's cold, I'll flag the waiter."

She drank half the cup quickly but not in gulps. "It's okay. Maybe a fresh cup later." He was quiet, allowing her to continue her story before commenting.

"I see them about once a month either at their home or mine." Her eyes brightened and she dropped her shoulders. "You may have wondered why I have a large house. They wanted it for me. Dad considered a 'good residential area' safest and somewhat permanent for me if I was going to stay single. He won't use the term 'old maid' but I suspect the two words lurk in his mind.

"Mom wanted to be certain there was room for them to visit without disturbing my privacy." Smiling, she continued. "She enjoys saying she has a suite at her daughter's house. She and Dad especially liked my house because it has two rooms with a connecting bath upstairs. One room is furnished in a bedroom style that both of them feel comfortable with, and the other has a three-quarter-sleigh bed and a cozy sitting arrangement with a small sofa and chair, even a writing desk and chair."

He interjected. "The rooms sound very comfortable and inviting." The second adjective registering as possibly being misconstrued, he added, "Amy has a room she calls Dad's room. And the open invitation is appreciated." He drank his coffee. "Did you always want to teach?"

"Honestly, no. I didn't decide until late in my sophomore year in college. Dad had great expectations of my going with the mill as office manager. You may have had chores to do on the farm in the summer. Well, I spent my vacations in the mills, learning the business. Not from the ground up as Jack had to do. However, I had to observe what went on in the mills, and Dad gave me errands that took me there frequently. I checked orders, compared items and costs from various vendors, read trade publications, and abstracted them for him. In other words, I became familiar with office procedures. In the evening at the dinner table, Dad would involve Jack and me in what was going on and projecting possible changes and so forth. He really tried to make us think businesslike. I appreciated everything he did to educate me himself. And Mom grew up in the same type of family and inherited a mill from her father. So, the two looked forward to my taking over Mom's family mill which, by the way, manufactured lingerie. Dad's was hosiery."

"Were they disappointed when you chose teaching?"

"They got over it and don't question my decision now. One night years after I had been teaching, Mom declared without preamble or any connection with our conversation: Well, we bore down on you and Jack every night educating you about our business, it is no surprise that you chose to teach something to others."

He laughed. "Your mom sounds like an interesting person."

"She is."

"Would you like some hot coffee?"

"Yes, thank you."

Bruce raised his hand, caught their waiter's attention as he was crossing the room. When the young man stopped, Bruce asked for hot coffee. The waiter noticed Nola's half-filled cup. "Yes sir." He removed the cups and the pot.

"So you went happily on to your chosen field after college," Bruce asked matter-of-fact but watched for a change in her expression. He saw it immediately – pain and hesitation. She lowered her eyes and again placed her hands in her lap.

Lifting her chin, she said without directly looking at him, "While the waiter is getting the coffee, I'll take a break." She picked up her purse and he stood as she walked toward the restrooms.

Bruce squared his shoulders before he sat back down wondering if he'd blown hearing what he wanted to know with either inference about college or happiness.

The waiter arrived with two steaming cups, set them down before asking if he could bring them anything else. Bruce replied, "Not right now, thanks."

When Nola returned, Bruce again stood. The custom of doing so allowed him to be more on eye level with her as she approached the booth. The glance she darted at him indicated a holding back but her facial muscles were not tensed. She eased into her seat, replaced the napkin in her lap, and poured cream into the coffee.

She took a sip and pronounced it just right. Giving her time to decide about continuing her story, he added cream and drank from his cup. "It's from a fresh pot, no doubt. I agree it's very good."

They continued to sip coffee in silence. Finished, she moved her cup well to the right and placed both hands, one over the other, in front of her on the table. She looked directly at him.

"Is there a particular question you'd like to ask?"

"Yes. It's unusual to see a woman so lovely, and obviously intelligent, single. There's been no mention of a former husband."

"I've never married." She interlocked her fingers. "In former days, the question or suspicion of sexual orientation would never have occurred, would it? To lay that thought to rest, that's not the case. I was engaged once. We met in college during our sophomore year; by our junior year we were in love and engaged our senior year. He wanted a year to travel in Europe, backpacking, camping out, or sleeping in hostels. Alone. So I signed a contract to teach a year back home."

She paused and looked at her hands. She sensed his shifting his position, leaning closer toward the table, his hands out of view.

"His letters became less frequent. A month before the time he had planned to return, a letter came saying he was going to stay in France and marry a French girl. We'd never set a date for the wedding, so there's was nothing to cancel."

"I'm . . ."

She interrupted quickly. "Don't be sorry, please. I won't lie to you. I loved him very much. The hurt had begun when the letters were less frequent, less Kyle – his name was Kyle Edgerton – less love letters and merely brief tourist descriptions. I applied for a position with the school system here, found an apartment and here I've stayed."

His concern for her was evinced in his eyes as her story unfolded; his pleasure was obvious as she concluded. Leaning forward, he pursued. "And no one since?"

"Dates, but no one of interest for any duration. And no affairs," she looked in his eyes for some reaction. Before any showed, she dropped her gaze.

He placed a hand over her clinched fingers. "Thank you for telling me."

Slowly, she raised her eyes to meet his. He saw a trace of pain and heard sorrow as she spoke. "I've never spoken of him to anyone since I've moved here."

"I'm honored." He squeezed her hands. Her eyes moistened. The waiter came and placed a black folder on the table. Bruce removed his hands and she looked aside. He pulled a credit card from his wallet and inserted it in the folder. The waiter collected it and transactions were completed.

Back at her house, Bruce pulled into the driveway and walked her to the door. She said good night, unlocked and opened the door, and quickly entered to press a code on the security alarm. He stepped into the hall behind her. She turned around.

"You don't mind that I came inside? I didn't want to give the neighbors something to gossip about."

"Gossip?" Her question brought a blush to her cheeks.

"Outside, it would be gossip. In here, only curiosity." He looked into her eyes that showed no apprehension. He placed a hand on each of her upper arms. She didn't back away. He bent and kissed her. She shivered. He drew back a few inches, rubbed her arms, and asked, "Cold?" She shook her head.

Slowly, she tilted her chin upward, her eyes never breaking the exchange with his. Encouraged, he pulled her closer and kissed her again with increasing pressure. When she circled her hands at his waist, he let go her arms and wrapped his around her shoulders. She accepted his kiss and responded to his warmth and ardor. She moved her hands and arms to his back. From unknown inner depth, passions ignited and hurled a blinding, churning heat that spiraled though her head, leaving her oblivious to time and body.

Holding her close, he fully savored her responsiveness. As he lessened the intensity, he moved the side of his face against hers. "I had to know."

She clung to him, thankful that Bruce was so steady on his feet, so strong of arm, and most of all so forward. Never would she have had the courage to make the first advance. "And?"

"It's right. You're right."

She managed a deep breath telling herself: Don't ask him to explain. Accept the moment. The rebirth of feeling passion.

They stood without speaking for minutes. "Are you free Friday evening?" Bruce asked.

"Yes." She leaned against him.

"Without consulting your calendar?" There was warm assurance in his voice.

"What calendar?" she coyly murmured.

He leaned back just far enough to look into her eyes. Did he read a sign close to surrender? With one hand he pushed her hair aside, curling his fingers amid the thick, soft strands, leaned, and kissed her ear. Again, she shivered. His lips caressed her cheeks and found her soft, parted lips again.

The pleasure of reunion was reciprocal.

He broke the embrace, slowly released her before stepping back. "I'd better go. Sleep well." In long strides he reached the door, opened and closed it without looking back.

Only after hearing the car leave the driveway did she move. She pivoted, took a few steps, and looked at her image in the hall mirror. Returning her scrutiny was a new face – flushed, vibrant, happy, content, challenged, and conquered. "Oh," she exclaimed quietly. She sensed a deep breath, held it in her chest and abdomen, and enjoyed the tightness.

Switching the lamp off and the overhead hall lights on, she walked warm in heart to her bedroom knowing that sweet dreams would be her companion tonight.

Chapter 10

Detective Jim Smith learned that Mr. Kester's car had been returned. No blood showed up in or around the car. The car was clean – no fingerprints except Mrs. Kester's nor strange objects or debris. The item that provoked questions was the ignition key discovered in the bottom of a small tissue box that was tightly wedged underneath the driver's seat. This place would be difficult for anyone sitting in the driver's seat to reach. It fit the Kesters' car. And he wanted to talk to the man.

The Kesters' car was now parked in the driveway up close to the rear of the 1930s-style one-story house. Privet hedges ran between most of the houses on the block. Large oak trees shaded the front yards. Grass was sparse. Detective Smith walked up the cement path and knocked on the front door.

It was jerked open. The elderly man hunched behind the screen door. "What do you want?"

"Good day, Mr. Kester. I'm Detective Smith."

"I remember."

"I'd like to ask you a few questions, sir."

With an exasperated, teeth-clinched face, he signaled with a stiff elbow and swivel of his head and stepped into the room. Smith opened the screen and entered.

"Close the door. A slew of people have been in for two days now. What do you need to know?" Kester barked, sat in a deep chair, and pointed Smith to one opposite.

"Was the spare key always kept in the car?"

MYSTERIOUS DEATH AT THE MALL

"It was. After Bessie locked herself out years ago, I had to leave work and go unlock the car. I had an extra one made to keep in there."

"And it was in the tissue box?"

"Her idea." He shook his head. "That's what the glove compartment is for. She said that would be the first place a thief would look. I told her she'd toss out that box someday, not remembering the key was inside."

"It was lodged up under the seat. Have you needed to use a spare recently?"

"Nope, I haven't. She never said so." Mr. Kester thrust his head forward. "Well, she had to unlock the door to get in."

"You always lock the doors?"

"We made it a habit to lock the car doors and lock them every night in the driveway."

Smith asked, "You said you have a son who lives in Arkansas. Have you been in touch with him?"

"Not yet. I keep trying. His office says he's on vacation. They thought he was coming to North Carolina."

"Is there anyone he would be coming to see other than you in the state?" Smith had his pencil and pad out.

"He has a friend in Groton he goes on vacation with some times. He doesn't answer his phone either." Kester offered with a scowl.

"May I have the home phone and work phone numbers and the supervisor at work of both your son and his friend. We'll try to locate them, sir."

Kester tightened his lips, wrote the information on the pad, and handed it over.

"Let me know if you hear from him. You said a number of people have been in. Your needs are being taking care of?" When Kester affirmed with a nod, Smith rose and bid him goodbye.

A woman in her sixties was sweeping a few dried grass clippings and foliage from the sidewalk onto the narrow right-of-way grassed area near the curb. She looked up and said hello as Smith approached. He paused and greeted her.

She held the broom upright. "It's so bad about Bessie. A terrible way to go."

"Have you been neighbors long?"

"Dear me, yes. Twenty years. Mr. Kester said he hasn't heard from his son. I do hope he locates him soon and in time for the funeral."

The last statement was a courteously spoken question. "Does the son visit often?"

"Oh my, no. Once a year at most. More like every two or three years." She stepped closer to Smith and glanced toward the Kester's house where the door was closed. "The three didn't get along too well together. Lots of arguing. Horace, that's the son, was a young teen when we bought this house. Then, he seldom brought friends home but had a good friend that moved to Groton. Horace left home at age twenty. Takes trips with his friend when he comes back for visits."

"Is there a particular place they go?"

"Varies. They camp out, I think."

"The Kesters are quiet people. Good neighbors." Smith stated evenly.

She drew back astonished. "Not exactly." Again, she looked around and at the Kester house before continuing. In low tones, she said, "Mr. Kester stayed inside most of the time while she was here, but soon after she left in the car, he'd come outside, walk around. Kept his cane at his side but didn't use it for support."

"Not a close family?"

"Not at all. But we do rally around when there's a death. When Horace is located, they can plan a funeral."

Smith said goodbye and got in his car. He wondered if Kester ever took a cab. Could he have done so Monday afternoon to the mall then another back home? A check with cab dispatchers to and from the house could be made, Smith decided as he drove off. And what about the son? Coincidental that he goes missing when his mom dies.

His cell phone vibrated at his waist. "Smith here."

"A call just came from the hospital. Cause of death for Bessie Kester was heat stroke. The body has been released to Howard Funeral Home on Center Street," said Detective Efrid.

"Thanks. I left the Kester house a few minutes ago. Mr. Kester hasn't located his vacationing son yet. Can you check out the cabs? Talk with dispatchers if they have a record of cabs to and from Kester's house and the mall Monday around four o'clock or 9:45 p.m.?"

"Will do."

The large green service truck idled on the busy street in front of a strip mall anchored by a fast-food restaurant. The driver watched for the policeman to signal an okay to make a left turn. When the young officer stepped from the curb onto the street, held his hand up, and blew his whistle, oncoming cars stopped. Outgoing cars exited the parking lot and the service truck pulled in. The driver with long, lank hair hanging below a gray cap with a visor guided the massive vehicle around the curved entrance and on the straight path to the large trash container.

Lunch rush over, only a few cars remained in the lot. From the restaurant, a young male worker ran from the back door with two large black trash bags in his hands, holding them shoulder high so the driver would halt before thrusting twin spearlike metal arms forward to engage slots in the trash container. Spotting him in the side view mirror, the driver grimaced but braked, stopped all forward action.

The worker plopped the bags on the pavement beside the container. He slid open the door in the top half. He picked up one bag to heave inside, stopped, leaned over, and peered at the contents. He looked away, then back to the interior before putting a hand in and pulling out a ladies handbag. As if he expected someone to be coming toward the container, he turned around. There was no one in sight.

The vehicle driver leaned out the window. "Come on, man. Put the bag in."

There was no woman to be seen nearby, but the worker knew the restaurant bagged all its trash and no one else was supposed to use the trash container. Thus, he tossed both black trash bags inside and with the handbag walked over to the driver.

"What now?" the driver shouted.

The worker held up the bag. "You saw me take this out of there, didn't you?"

"Yeah, yeah. Who cares? Move on!"

"I don't want anybody to say I took it. I'll give it to that police officer." He pointed toward the street then headed toward the walkway beside the restaurant. He bumped into someone rounding the corner.

Hector Turner frowned at the bewildered, young man holding a pocketbook.

"It's not mine. It was in the trash." The worker spotted the officer walking from the street toward his patrol car. "Hey, wait a minute." He shouted and waved and hurried toward the car.

Hector scratched his head as he saw the young man waving the pocketbook in the air. What does that remind me of? The shape, size? By jimmy, the dead lady's missing bag. Quickly, he ran after the worker. "Wait!"

The officer stopped beside his car. The first young man reached him, excited and shouting. The second one was close on his heels, also shouting. "One at a time, guys."

"I found this in the trash container. The driver saw me pull it out. Here, take it!" he shoved it toward the officer.

The officer held up his hand and pulled some plastic gloves from a shirt pocket before accepting the handbag. He looked it over carefully then opened it. "What's your interest?" he asked Hector who was pacing a few steps, trying hard to control himself.

"It could be the handbag we've been looking for. The one a lady shopper should have had with her Monday night. The one who was found dead in her car in Saunders Mall."

"How do you know about that?" the officer stared at him.

Hector drew up his full height, threw his shoulders back, and said, "I found her. I'm with security there. That fits the description Mr. Kester, the woman's husband, gave us."

The officer peered inside the bag. He tilted it to shift the contents. There were a set of keys, a wallet, a small bag with a pharmacy logo, and an assortment of items women use: lipstick, compact, comb, and mirror. He closed the bag.

"I'll take it with me," the officer said.

"Let me take it. It's not far to the mall," Hector said.

"I'm going to the station. It'll be turned over to the division handling the report."

Hector stopped just short of stamping his foot and speaking disrespectfully. He swallowed. "There might be a clue in there."

The officer opened his car door, got a plastic bag, and dropped in the handbag. "Might be." To the worker he said, "Thanks, for turning this in. What's your name?"

"I didn't steal it. Never opened it." The young worker looked frightened. "This is my first week. I need this job."

"I need your name for the report." He opened his notepad and jotted the worker's name and address. "Your manager may commend you for being a good citizen."

The young fellow sighed and headed to the back door. Hector and the officer drove off in their own cars.

Mr. Kester grumbled as he reached for the telephone. "Hello."

"Dad, this is Horace. I just read about Mother's death. Aubrey and I were eating and looking at a newspaper. I'm real sorry about Mom. Sorry I didn't know sooner."

"I've been trying to get ahold of you. Called Aubrey's apartment. Left a message on his answering machine."

"He didn't check it until this morning after we read a day-old paper. There was nothing about the cause of death in the paper."

"They haven't told me yet."

"All of this is terrible. Did she suffer or anything?"

"She died, Horace. She didn't look happy. I identified her right there in the parking lot. On a stretcher and then they took her to the hospital."

"Where is she now?"

"At the funeral home. Where are you, Horace?"

"We're at the campsite. We're breaking it up, leaving as quick as we can."

"Is Aubrey bringing you here?"

"No. We'll go to Groton and I'll rent a car and drive over later today. Anything I need to know now?"

"I'm thinking of a private burial Friday morning. Just us, son."

"But Dad, wouldn't Mother have wanted a service in the church?"

Mr. Kester sounded exhausted. "I've been busy these past two days and nights. The phone ringing, people coming to the house. Everybody wants decisions now."

"Well, Dad, I'll help when I get there. I didn't know any earlier," Horace's tone was as if he were justifying his situation.

"I hear you. Next time, let somebody know where to reach you.

Come on when you rent the car." Mr. Kester hung up without waiting for a goodbye.

The young traffic officer took the plastic bag with the ladies pocketbook to the police station and asked for the detective handling the Kester woman investigation.

"Detective Smith isn't here. Expect him later this afternoon. I'll label the bag and see that he gets it soon as he returns." The desk officer put out his hand, and the young officer gave him the plastic bag. The transfer was recorded with officer's name, item, date, and time.

Chapter 11

Bruce filled the dishwasher after Amy and Lou left for work. The three of them had lingered over a second cup of coffee, and Bruce assured them he was not in a hurry. While making his bed, he recalled how surprised Amy had been at his requesting this room again Friday and Saturday.

Wide-eyed, she murmured, "Sure. Anytime."

The question "why" only showed in her raised eyebrows. He responded. "I've asked Nola out again." He watched the fact register and was pleased at her grin.

"Great going, Bruce." Lou commented heartily and pressed his knee against Amy's. "I can fire up the grill."

"No need. We'll go out. Maybe catch a movie later."

Bruce snapped his laptop in the case, zipped his luggage, and visually checked that the room was in order prior to locking the house back door and pocketing his key. Before leaving the driveway, he punched in Robert's office number in Groton.

"Hi, Dad," he answered on the first ring seeing Bruce's cell phone number on the caller ID.

"I'm leaving Amy's. Will you be ready for a coffee break in about forty minutes?"

"Sure, I can manage that. What's up?" Robert scanned his calendar and jotted a memo.

"I'll bring you up to date when I see you."

"Okay. Oh, did Amy agree to the farm sale?"

"Let's talk over coffee. I'll ring when I reach your office building. The coffee shop there a good spot?"

"Yes. Look forward to it." Robert hung up feeling uncertain that Amy was ready to part with the property. If she had agreed easily, then Dad could have told him on the phone. No reason to have to meet unless she was reluctant. I love the place, too, but hey it's time to sell if Dad wants to. He's the one with all the responsibility.

When he walked into the coffee shop, Bruce was seated over by a window. A waitress was approaching the table. With a salute of a hand, Robert pulled a chair from under the table and sat down.

Bruce ordered coffee and Robert told the waitress to make that two. When she walked off, Robert asked about his visit with Amy and Lou.

"Enjoyable as always."

"Did you luck up on another client that held you in Windermere a second night?" Change in habits of his father interested him.

"No." Bruce put his elbows on the table. "Amy was surprised that someone had made an offer on the farm. She said she didn't know it was for sale. I told her how it all came about. She remembers the Spruills. It'll take a little time for her to adjust to our not having it."

"You think she will though. What did she say?"

The waitress put the coffee mugs and the bill on the table and moved to a table where a man had seated himself.

"She spoke of things she liked to do. Mostly routine actions such as swinging under the big tree and walking on sandy paths. Childhood memories. Those she'll keep."

"Dad, we're not making memories there now, are we?"

"No, we aren't. It was a good homeplace. I'm glad someone we know, someone who loves the area, wants it for his family." He drank a couple of swallows then pushed the mug aside. "Amy introduced me to a friend of hers. She came over for one of Lou's fabulous steak cookouts night before last."

Robert noticed his father moving the mug as if getting it out of the way and wondered whether the coffee was bitter or not hot enough to suit him. He started to inquire about the evening, but his father's serious expression was an alert to wait. Let him tell what he had come to say.

He felt it wasn't about Amy. He watched Bruce over the rim of the mug as he took a swallow.

"Robert, I liked the woman. We took a drive in the mountains yesterday afternoon and had dinner out in the evening."

"Well, sounds like you have a friend in Amy's friend. Maybe not a client, but . . ."

"I'm going to marry her," Bruce said bluntly.

"Dad!" Robert uttered in a shocked voice. Quickly, he put the mug down.

"I am." Bruce sat back, folded his arms across his chest and the biggest smile spread over his face. Relief at the announcement was instantaneous. "By Jove, I am."

"Golly, Dad. You've seen her twice and you're making this major decision?" Disbelief showed on Robert's face. "What's she like?"

"She's lovely. When Amy told me she had invited a retired schoolteacher to dinner, I imagined a bad-dream evening. She's elegant, graceful, like a model." For the moment, Bruce's eyes were unreadable to Robert. He was witnessing a man enjoying his own mental pictures in pleasurable seclusion.

"Was she out to captivate you, Dad?"

Quickly, Bruce's attention reverted to his son. In refutation of the remark, he answered, "Not at all." His tone softened. "But she did. I know I don't have to explain it to you."

Robert leaned over the table and spoke in a low voice. "Dad, marriage is a major step."

"Yes, I know."

In an uncomfortable intensity, Robert continued. "How can you be so sure? If she's old enough to retire, well . . . there are considerations."

"Such as?"

Robert sat up and probed. "Granted, you'd know a lovely woman from one who isn't. And a teacher should be able to hold her own in conversation. But . . . Dad, did you . . . you know?"

"Go to bed with her?"

Robert blew out a deep breath and pulled back a few inches and shook his head. "Damn, this is like I'm the father and you're the son."

"Do I seem so old to you? I'm aware I've been no ladies' man these past ten years."

"No, that's the point, Dad. You don't look old." Squirming, he said, "Lifestyles are different now. Gad, what do you know about her? Did you ask questions?" Bruce glared, but Robert continued. "Oh, come on. Health questions?"

Bruce looked down and couldn't hide a smile, but he lifted a sensible, confident face. "Robert, she's single, never been married. And I'd bet my last dollar she doesn't play around or sleep around."

"Well, she may take your dollar!"

Sternly, Bruce retaliated. "I resent your prejudgment of the woman I plan to marry."

"She said yes in a hurry!"

"I haven't asked her!"

"What?" Disbelief spurt forth.

"No. I'm telling you first. I want you to know my intentions. What I do from this day on will be with Nola in mind."

Leaning back against his chair, Robert appeared in shock. After a few minutes, he said, "Tell me about her. And I'll keep a placard up there: Amy's friend." He ran his thumb and index finger parallel over his forehead.

"Nola Gilbert. I never asked her age. She told me she started teaching the year she graduated from college, taught twenty-five years and retired a year ago. Your guess is as good as mine. Her family was in textiles. Her only brother still runs one of the family mills. Her parents live in an upscale retirement village. Nola has a large two-story house in an affluent neighborhood. So, she is not in need of anyone to support her. She's active, intelligent, and more cultured than I am."

Not wanting his father to compare himself in a negative manner, Robert rallied. "With all this going for her, why no men friends?"

"I didn't say she has no invitations for evenings out. I'll tell you this now then leave the matter be. She was engaged during college. The young man took a year off when they graduated to do the European tour. Solo. At the end of the year, he broke the engagement and married a French girl and stayed in France."

"Dad, that's been a long wait." Robert was silent, thoughtful, assessing the story. "Amy doesn't know?"

"No. She's wrapped up in her work, some problems at the center including the death of a member of her program."

"The one found dead in the parking lot?"

Bruce nodded.

"I saw it on TV. Gad, that's a blow to someone as sensitive as Amy is. When will you tell her?"

"Not until I ask Nola. They're close. It's a good friendship."

"Do you know when?"

"Soon. I don't want to wait."

Robert detected a note of longing in his father's voice and an enlarging of his whole persona. And Robert remembered his feelings when he first knew he wanted Susan.

"Are you going to find out first if ... if you're compatible, you know, in all ways?"

"Let's not worry about incompatibility. Trust me?" The message he conveyed was received and acknowledged with a positive shake of the head.

"Well, Dad, there's nothing on my calendar to top this meeting!" He stuck his hand across the table. When Bruce firmly clasped it, Robert said, "Congratulations! When can Susan and I meet her?"

"Saturday evening, if you're free."

"You don't lose any time, do you?"

"I try to accommodate quick as possible. Would you like for us to come over here or would you like to set up a family gathering with Amy and Lou?"

"Let's just have a foursome Saturday at our place here. Okay?"

"Great. And thanks. I mean it."

"Dad, you've never made me feel prouder than at this moment. Being privy to your plans is an honor."

Both men stood. Robert picked up the check. "Not champagne. We'll do that whenever. It's a promise."

Midmorning Nola heard the phone ring. Quickly finishing a notation on a shopping list, she picked up the receiver. "Hello."

"Good morning, Nola."

"Janet, it's good to hear from you."

"If you aren't busy Friday evening, how about let's go out to eat?"

"Janet, I'd love to, but I do have plans." Nola spoke with enthusiasm as she circled roses for the living room on the shopping list.

"Oh, we'll do it some other evening." After a moment, Janet asked, "How about Saturday?"

Nola peered at the desk calendar. In Saturday's block was Bruce with a question mark. Bruce hadn't exactly said to hold that night, but she preferred to leave it free. "Can I have a rain check?"

"Of course. Are you doing anything interesting these days? It seems weeks since we've touched base."

"A few things. A lot of volunteering at the health center and a couple of evenings with the director and her dad. Amy and her husband invited me over for a cookout when her dad was in town last week."

"Would it be impertinent if I asked is the dad still here?"

"Not at all. We generally know what's going on with each other, don't we? No, he's not in town. And his name is Bruce Braddock. But he is returning Friday. He's an interesting man."

"I would say this situation is interesting. Four evenings in one week! Next week, we will have lunch together. I want to hear about this dad when we're face to face. Call me."

Nola promised. After hanging up the phone, she penciled Janet's name on the next Tuesday noon. She traced her fingers lightly over Bruce's name at six thirty Friday then over the Saturday entry. She closed her eyes and relived the series of contacts between them.

What may have first been accidental touching was later intentional, she felt certain of that. She asked herself: "Did I touch him at any time first? Did I flinch, jerk my hand away, or telegraph signals not to repeat the gesture?" Smugly, she confessed: "No. The touches had been pleasing, exciting, warm, firm, yielding, and protective. Not possessive. But would I have minded that Saturday in the hallway here?"

Recalling the kiss brought a sharp intake of breath that dried her lips, and she moistened them with her tongue. She mused, "Will he be expecting to kiss me again Friday? He won't be returning in a stoic posture. If the parting had been without responsiveness, and was certainly not so, would he be back so soon? No. Or would I be so ready to see him? I haven't felt physical excitement like this in . . . since. Maybe he hasn't either. Didn't he say he hasn't been out much? No, Nola. Don't think like this. Amy would have told me if he was seeing someone. Why, she wouldn't have asked me to dinner at her home without tagging that information onto the invitation.

"Today when I see her at the center, oh my, what time is it? I need to get ready to go. I'll mention he's coming if she doesn't say something first. She's so honest that she'll tell me if he's interested in someone else."

She ripped the shopping list from the notepad and hastened to finish chores before going to the health center.

Hector Turner was scheduled for duty tomorrow at four o'clock, but he felt antsy loafing around the house. Before his mom left early for work, she reminded him of his chores. Already he had mowed the small yard and dumped the clippings in the compost pile. Her parting words every mowing day were "Turn it, son; it'll decompose faster and make the vegetables grow into those good potatoes, beans, and tomatoes you and your dad love to eat."

Well, I've done all that. Now what? He clicked through the TV channels. Man, who wants to listen to all those characters shouting at each other or laughing like they're crazy or high on something. He put the remote down and rambled around the small rooms, shrugging his shoulders and scratching the short hair on his head.

"Heck! Enough of this place. I'm going to the mall. Hang around. Maybe pick up if there's any news about that dead woman."

He started his compact car, adjusted the mirrors, and backed out of the yard. Feeling pleased that he had mastered staying in the parallel tire-size tracks with hardly a miss, he straightened out on the narrow street. Since he had to do the yard work, he protected the grass, got praise from his mom, no flack from his old man, and less labor in the process.

Yeah, protection was the name of the game. He turned the corners of his mouth in a self-satisfied tilt. After giving a what-for to the gang of brats that had ridden their bikes onto his yard, he'd had no more trouble from the kids in the neighborhood. Hector liked seeing the awelike respect on their faces when he drove by them in his security uniform. He was mindful to let the emblem on his sleeve show above the window and at times to nod his head, reinforcing his official status with the regulation hat.

Today the street was empty. As he drove to the mall, he was careful to stop at red signs, intersections, and give proper turn signals. He fretted: what if somebody I know asks why I'm at the mall on my day off? Answers didn't come to Hector quickly. It annoyed him now not to have one ready. Suddenly, a car stopped in front of him and he had to act quickly. Blast that stupid driver! He had his hand raised above the horn to do just that. Then, he saw a pedestrian with crutches slowly crossing before the stopped car. The elderly man paused briefly on reaching the other side of the road and waved a thank-you.

Hector was glad that he hadn't honked. As he entered the mall area, a large garden shop entrance sign caught his attention. Parking, he smirked for he had his answer. "I came down to get some lime for the compost pile. Maybe I'll say 'lime for the yard'; not everybody knows what compost is."

First, he checked on lime and decided to get it on his way out. On the main corridor, he kept alert for a security officer. He soon spotted one he had taken his training with.

"Hi, Lemuel. What's up?"

The dark-haired officer same age as Hector sported a crew cut, wore his white short-sleeve shirt fitted tightly so that his muscles showed the time he gave to weight lifting, and slowed his swagger for Hector to fall in beside him. "Not much today. Calm."

"Pierce'll like that. Not like night duty, is it?"

"Not today anyway. Too early in the week. You prowling the mall on your day off?" Lemuel asked.

"I came in for lime for the yard. Hear any new development about Mrs. Kester?"

Lemuel turned to Hector, but continued his steady, unhurried pace. "You mean that woman they found dead? Oh, yes, you found her, didn't you?"

"I did. Man, that was weird."

"Bet it was. I haven't heard any reports today. Do you think it was a natural death?"

Shrugging his shoulders and keeping his expression serious, Hector replied. "Couldn't say. Got my first experience with dead people early on in security."

"Yeah, bet you want it to be your last."

Three young women were rushing along the corridor. They were giggling and darting around slow walkers in front of them. Approaching the officers, the group parted two to the right and one on the left. After they passed and regrouped, one woman put out an arm and stopped the other two.

"Hey, I think I know that guy with the security fellow." Quickly, she retraced her steps. "Hector. Hector Turner."

Quickly, Hector turned around surprised to hear his name.

"Hi. Remember me from school. Shirley Redfield."

"Sure. Hi." Hector was obviously controlling his facial muscles before hearing any other comments. Girls didn't call out to him.

She said with awe, "I heard about your finding that woman in the parking lot. It was on TV. You're mighty brave, Hector."

The two girls were fidgety and called, "Shirley, come on, we're late to work!"

Shirley said, "Coming. Sorry, Hector, got to go." She turned, rejoined the girls, and they rushed on down the corridor.

The smile Hector had held under control now spread across his face. Lemuel said, "Well, you've got a fan, now. Saw you on TV, eh?"

"Well . . . I'll see you later." Hector said

"Don't chase the skirts, man." Lemuel nodded.

"What?" Hector showed surprise. He glanced where the girls were seen far down the hall. "Oh, them. No time. Got to get the lime."

"Yeah, buddy," Lemuel turned and resumed his surveillance stroll.

Hector glimpsed his image in a store window, lifted his shoulders, and threw them back. Hey, man, you're looking good, he thought.

There was a knock at the door. Who's that now? Mr. Kester muttered to himself.

Grabbing his cane, he hoisted himself from the deep chair. He opened the door slowly. "Back so soon, Detective Smith? Better come on in."

He shuffled back to his chair, and Smith took the one he'd been shown yesterday. He held the handbag at his knees. Suspiciously, Kester eyed it then Smith.

"Do you recognize this handbag, sir?"

"It looks like the one Bessie carried wherever she went. Is that hers?"

"It has her wallet, some prescription refills, and a set of keys that should fit your car and perhaps your house door." Kester merely continued to stare at the handbag. Smith asked, "Do you want to see the contents?"

"Where did you find it?" Mr. Kester clinched the head of the cane but made no move forward.

"A new worker at a fast-food place spotted it when he was tossing some trash bags in a trash container yesterday. He turned it over to a policeman who was finishing lunchtime traffic duty."

"Any prints on it?" Kester narrowed his eyes.

"Only the worker's."

"Huh! He stole it, did he?" The crabby tone returned.

"A driver waiting to empty the trash container into his truck saw the worker discover the handbag. A mall security officer was leaving the restaurant and says the worker didn't open the handbag. The fast-food worker was very public service oriented and willingly had his fingerprints made today."

"Strange. No other prints. Not Bessie's?"

Smith said no and offered the bag. Debating a few seconds, Kester finally reached for it, pulled it on his lap, and released the top catch.

He shook the bag, looked at the contents, and then turned them out on an ottoman beside the chair. "Guess I can touch 'em?" he sounded quarrelsome.

"You may." Smith watched the old man open the wallet to check the bill section and the various cards. "Is that what your wife usually carried?"

"Huh," he grunted. "I never looked in this bag. Driver's license, registration, and insurance cards. The cards she'd needed for identification are here." He continued to look at each one. "Library, grocery store, drugstore. She knew the cost of prescriptions before she picked them up. Never took more cash than she needed. Our one credit card stayed here unless she was doing special shopping. That's right where it's always kept here. She'd left her checkbook here, too. I saw it last night in a drawer."

"Are you saying that no credit cards of any kind or cash or checks are missing? And no valuables that you know of were in the purse your wife was carrying?" Smith had his pencil ready to list any items.

Kester shook his head. "Right."

"I saw the two prescriptions are for you. Did you have enough these past few days?"

"I did. I run out tomorrow. The druggist can tell me whether or not these are safe to take," Kester said as he turned the two brown plastic containers round and round.

"Do you need a ride to the pharmacy to have those checked?"

"My son, Horace, will be here this afternoon. He read in a newspaper up at the campgrounds about his mother. His friend Aubrey Dinkins will drive them to Groton. Horace will rent a car, drive over."

"You're planning a graveside service Friday early afternoon?"

"It was about time your men finished whatever they had to do. A heat stroke shouldn't be hard to diagnose." He spoke grudgingly.

"Circumstances were unusual. The coroner wanted to be thorough. Follow-up with her primary physician and pharmacist were necessary for determining her condition and her filling her prescriptions. The lab is checking the tablets for high blood pressure that were in her purse. It was a hot night and the car had been in the sun for several hours."

Kester waved his hand as if to stop the explanations. "I know, I know. And the keys and handbag were missing. Well, we have those now. That seems about all we're gonna know. Add this case to your unsolved mysteries!"

"We'll be in touch. Something may turn up." Smith stood. "I'm glad your son will be with you, and in time for the service tomorrow."

Chapter 12

Detective Smith considered the graveside service for Bessie Kester the shortest and simplest one he had ever seen or heard of. Two men from the funeral home stood several feet from the open grave with the casket on supports over it. Mr. Kester and Horace stood quietly with bowed heads. The husband spoke a few words about the length of their marriage, and the son quoted her favorite Bible verses.

When the two men walked away, the funeral directors headed toward the hearse. Smith approached and extended his hand to Mr. Kester. After a quick handshake, Mr. Kester introduced Horace.

Smith shook his hand, too. "I'm sorry about your mother's death. It's good you were nearby."

"Thank you," Horace said. He seemed tense. The frown lines on his forehead were deep, similar to his father's. His stance was straighter, but there was an air of uneasiness about him. Horace looked at Smith. "Thank you for coming. We didn't invite anyone for the burial. A short memorial service will be Monday morning at ten o'clock at the church she belonged to."

"Relatives and friends like to pay their respects. And your friend from Groton, Aubrey Dinkins, will he be coming?" Smith inquired.

"He plans to," Horace replied, his frown deepened, his lips tightened.

"Will you be staying on?" Smith asked.

"I'll be leaving Monday afternoon. I changed my flight out from Sunday. My company is short-staffed."

Mr. Kester said, "Says his vacation is up. He's in such a hurry we need to move on. Take care of some things during business hours today." He leaned heavily on his cane as he headed toward a black limousine where one of the directors stood and opened a door.

Horace spoke. "The car was in the plan Mother had paid for over the years. Dad said we'd use it. Grave digging cost more on the weekend, so we rushed the burial once we had the okay."

Smith nodded. Horace clinched his teeth. Smith speculated there was more the son would like to say.

Friday evening, Bruce parked his Mercedes-Benz in a secure lot near the theater. Nola had been down earlier to pick up two tickets to the foreign film series.

"This is a thirties British film, considered a classic but is seldom shown." She paused as they looked right and left for any passing traffic. Resuming, she added, "Many films have borrowed from the plot over the decades. Now, we have the opportunity to see the original."

"Sounds interesting. Do you come to the series often?" he asked as he held the theater door open and they entered the lobby.

Walking up the carpeted stairs, she answered, "No. Occasionally, a friend and I come if there's something special we want to see and tickets are available."

Waiting in a short line for a program from an usher were Dr. Belding and a woman. He turned and recognized Nola as she and Bruce joined the queue. "Hello, Miss Gilbert."

The woman looked around to see to whom he was speaking. "Alice, this is Nola Gilbert, the lady I told you about who was so kind to allow me a seat at the concert last week. She's a hostess at seminars at the health center."

"Good evening, Dr. Belding and Mrs. Belding." Nola said pleasantly and turned toward Bruce. "This is Bruce Braddock. Dr. Belding, Bruce is Amy Umstead's father."

Dr. Belding put forward his hand. "You have a fine daughter, sir. She is a capable director and very pleasant to work with."

"Thank you."

Alice spoke to the others. "Jonathan enjoys the lectures at the health center. What an innovation – taking health education to the mall."

The line had shortened and the usher handed programs toward the Beldings. Jonathan showed the young man the ticket stubs with seat numbers. Before moving on, Alice leaned back and around Jonathan. "Thank you so much, Miss Gilbert, for offering Jonathan the seat. He would not have wanted to miss that concert. It is one of his favorites. Maybe he can return the favor some evening. I have to be out of town, with our daughter . . ."

The usher was waiting, and Jonathan was gently urging her on with a hand at her back. She hastened to move forward.

Bruce leaned close and spoke quietly to Nola. "Um. How generous the lady is to share her seat with a stranger, to her, if not to her husband."

Nola kept her lips together but the corners spread. "He's a prominent cardiologist and had lectured that afternoon at the center."

"Oh. You were kind and he is grateful," Bruce teased.

"And we must keep Amy's good speakers happy. They volunteer their time."

After the usher seated them, Bruce scanned the audience and spotted the Beldings two rows ahead of them. "Are these your regular seats?" "When they're available." "And those are his?" "I believe so." "Interesting."

Nola, sensing a bit of jealousy, kept her body still neither displaying pride nor pulling her shoulders in pleased. After the lights dimmed, Bruce sought her hand in her lap and held it firmly while the title, cast of characters, and credits were projected on the large screen. The sound track had been improved, but its age still screeched through.

The following morning, Nola was busy with a project, and Bruce was helping Lou move some furniture to clear space for a new filing cabinet for Amy.

After lunch, Nola and Bruce drove to a nursery and selected a flat of pansies for her and another for Robert's wife Susan. Returning to Nola's house, they placed the flats on the patio. She pointed to the urns where she would repot her pansies.

As he stood behind her, he inquired. "Will you need some help?" He put his arms around her and pulled her close.

"I'll wait until tomorrow evening. You'll be on your way home when the sun is off the urns. But I thank you." When he leaned forward and kissed her ear, she sighed. "I'm going in now. I need to change before we go to Groton." She pulled his hands apart and moved away.

"I'll be back in a couple of hours," he said and walked to the front drive.

Nola found Robert and Susan very comfortable people to be around. She was coming to expect that from knowing Amy and Bruce. Robert resembled his father in coloring and height. He was several pounds heavier, and Nola thought he may spend many hours at his desk. His manner fluctuated between intensity while he listened and spontaneity while he talked. Bruce tended to weigh his words first. There was a strain between the two men that surfaced occasionally into what apparently was otherwise a solid relationship. She pondered what issue lay unresolved.

Susan invited Nola to join her in the kitchen for the last-minute food preparations. The men remained on the porch.

Immediately, Nola found an understanding ally in Susan, who was a librarian. At one time, she had worked in a public school but now was with the city-county library system.

"I hope the teachers didn't drive you away. I was guilty of assigning many papers." Nola reflected a moment and added, "Our librarian was always so efficient and accommodating that I didn't realize she could be overwhelmed. After all, I wasn't the only teacher who expected her to be the keeper of reference books and the very ready source of guidance through the stacks."

"Oh, I'm sure you thanked her in your own way. And we know it goes with the position." Susan placed rolls in the oven.

This being the last task, Susan leaned back against a counter and talked to Nola about the excellent North Carolina room on the floor where she was assigned. Also, she was enthusiastic about the financial world. Among her tasks were keeping periodicals and investment journals in order, replacing magazines with the latest issues, and inserting updated investments guides in large binders. During any lag time she scanned articles of interest. An ability to speed-read she considered a blessing.

"And I'm really getting speedy with the computer." She grinned. "I was a slowpoke until I had to help patrons learn to use programs in the library. I've logged on to so many investment sites and pulled up all kinds of research data for students of all ages that I'm getting to be computer competent." She paused. "You know, it gives you a good feeling to learn something new, to take on a challenge, or to do something unexpected."

Nola, watching Susan and hearing her expound, mused: She's feeling a confident young woman. And there's a glow about her as if she has conquered something major. She asked, "There were no computers in your school library?"

"No. There was a computer lab. It was a middle school. Students could take computer as an elective. They would have had simple software programs throughout the elementary grades. But learning to research on the Net was more a challenge."

"Did they have research papers or projects in their classes?"

"They did. And computers, too." Susan turned to open the refrigerator and took out two bottles of salad dressing. "Still, I pulled many resources for teachers for a reserved shelf for an assigned paper. In fact, projects became such a major feature in so many classes that getting materials together and assisting students, I was always exhausted at the end of the week." She laughed. "What am I saying? At the end of the day."

Nola joined in the laughter. "I understand. I researched for sources the students needed and read their papers. Sometimes, I had to check their work against the footnote and bibliography. Researching is a way of education and of life."

"Well put. Let's see, what I have forgotten to set out?" she scanned the countertop of service ware and food dishes. The timer rang. The rolls ready, the men were called in.

The evening was at turns relaxing during dinner and stimulating with conversations ranging from days on the farm, in Raleigh when

Robert shared the apartment with Bruce, and during Susan's interjections of global financial enterprises. Nola related the change of pace during a year of retirement.

On the return to Windermere, Nola, snug in her seat and shoulder belts, told Bruce what nice adults his children were, and congratulated them on their choices of spouse. "I feel as if you've given me a special treat the past two weeks, meeting such nice people. Too much negativism about family relationships is featured in the media. Often, the talk of people tends to be on wrongdoings such as crimes and conflicts, a lot of fault finding. So, this time with you has been refreshing and reassuring that families get along and love each other."

She started to say that Susan seemed a bit young, thinking she was thirty, to have been overwhelmed with the school library work. Susan appeared so together and enthusiastic that taking an easier position somehow didn't jibe since it was probably at reduced pay and benefit package. On second thought, Nola chose to keep the opinion to herself. Such an observation may come out as a negative trait, which was opposite of what she wanted to convey. She looked at Bruce whose facial expression she couldn't quite decipher at the moment: only it appeared one of positive and pleasant thoughts.

Thus she gazed at him. "Thank you." After a moment, she added. "You're very nice yourself."

"You are, too." Driving the interstate highway, he could only occasionally glance her way. He wished right now for a back country road that one could travel slowly, where traffic was light, and the days before seat belts when he could pull a girl close to his side, his arm around her shoulder. Pull over onto a side road and kiss her soundly. Then move on, both revved up and content.

For a while longer, he could be patient for he knew where he was headed and what he was going to say. And he felt his heart racing as fast as the speedometer needle.

This Saturday night, three security vehicles slowly circled Saunders

Mall parking lots. After several laps, Chief Pierce would pull up beside one of the other white vehicles to ask if everything was quiet.

An older guard tipped his hat back and said. "Yes, no problems. Looks like everybody's out of the mall. The only cars are up around the theater." He stuck his hand out the window to read his wristwatch with the overhead lights. "Another ten minutes and the last feature should be over."

Pierce said, "After a couple more turns, write out your report. Bring it to me. I'll wait around until the movie lot clears. Hector is over that way."

The older guard laughed. "He might be scared of every car for a bit yet. He'll keep that flashlight handy and his cell phone on."

Pierce agreed and renewed his surveillance.

Hector was driving very slowly up and down the rows of cars parked outside the theater. He likened himself to an alien in a strange land. Their means of travel raised on four dark wheels, no wings to lift them off in a flash, all real spooky terrain swathed in leaden colors under tall iron towers with glowing orbs atop. He'd seen a science fiction show with a scene like that.

His attention was drawn to an older couple coming out of the theater. They looked toward the lot. As if not seeing a car they recognized, they huddled together against the building. The man left to look for the car. Hector pulled into a vacant space. From there, he watched the man go from one row to another. The woman stood tiptoe to keep him in sight.

Hector switched the engine off and got out of the car. He straightened his hat, squared his shoulders, and moved toward the theater.

"Ma'am, do you need some help?" Hector asked.

"We can't find our car. My husband's over there looking for it," she spoke anxiously and pointed her hand.

Not seeing anyone, Hector asked, "What type and model of car is it?"

She gave him the make, year, and color. "Where could it be? I don't want my husband to wander too far. Remember what happened to that lady not long ago."

"Well, let's us have a look, too."

"Thank you. That's a sound idea. Mind if I hold your arm as we walk?" She put a hand on his upper arm before he replied.

Running footsteps sounded behind Hector and the woman. Both glanced back but kept moving forward. Two teenage girls each spiffy in tight jeans and tee shirts caught up with them and followed closely. "Can we walk with you to our car?" asked one. "We feel safer with a security guard," declared the other girl.

Hector was overwhelmed. His emotions were excited with the rush of attention. Both admired his uniform and praised his bravery.

Hector soaked it up. He didn't trust his voice to say more than a syllable or two. Spotting their car, the girls said together, "That's it". Before crossing toward the car, one of them eyed the emblem on his shirtsleeve. Coyly, she said, "Nice uniform." The second asked Hector if he patrolled every night.

"Sometimes" was all he could mutter.

As they got into the car, someone behind Hector shouted. "How're you doing, girls?" Before driving off, the girls waved to the boys now standing beside Hector.

Walking on, Hector overheard the guys. "Girls admire uniforms, don't they?" "Yeah, after trouble, a death right about here makes 'em feel safer." "Your friends are good-looking, man. Do you know where they'd be headed?"

That was all Hector could hear of the conversation, but that was enough to put his ego over the top. Hector Turner never had it so good. He and the older lady spotted her husband unlocking their car. She thanked him for escorting her.

In Cambridge neighborhood, the summer evening was warm but a breeze was stirring. Occasionally, a rustle of drying tulip poplar leaves could be heard among the swish of green pine needles above long stems of forsythia and lobelia quite supple and sporting foliage. Roses by the roadside and in residential gardens were silent: their contributions to the senses were heady fragrances, and where the moonlight sifted through the tall, full-leafed trees, the buds and full-blown blossoms glowed like magnified fireflies.

Returning home after a leisurely meal out, Amy and Lou stood on the deck and looked at the view.

"Doesn't everything smell so divine?" Amy said softly.

Lou sniffed. "It does. All the vacant land out there," he waved his hand easily toward the rear fields, "reminds me of summer nights back around Acorn."

"Yes. Our first dates in the evenings. We walked a lot then, didn't we?"

"Honey, how about we do that right now? Take a walk down Hunt Road. Maybe meander round Cambridge."

"Are you sure you want to?" She was surprised at the sudden suggestion.

"I do. Let's put the parcels inside. Change shoes. How about it?" He peered at her and put forth his best-selling smile.

"You're on!"

They ambled down Hunt Road and surveyed the general appearance of their neighbors' yards. They stopped and listened to an owl hoot and waited for an answer. It came rather quickly. As they focused on a tall pine tree, they spotted a large owl that they labeled a barn owl by its shape. Lou squeezed her hand. She returned the gesture.

They walked on in a comfortable mix of small talk and silence. As they neared their house, Lou asked if she was tired or did she want to watch a video.

"Um. I'm fine. The delicious dinner that neither of us had to prepare and no dishes facing us to do. After this special end to our outing," she squeezed his hand, "I prefer a soaking bath and dreamy music."

"Sounds relaxing." He gave her a brief kiss before they started up the deck steps. "You deserve whatever you want. It's been a busy week for you. Go soak in your bliss. I'll find some romantic CDs and put the portable player in the bedroom so you can hear. And you won't have to think a moment about the center or the mall. It's Saturday night."

Amy submerged all except her head in the mounds of lemon-scented bubbles and the warmth of the deep water. With her head on a terrycloth bath pillow, she closed her eyes and let the music further soothe her.

Lou turned down the bedspread and plumped the pillows. He knew she would emerge relaxed and glowing. He switched off the overhead light, leaving only a lamp on the dresser burning. Slowly, the room brightened. Lou walked to the window and stood in a path the moon was creating as it traveled in the sky.

The country-bred boy hailed his old friend. "Thanks for appearing."

Lou eagerly awaited the remainder of the evening. They had the house to themselves. Surely, Bruce would stay awhile at Nola's after they returned from Groton. But the expected father returning, the hour unknown did add an element of drama and perhaps urgency to the evening.

On Glamis Drive, the moon was also at its zenith for the evening, shining between gaps of giant oaks and maples. But it was a hall table lamp that shone on Bruce's face as he spoke to Nola.

"I want to be with you always." As Nola opened her mouth, Bruce raised a hand gently. "Don't say anything yet. It's important for me to continue. For you to know the future from my point of view."

A slight tilt of her chin communicated all right, go on. He made a soft fist under her chin, bent, and kissed her lips briefly.

"I want to marry you. I want us to live together. Tomorrow wouldn't be too soon for me. But I'm sensible and to a degree, patient, and I know getting all this arranged takes time. You haven't said how you feel about me or if you have plans for the future. I hadn't thought a great deal about what lay ahead for me. I thought I had a good life. But life has changed because of these few evenings together. With you, I feel ageless. You give warmth, energy, laughter, excitement, friendship, and peace. Peace, does that sound strange? But it's a peace of comfort and knowing you're the only person I've met for whom I'm willing to trade in my single lifestyle."

As he paused, she asked, "Do you love me?"

Kindly, he answered. "If wanting to be a companion to you, a friend, a partner, and my dear, Nola, a lover, then yes I say 'I love you.'"

She circled her arms around his back and filled the space between them, her head on his shoulder. Her breathing was even and deep and rhythmic against his chest.

Her embrace brought a feeling of hope that registered on his face.

That emotion began to shift into one of concern then replaced with a drawn brow and fear of rejection. Sensing his tension, she raised her arms upward and her hands clinched his shoulders.

"Bruce," she uttered with emotion, "I had forgotten love could exist." She lifted her head and curved her neck to see his face. "Please, kiss me."

Lowering his face, he halted almost immediately. "Nola, do you care for me?"

"Yes, very much. I love your passion for me. And the responses you create in me." And swiftly, her hands released his shoulders and sought his neck and pulled his face down to hers.

After a long embrace, they separated and stood somewhat breathless. "God, for two long-deprived lovers, we really communicate," said Bruce.

"A feast." Her eyes sparkled and her words lilted. Then earnestly she asked, "Can I have a week to answer?"

"That you love me?"

"About getting married."

"Doubts?"

"It's selfish of me, but give me time to revel in unabashed joy of the beautiful proposal. Let me astutely query myself and sagely and impishly. Give me that length of days and nights to secretly carry your most precious gift." She took his hands in hers and crossed their arms, interlocked her fingers around his. Rising on her toes, she kissed him then murmured, "Thank you."

Quietly, he said, "I love you. I feel . . ."

"I feel your strength, your warmth. Your heart throbbing against my arms. And your words echoing in my head."

"And I, your strength and your gentleness. Your words I wait for."

Chapter 13

The brick church built thirty years ago to serve the residential neighborhood was set back from the street and surrounded with a neat lawn and pruned evergreen shrubbery. Inside, the walls and woodwork were painted a soft white. The backs and seats of the pews were a maple color that matched the wooden floors. The windows had clear panes except for one of stained glass behind the pulpit and choir area. A red carpet ran from the altar to the vestibule door.

Detective Smith was running late. He was a punctual person and preferred being seated early at services such as this one. The organist played the refrain of a typical hymn for funerals as Smith edged into a vacant pew several rows from the back of the sanctuary.

Picking up a hymnal, Smith located the page and heard the words beginning the second stanza. I'm not very late, he affirmed. He knew the hymn and could sing and survey the crowd, moving his eyes, scarcely shifting his head or shoulders. His height was a disadvantage when he needed to blend with a crowd, but an advantage whether standing or seated when he wanted to look for someone.

The sanctuary was about half full. He had heard that several cousins were to attend as well as neighbors and church members. Likely, former supervisors where both Mr. and Mrs. Kester worked would be here.

On the first row of the left-hand side, tightlipped Mr. Kester stood, probably supporting himself with his hands on the rail in front of him. He held no hymnal and did not peer at the one Horace was using. Immediately behind Horace was a man of similar age with the songbook opened; he could be Aubrey Dinkins. Mr. Kester wore a dark blue suit.

Horace wore a tight-fitting tweed jacket that Smith assumed had been in his wardrobe years ago and now pulled out for the service. Economical trait, Smith noted.

Seated halfway back, he recognized Amy Umstead who was sharing a hymnal with another woman. Nice of Amy to come, he thought recalling her compassion when he interviewed her.

Then he thought of two other interviews made by the telephone. First was with Bessie's doctor. With her records in hand, the doctor stated her health was generally good for a woman her age. However, she had a hyperthyroid condition controlled by medication, and hypertension or high blood pressure as most people referred to it also treated with a prescription. The two medications have been adjusted several times. There was no problem at her checkup four months ago. When Smith had asked if she was depressed, the doctor took a few seconds to respond: "I made no comment that she was. Now in retrospect, she could have been." The doctor didn't want to answer questions about Mr. Kester, but he did say he had no prescriptions similar to Bessie's, so pills would be noticeable if wrong bottles were opened.

The second interview was with the pharmacist, named on the receipt for two prescription refills for Mr. Kester the date Bessie died. Pharmacy records had no entry that Bessie picked up any other prescriptions that day. Smith asked the pharmacist if Bessie had any medications that were counteractive. He replied decisively, "No. We would have pointed this out to her as well as enclosed a printout stating the same cautionary information."

Smith posed another question. "Would she have taken either medication or both in late afternoon?"

The pharmacist informed him definitely that medication for hyperthyroid condition was taken once a day and usually in the early morning for it needed to be taken on an empty stomach. And the hypertension medication that she was prescribed was to be taken twice daily at twelve-hour intervals. So, she would not be taking either of those at four or five o'clock in the afternoon.

"Are you the only pharmacy that fills prescriptions for the Kesters?"

"Yes, to my knowledge," he responded a bit short. It wasn't just condescension to a police officer; it was as if no one should question the professionalism of a pharmacist.

The interview that left Smith with doubts was when he talked with the doctor who filled out the death certificate: cause heat stroke. Smith concurred that the day was hot and sunny and that the car had been parked at least five hours as accurately as they could determine before she died. The car was parked under a small tree, but during the daylight hours the shade varies. The windows were closed. And Bessie's facial expression showed strain or fear. Was she bent forward groping for the tissue box with the key? Did she panic when she couldn't feel it? Did she slump over the wheel trying to calm herself – to catch her breath? Was someone she was afraid of trying to open the door? There were no fingerprints found except hers.

Smith could visualize various scenes. Which was the truth? Would he ever know? He certainly wanted to. Heat stroke didn't explain the whole picture to his satisfaction. To the medical personnel it was deceased's physical condition. To Smith it was *what wasn't there*.

The service was brief with a eulogy by the minister of the church. Neither Mr. Kester nor Horace spoke. After one song from a soloist and a closing prayer, the minister said that the family would receive people at the altar after the service.

The people grouped in twos and threes and slowly walked down the aisle. The young man seated behind the Kesters was the first to shake hands then moved up the aisle toward the vestibule.

Smith left his seat and joined him. He introduced himself and asked if he were Aubrey Dinkins. "Yes."

"I checked with your office and your vacation time was confirmed. Also, you and Horace signed in the campsite and left at times you both have given us. Horace indicated that you would see him off at the airport."

"I will."

"Did either of you leave the campsite from the time you signed in and signed out?"

Aubrey appeared vexed by the questions. "Yes. We drove to a town five miles away for breakfast Wednesday. That's where we saw the newspaper and learned of Mrs. Kester's death. Horace was distressed.

He regretted he hadn't called the family when we first arrived." Aubrey softened and dropped his head slightly.

"I understand. Having a friend nearby is a help at these times." Smith saw Amy and a woman approaching and wished Aubrey and Horace a safe trip to Groton and the airport.

Aubrey walked toward the vestibule, and Smith waited and said hello to Amy. She introduced Nola.

"You're the volunteer who assisted at the Healthy Heart Seminar last week?" Smith asked Nola.

"Yes, sir."

"Did you notice anything unusual about Mrs. Kester that day?"

"Her behavior during the seminar was typical. She asked several questions."

"Did you see her after the seminar?"

Nola thought a few moments before commenting. "Yes. I do not know if what I saw was typical or unusual for her. I was talking with a friend in the reception room. I was facing the beverage area. Coffee and water are always available. I saw her close her handbag then she drank from a water cup. She tilted her head back. She threw the cup in the trash container."

Smith looked curious but asked calmly; "Did she take a pill? Maybe a medication?"

"I did not see her take one from her bag. It's possible she could have done that before I noticed her. She did toss her head back as many people do when trying to swallow a pill or tablet."

"Did she throw anything else in the trash bin?"

"Not that I saw. Could I ask, Detective Smith, if there's an indication she may have been medicated – taken too much medication that afternoon?" She focused on his expression.

He maintained a professional attitude. "That wasn't noted by the doctor at the hospital."

Nola turned to Amy. "Did Joyce say whether Bessie had her blood pressure checked that afternoon?"

"She didn't."

Smith interjected. "Joyce didn't say or Mrs. Kester did not have it checked?"

Amy replied quickly. "I'm sorry not to have been clear. Joyce said Mrs. Kester did not stop to have it checked. She usually does." Amy looked at Smith then Nola.

"Maybe she had monitored it at home or at the drugstore. Many of the members do that if they're picking up prescriptions, especially if several people are waiting at the center," Nola stated. Seeing groups of people walking up the aisle, Nola turned toward the door then Amy and Smith followed her.

He asked Amy, "How often is the trash bin emptied at the health center?"

"Whenever it's full. But always as soon as the center is closed. It's taken outside to the waste container at the loading dock." She paused. "We tie the drawstring together. We never search inside."

"Thank you." He nodded courteously and Amy and Nola left the church. He waited until Horace came into the vestibule. "It was a nice service."

"Thank you."

"I trust your father is feeling well?"

"Yes. We've arranged for a professional home nursing service to come in three days a week to check on him. Work with him in therapy. Strengthen his legs so he can get about and drive again. Be more independent. She'll view his medications and leave a new chart each week. He is to check when he's taken his medication. She counts the tablets. Initials the charts and takes the current ones, leaves him the carbons. She inspects the house topically including the bathrooms even though a cleaning woman comes twice a week. The woman who cleans also prepares some meals for the freezer or refrigerator and does the laundry."

"Thorough planning."

Horace shrugged his shoulders and spoke with slight exasperation. "If he doesn't fire them before the week is out. He's not fond of having a nurse."

"Well, we do what we can for our parents." Smith extended his hand. "Have a safe flight back."

Horace shook hands then looked back at his father, who was supporting his weight with a cane as he walked up the aisle.

Chapter 14

During the following week, Bruce telephoned Nola nightly at nine o'clock. She picked up on the second ring, each time in the den and settled on the couch. They briefly summarized their day's activities. Bruce never mentioned the proposal, but she felt it lay beneath his saying that the maid service was coming an extra day to apply a hefty application of elbow grease to windows, walls, and floors, and to shampoo carpets and upholstery.

When she pronounced that was a regular fall cleaning, he replied, "Well, there may be a visitor coming and the apartment wants to pass inspection."

She confessed, "I've been thumbing through the new seed catalogues. The rose sections are full of new varieties. And I've been inspecting rose gardens on my walks."

He visualized the scenes but cautioned himself not to be overly optimistic yet.

She asked if he were coming on Friday. "Not until Saturday." She was silent. He inquired, "That is all right, isn't it? About coming Saturday?"

"I shall miss you on Friday. But you'll be welcomed on Saturday. How does eating here sound to you? I have a fabulous recipe in mind," she said as she sank back onto the cushions.

"This will be an occasion to look forward to. I am still learning of your many talents."

"Are your projects going well? Are you trading many stocks? Is the staff surprised to see you in town for a full week?"

"The projects are on target. Activity as usual. It's near the end of the third quarter so there're portfolios in need of review. It's been amusing to hear my partners probing about my prolonged stays in Windermere. Curiosity, as to who my new client is, is killing them. I told them to hold their horses – in due time I'd make my client announcement to the office."

She basked. "I, too, have been grilled by my girl friends. It's hard to eat lunch with them and not broadcast the lovely words of last weekend." She wondered if he could sense her mood. That was her only reference to his proposal.

During Friday evening's call, she asked if he had commitments for Sunday. He hesitated before replying. "Nothing definitely."

"Good."

On Thursday, as Nola was returning the box of pencils and seminar roster to the reception desk, she heard someone speak her name. Looking up, she saw a burly young man in his late twenties. He had a questioning expression as if reassuring that he had identified her correctly.

She responded in like manner. "Matt. Matt McDowell?"

He beamed. "How are you, Miss Gilbert?" He glanced around the center. "Do you work here now?"

"No. I'm a volunteer."

"I heard you'd quit teaching. They sure will miss you."

"Thank you. I retired a year ago June. What are you doing now?" She noticed the basket of flowers he was holding.

"Delivering flowers."

"You liked flowers when you were a student. You wrote a paper on grafting roses. So you followed your interests."

He shook his head and muttered in awe. "What a memory! You must have read thousands of reports. For a few weeks, I'm helping out a friend who has the flower shop on the first floor inside the main entrance."

"What else keeps you busy?"

"My greenhouses and the nursery. I supply this shop and others with cut flowers and some landscaping outfits with outdoor plants."

"Matt, I'm pleased to hear of your successes." She noticed his muscular arms, tanned skin, and work-hardened hands as well as his tightened woven twill blue work clothes. She recalled reading of his playing several sports during high school in the Windermere newspaper. He might have been labeled typical teenager. In reality, there seemed to be few of those. He had a good mind for practical things, a tender quality apparent in his love of growing things, and an affable nature that his classmates and teachers appreciated. Steady, reliable, and successful. She felt honored to have had a part in his education. "And these flowers are beautiful."

"Thank you, Miss Gilbert. Right out of the greenhouse." He noticed Phyllis approaching from the office area. He took a step toward the desk. "Phyllis, your special order."

Phyllis inspected the bouquet and basket then exclaimed. "Matt, what a colorful selection. And so fresh and sweet smelling. My mom will love them. When she was in the hospital, she admired your arrangements. Declared whatever came from your greenhouse was the freshest she ever saw and smelled. Thank you for bringing them up here."

"Glad to do it." Phyllis took the flowers to the office area.

Nola commented. "Will you be helping in the flower shop all week?"

"For a few weeks. Most afternoons. My friend is on maternity leave. We met in a horticulture class in the community college." Somewhat bashful, he added in lower tones, "It's their first baby. She waited until the shop was doing well. She's thirty."

Nola spotted Amy crossing from the auditorium to the offices. "Matt, it was so good to see you. I need some flowers for Saturday and will drop by the shop tomorrow."

"See you then."

Midafternoon Saturday, Bruce entered the interstate and headed toward Windermere with great expectations mildly tempered with the age-old masculine dread of having his offer of marriage turned down. Her cheerfulness and tantalizing references to roses and preparing dinner for him were not definite signs of acceptance. And there would be an hour plus of driving and then of conversing with Amy and Lou before resuming his destination on Glamis Drive.

His purchase from the jeweler was safely stored in his luggage. He wished it were fall and jacket weather so he could carry it less noticeable this evening – it could create a bulge in his slacks pocket. A little late thinking of that, he chided.

After leaving Amy's, Bruce made a quick stop at a drugstore and arrived at Nola's at the invitation hour for dinner, seven o'clock.

Immediately with the first doorbell chime, she stepped from the kitchen into the hall. She wore a long, flowing dress of taupe and gold color, with a gold sash tied about her waist. The sheer, taupe bodice featured a simple scoop neckline and three-quarter-length sleeves. As she passed under the overhead light and beside the table lamp, he admired her graceful carriage and the silhouette of her long, slender legs.

"Hello," she greeted him warmly as she opened the glass door.

"You look lovely." He entered and closed the door, latching it.

She held out her hand. He took it. A small candy box was in his other hand. "A small treat for later. Nothing to interfere with your dinner," he commented and placed the box on the hall table. Looking into the dining room and seeing the chandelier lit, he commented. "My, you have been very busy yourself. The room is gleaming." He turned an admiring expression toward her.

"You inspired me with your talk of elbow grease. Tonight we'll dine in here. It's all ready. I shall treat you as a proper guest and invite you to have a seat in the living room while I put the finishing touches on the plates."

"No appetizers?"

She walked with him to the doorway of the living room, paused, and gently kissed his cheek. "How's that?" She flirted then pivoted to swish down the hallway again.

He realized another aspect of her nature, a flair for drama. Well, he'd see how this play unfolded.

He sat where he could watch her enter the dining room. First, she brought salad plates, next dinner plates, and finally a bread tray. Butter dish, water and tea goblets, salt and peppers were already placed.

Standing at the dining room entrance, she said, "Please, come in, sir."

"My, what formality. I pray this isn't my last meal."

She walked behind a chair and indicated the opposite chair with a hand.

He seated her before himself.

"I checked with Amy that you liked crab and shrimp, and I wanted to serve it piping hot." She unfolded her napkin. "And Italian dressing she said was your favorite with seafood. And the tea is sweetened. The rolls are fresh and hot."

"After a hard week in the fields, what more could the farmer ask for than his favorite foods." He smiled at her. He watched her lift the first fork of shrimp to her mouth. Similar colors in the centerpiece drew his attention. "The talisman roses and yellow lilies are exquisite. The gypsophila is a delicate addition."

She entertained him with small talk of the center, her spying on the neighbors' gardens, and her shopping forays. He asked trivial questions matching her lighthearted mood. After finishing the main course, she removed the dishes and tea goblets. The swinging door, separating the dining room from the breakfast room and the kitchen, was closed and he could hear no sounds.

Returning, she carried two plates. "One of my few desserts I can count on coconut pie."

After they finished the pie, she removed the plates and was back in a few moments with a coffee service. She poured coffee and handed him a cup and the creamer.

They sipped hot coffee and she asked about Amy and Lou. He told her about their day then put his empty cup down.

"More," she said reaching for the pot.

"Not now. Maybe later."

"Then I shall excuse myself for a few minutes," she began to rise and he immediately pushed his chair back and walked around the table to assist her.

As she stood, he said, "Thank you for the delicious meal. You were very thoughtful to discover some of my favorites and prepare this very gracious occasion."

He stepped back.

"It was my pleasure," she said and moved into the hall and toward her rooms. He went to the guest bathroom and washed his hands.

Since she had ushered him first to the living room, he returned there. He walked around looking at the pictures. From a large mirror he noticed that no curtains covered the windows; and while the house sat back a number of feet from the sidewalk, anyone standing inside would be clearly visible to people walking by or neighbors standing across the street for a friendly chat. He realized these front rooms were primarily for formal usage. The high visibility would prevent young people from too close encounters. And he deduced adults also. He heard Nola's soft step on the carpet.

She paused in the doorway. He spoke. "You are absolutely lovely. A marvel. You stand there as if you haven't been busy for hours."

"The compliments are appreciated." She walked toward him. "It's been a long week."

He met her halfway. "It has."

"And I know I asked for a week and a week really should be tomorrow. But may I borrow a few hours?"

"Yes."

She put her hands out, keeping them low. "Yes."

"Yes? Yes, is your answer?"

"I accept your proposal of marriage."

He brought her hands to his lips and kissed them. "And?"

"And yes, my dear Bruce. I love you. I love you more than I ever thought I could love anyone."

He swung around with his back against the doorway facing and pulled her close to him and kissed her firmly and hugged her tightly. "Dear God, I am so happy. So complete." He spread his arms outward, holding her hands, his face lit with excitement. To her, he stood taller, his whole being expanded as if needing more room to contain his joy.

"So am I."

"I feel like we're showcased between the door and the windows to the world. May I close the front door?"

"Please, do." After he did, she took his hand and started down the hall. With his free hand, he grabbed the candy box on their way to the den.

They stood and happily embraced each other in the middle of the room before settling on the couch. He handed her the box.

"Oh, I couldn't eat anything else at the moment. I am so full."

"At least open it," he implored.

She untied the narrow ribbon and lifted the top. Inside was a square velvet box. "Ah," she exclaimed then carefully removed it and opened the hinged top, exposing a large, faceted diamond, clear and brilliant, flanked on either side with three small diamonds in a platinum setting.

"I could only guess at the ring size, and it can be sized to fit you."

"Will you put it on?"

He took the ring and slid it on her third finger left hand. "A bit loose, is it?"

"Bruce, it's absolutely the most beautiful ring I ever saw. I love it." She put her hand out and admired the gem. "How dear of you to bring it tonight. My heart is so full. And I am indescribably pleased that you thought I would say yes. How long has it been? Three weeks? And we're both so committed!"

"Committed, yes." He almost added that he knew within twenty-four hours but decided that could wait.

They talked and held each other and then repeated the pattern for a couple of hours. "Bruce, can we visit my parents tomorrow and tell them? It's too important for a phone call. It will be such a shock. I want us to tell them together."

"A marvelous idea. And next weekend, we can do the same with my parents and sister. And if that's okay with you, I think I'll ask my sister to invite my parents to her house for the weekend. It will be easier for Mom to have Sis for support and reassurance."

"There is so much to do and so many people who will want to know. Bruce, will you tell your partners and staff that I'm your important client?"

"I will. What a surprise, a welcomed one for them! They have despaired endlessly about my single status. Now, we need to set a date. I told you ages ago that tomorrow wouldn't be too soon for me."

"Or me, I must confess. But, Bruce, can you understand I'd like a wedding? Not a very large affair but a real service. I know my mom would relish it."

"Anything you want. Just soon. As I admitted, I am patient, but . . ." and he pulled her into his arms and held her close. "Or we may have to live like so many lovers are doing these days."

"Bruce, we've had a void in our lives. Now the promise for future happiness and fulfillment is so close, can we try to abstain from . . . until we're married?" She gazed into his eyes intently and saw his yearning that matched her own. "This is September. Can we get married in November?"

"November?"

"The week before Thanksgiving? That's such a short time to plan a wedding."

His expression showed disappointment, but when he answered, it changed to one of compassion. "Let's set the date. And we'll work on self-control. My dear, you drive a hard bargain. Are you sure you didn't miss a calling as a negotiator in the business world?"

She laughed and squeezed him then stared at her ring. "Two months and there will be two rings on this hand."

It had been over three decades since he had approached parents about marrying their daughter. Back then, he knew the future in-laws well; they had been pleased, looked forward to his being officially a part of the family and not a'tal surprised. Today, the Gilberts were shocked as Nola had predicated. Once they regained breath and composure, both eagerly listened to Nola's revelation of the quick courtship.

Bruce watched and listened. The three had good chemistry in listening and responding. Their voices were regionally cultured and appropriately controlled. Nola inherited her height and coloring from her father, but not his very masculine build or presence. Her feminine qualities and enthusiasm reflected her mother's influence. Mrs. Gilbert was shorter and bit more round than Nola. He guessed Nola gained her business acumen from both parents.

Mrs. Gilbert admired the ring then raptly sought the news of wedding plans. The idea of only eight weeks to prepare at first sounded preposterous; however, as Nola was adamant, her mother adjusted her attitude and delved into the planning. After hearing the women chatter for a quarter an hour, Mr. Gilbert asked Bruce if he'd like a tour of the grounds. Nola and her mother encouraged them to go.

Bruce expected that Mr. Gilbert wanted to know some facts about this man who was in a hurry to marry his daughter. Thus, as they strolled, Bruce, who was accustomed to reassuring potential clients his credentials, talked about his youth, his marriage, his wife's death, meeting Nola via Amy, his college education, and his business.

"So, you're considering giving up the farm?" Mr. Gilbert asked.

"Yes, we're in the discussion stage with the realtor and the banks. Neither my brother nor sister has any interests in buying the place. Amy and Robert are pretty much settled on Windermere and Groton."

"Have you and Nola decided where you will live? Windermere or Raleigh?"

"For a while we'll be in both cities. My apartment is spacious, two bedrooms, and baths. Next weekend she'll get to check it over. We're going to drive east for her to meet my parents and my sister's family."

Mr. Gilbert nodded approvingly at the statements and in the manner they were conveyed.

Mrs. Gilbert delayed Nola and Bruce's departure even as the two stood beside his car. She posed one question after the other about the plans for November. Finally, Nola assured her mother that she would write down a full schedule in a couple of days and send it in the mail. She further promised to telephone her frequently.

Her parents stood beside the driveway and waved until the car was out of sight. He put an arm around her shoulders. "Well, dear, our daughter has made a choice."

"And a long time it took her!" she stated firmly.

"I'd say she made a pretty quick decision, my dear." He rejoined giving her shoulder a bit of a squeeze.

She lifted her shoulders and patted his hand. "Sorry. I was thinking how long it has been since Kyle. Yes, she's known Bruce only a few weeks. What do you think about him? Bruce? You're so keen in first interviews." She kept her eyes forward looking.

He answered. "I like him. He's got sense. He knew what I needed to hear. He was direct, forthcoming about his past, his marriage, and his children. It sounds as if he has had a happy life. And he's been in his current business for many years. Investment brokers have done well. I think he can take care of our girl."

"I knew I could trust your judgment as always. Let me breathe in this quiet sane moment. It may be my last deep inhaling until after the wedding."

He flung his head back and laughed then pulled her toward him and embraced her with vigor. "What a self-appraising woman." After a close moment, he asked with care, "But do you like him?"

She lifted her chin and stared at him. "Oh, yes, Papa, I do. I feel I can grow to love him. Anyone that could put the sparkle, the glow, the loving look in her eye that he has, is a very special person. She's the happiest I've seen her since . . ."

Mr. Gilbert's response was so immediate it would hark on being an interruption to anyone who was not familiar with two people who were so in tune to each other's thinking. "Shall we opt to say she looks the happiest we've ever seen her?" The upward vocal pitch and outlook ran customary in their conversations.

"Right, you are. Now, let's go in and start planning."

A few miles down the road, Nola said, "Bruce, they loved you immediately. I knew they would. Thank you so much for coming with me to tell them."

"They are very nice people. Cordial. And enthusiastic. They obviously are fond of you. So we begin our association in mutual admiration." He turned to smile at her. He reached for her hand and brought it to his lips.

Strapped in as she was, she managed to lean over and kiss his cheek.

Nola enjoyed the visit with his family even though they were not as outwardly elated as her parents were. She considered that assessment might well be because they had memories of his first marriage and possibly recognized the vulnerability of sorrow and hurting again. She sensed the family's deep love for each other, thus she looked forward positively toward their acceptance of Bruce and her relationship in due time.

His sister was very much like her mother, both in appearance and temperament. Women of medium height, fair skin, brown eyes, and brown hair, rather his sister's hair was definitely brown but her mother's had grayed considerably around her face. They spoke more slowly and softly than Bruce and his dad. The three shared a strong trait of kindness. She could hear it in their voices. Nola had no doubt that the entire family rose to the tasks before them and stayed until results were the best they could bring about. Perhaps, the farming had been very strenuous and prompted the parents to move before their health broke. She was pleased that their daughter lived close by. That arrangement had to be a comfort to Bruce, she thought.

The family asked simple, direct questions about the wedding and where they might live after the marriage. Nola responded to the first question and Bruce, the second. As with her parents, Nola and Bruce promised to keep in touch about the November wedding events.

It was dark when they arrived at his apartment in Raleigh. The streetlights were on. As Bruce opened the car door for her, he pointed to his place.

"The lights are on?" She noticed.

"Timers." He unlocked the door and bid her come in. He walked ahead and switched on more lamps. "Take a look around."

He followed her about the rooms, enjoying the exclamations at his comfortable furnishings, the framed prints on the wall, the immaculate kitchen, the charming dining room, and the large bedrooms. He paused between the latter two rooms. "Which one would you like tonight?"

She had brought an overnight bag just in case they decided not to make the trip in one day. Still, she peered askance at him.

"Last Sunday, I told your dad that I had two bedrooms and two bathrooms. Trust me, love, an understanding passed between us." He moved across the narrow hall and placed both hands, palms on the wall either side of her. "It will take more will power not to cross this hall or put a hand on you between these rooms or in these rooms, than it used to take me as a kid to stay out of the river until I had permission."

"I'll take the guest room. Until Thanksgiving. If we mosey back to the den, may I hug you?"

Chapter 15

Nola stopped her car near the front walk at the Umsteads', gathered a tote bag and her purse, and walked up to the house. Even though she and Bruce had been engaged some weeks, she didn't presume to go around to the back door like a family member.

Lou appeared in the hall as her second push of the bell sounded. He smiled broadly and opened the storm door.

"Come in. We're the only ones here. Amy called she'd be a bit late."

"Was there a lecture scheduled this afternoon?" She walked with Lou toward the kitchen. "I forgot to check the center's calendar." She spoke as if that were a grand omission.

"There was. Or is." Lou glanced at the clock on the microwave. "Should be over soon."

She placed her tote bag on the center counter and pulled out a box of doughnuts and a bag of coffee. "I couldn't resist the glaring, red neon light as I passed by."

"That does take some doing. How about I make a pot of coffee?"

"I would welcome a cup." She perched on a tall stool. "And Bruce? Is he on his way?"

Filling the carafe at the faucet, he half turned and grinned. "I thought you'd never ask."

"Lou, you are truly a tease. But a happy one." She waited.

"Yes, he stopped in Groton but planned to leave about half-hour ago."

Nola watched him as he went about the coffee making with ease. He appeared a man who was comfortable with himself. No pretense of being awkward in either kitchen or brandishing bravado gestures grilling on the deck. He went about life with an agreeable self-assurance. Nola relaxed in his company and enjoyed the easy banter.

"Do you mind a personal question?"

"Fire away!" he replied and pulled a doughnut from the box.

"Did you ever think about being a farmer?"

Swallowing a hunk of glazed doughnut, he reached for a mug and poured it half full, then drank some coffee. He raised a hand toward her. "Sorry to serve myself first. Here," he said as he handed her a full mug. She reached for the creamer. He continued. "As a youngster, I thought that was what I'd be. There was always something to do. Some folks may think it's boring having routine chores. But with our change of seasons, the routine varied. Some tasks were constant, and we needed those to give a rhythm to the day."

When he paused to pour more coffee, she commented. "I understand that. The school day also had its regular format but we varied the content and the presentation."

"Farm life was all I knew till I was a teenager. We went to the county school and most all the students lived on farms. Then in high school we were thrown with teens from nearby towns. It was a huge school and a really new experience for me. And I got involved in sports that gave me another dimension in groups." He shook his head. "I didn't realize how busy a guy could be keeping up with the consolidated education program and pulling his weight at home."

"Was that when you started looking at other occupations?"

He lifted his shoulder, grabbed another doughnut, and leaned back against the counter opposite her. "Do you know what really changed my direction?"

Nola shook her head and showed interest in her expression.

"Bruce."

She smiled. "Bruce? How?"

"It was in Raleigh. Those weekends I dated Amy and we'd go over to his apartment. Really, theirs. She stayed overnight a lot. I asked him about his work, his years in college, and in the brokerage firm. I knew he loved the farm, but I could see he was enthusiastic about his work in the city. His business isn't like something you can grab hold of, not like reaching down into the earth and curling your fingers around a handful of soil. Or pulling leaves from a tobacco plant. Nor . . . well, you know all those tangibles."

"I do. Like seeing the spool of thread on the mill looms and watching it grow into yards and yards of cloth. It has a smell and a hand that are real."

"Right, you are. And Bruce's world is one of paper and pencil and computers and drives and disks and is driven by a desire to see your figures shoot up on the graphs. Not just his, but also his clients. He's really a good guy. He looks after his clients."

"And how did his work help you into what you're doing?"

"Well, during high school he listened as I told him some of the key facts I was learning and to me ranting on about ideas I was forming. He'd ask me a few questions that redirected some of my suppositions. He never lectured, merely made it easy for me to talk. And he got me a job in Acorn with the weekly newspaper. Writing local sports and selling ads. Can you believe an eighteen-year-old talking with the businessmen whom I had known of all my life – selling them an ad? And others who were strangers."

"Well, I can. You have a natural talent, so I hear."

"My junior year in college, he got me an interview in Raleigh with a businessman who had a new product line that he wanted to test-market in a few towns. I got the job and that directed me toward selling as a career. And I had a better perspective for weighing my options."

"It was good to have those opportunities and experiences."

Lou propped his arms back and cupped his hands over the smooth edges of the counter. "Bruce had been a broker for a number of years and I could see he was very prosperous. He had a good life. In many ways better than what, he would have had if he'd tried farming full time. He could give Amy and Robert many advantages, especially college education. They didn't have to work jobs during those years. Oh, they worked, but it wasn't the pressure of being necessary." He laughed genially. "And he had time to watch out for them. I won't say watch over them. He didn't give us, Amy and me, much opportunity to get into trouble."

"Oh," she hummed. "Just kept you working."

"Yeah, Bruce, set high standards for his children. And it paid off. I have the best of wives." He became introspective and drew his lips into a firm line.

"She is a jewel, Lou. I'm glad you've shared this with me. I think your whole family is very special."

Focusing again on Nola, Lou said, "Mrs. Umstead was an upright woman. She loved her home, her family, and her farm. She was what one calls a homebody. That's where she was happiest. They all loved each other." He looked down at his shoes, his forehead in a frown. "As far as anyone knows, Bruce was always loyal to her. It was hard for all of them, me too, when she was sick." He raised his eyes. "After she died, it was good he had a place in Raleigh and work he could dig into. Ten years is a long time alone. We're all pleased as can be he has found happiness again. Thank you for . . ."

"For loving him? I do. And I love his family, too."

Car doors were slammed outside. Nola wiped her eyes. "Will this be our sweethearts arriving?" She stepped the few feet between Lou and her and leaned over and kissed his cheek.

The back door opened and Amy came in with Bruce close behind. Amy called out. "Sorry we're late." Bruce spoke with a mock rebuke. "What have we here?"

Nola sensed that he had witnessed the affectionate peck on the cheek. "I'm thanking Lou for making a delicious pot of coffee. Do come and have a cup."

Lou added, "And a doughnut. Nola brought her own treat. Shall I mic the doughnuts so the sugary glaze delights your nose as well as your palate?"

The phone was ringing as Nola finished dressing for the day. "Hello," she answered.

"Nola, I hope this isn't too early to call," said her neighbor Mary Few.

"Not at all."

"If you have a couple of minutes, I'd like to come over for a chat."

"Now is a good time. I'll perk a fresh pot of coffee." As Nola hung up the phone, she prepared the coffee and a serving tray. Mary's voice had a mix of friendliness and uncertainty. Having not talked with her in a week or more, Nola chose not to play guessing games.

When the two were seated at the breakfast table and Mary finished a first cup of coffee, she looked as if she didn't know quite know how to phrase what she wanted to say. Finally, she decided. "Nola, I don't like to be a pessimist, but I want to tell you about a man who was in the neighborhood a few days ago. He was asking if there were any odd chores he could do."

"Oh?"

Mary continued. "Usually, anyone seeking work asks about yard work, cleaning gutters, even painting, but this one was vague. He didn't have a truck. He may have had a car somewhere down the street, but I didn't see one. No card, no flyers. He didn't smile or have a practiced sales pitch."

Nola asked, "Did you have any work for him?"

Mary shook her head. "If I'd had any, I wouldn't have given it to him."

"He didn't look reliable?"

"Not a bit. Rather spooky. Nervous. I don't expect men who have to knock on doors to be dressed like office workers, but their clothes usually fit, and they have an attitude of being willing to work. This man may well have needed a job, but . . ." she frowned and slightly drew up her shoulders.

"He wasn't someone you wanted in the house or the yard," Nola offered.

"Right," Mary sat back, relieved to be instantly understood. Nola refilled their cups and waited for Mary to add cream and sugar, then poured cream into hers. "I saw him knock at your door. He looked in your front windows while on the porch. I thought you'd like to know."

"Thank you for telling me. Has he been around again? Did any of the other neighbors say he had come to their houses?"

"I only saw him once. No one else on the block talked with the man. After he left my house, I watched him go to yours and the Gibsons'. They weren't home either."

"What did he look like?"

"A small man, with a quick, jerky gait. Thin, scrawnylike, his clothes kind of hung on him, not ironed. He had on an old hat, like a fisherman's, narrow brim around."

Nola was quiet a moment. "You're right he doesn't sound like the typically odd-job person we see. But there are more laid-off people right now with factories closing in many nearby counties and people doing more of their own yard work and such. You didn't say he was a foreigner or immigrant. The increase in their numbers could be forcing local men to look elsewhere for work."

"Humph! If more Americans were willing to work, then perhaps there wouldn't be such a surge of crossing the borders or trying to swim ashore from outlying boats."

Nola had heard this talk before and turned the conversation to comments about the lovely fall morning.

"Yes, it is. Now, what I really came to chat about is I want to have a bridal luncheon for you." Mary's smile returned, as did an enthusiastic tone. "We must celebrate this marvelous occasion. I would love to have the women in our neighborhood and any special friends you'd like to invite to my home. Early – to mid-October is usually still colorful and the weather pleasant."

"How very nice that will be," Nola responded. They discussed the event, and Nola promised to checks dates with her mother who was coming for the weekend.

Nola became more careful to lock the outside doors even while she was in the house and the front and side doors when she was out back. The neighborhood had always been so secure; she had the alarm system installed at her parents' request. Recently, she was warned that prior to a wedding the bride's house was a good target. Thus she was doubly glad she had the alarm.

She had no intention of mentioning either or these two remotely possible threats to her parents or anyone else.

The visit overflowed with lively conversation from the Gilberts' early-afternoon arrival on Friday until their departure Sunday afternoon.

Mr. Gilbert joined in the talks that pertained to his responsibilities, and he listened to general plans being formulated. Otherwise, he watched a few newscasts on television, read the sports and business pages of Windermere newspaper, and rode around the city with Bruce.

Nola offered to prepare dinner at home on Friday night, but her father offered to take the four of them out. Everyone accepted his invitation. Bruce wanted to be a host at a restaurant that he and Nola liked on Saturday night. Amy and Lou invited the four of them and Robert and Susan over for Sunday brunch. It was a full weekend with everyone delighted to be in on the planning for the Thanksgiving wedding.

"Next visit, Mom and Dad, we will go to the eleven o'clock worship service. Then you can get a feel of the church and the congregation, hear the minister and the marvelous choir. The sanctuary is magnificent. You can imagine how floral arrangements would look in it. Then we'll take another look at the chapel. It is quite lovely. I believe everything we've planned will be just perfect."

"That's a good idea. We'd better do that soon. We have really set some set dates this weekend. The neighborhood luncheon, Amy's barbecue, your friend Janet's shower, the photography sitting. Oh, and the shopping. And Nola, do have the maid for those last days before the wedding?"

Nola placed a hand on her mother's arm. "Mom, I've made notes and will keep a to-do list close by and update it often."

Mrs. Gilbert patted Nola's hand. "Right, dear. I know the men don't want to hear each detail. But I'm just so excited and I want to help all I can."

"You always do and I appreciated your caring."

Amy stood at the tall counter in the auditorium stacking the filled-in evaluation forms while Nola collected pencils and replaced them in the box. Amy clipped the papers together.

"Good responses?"

"Yes. And they give checks to the professional and polite registration. Thank you," Amy answered and smiled.

"The doctor had a very good presentation. The audience was especially attentive."

"So many people have shoulder problems. Though this was geared toward our older members, especially those who play golf or tennis, everybody could surely get a better understanding of what young athletes face. The injuries and treatments."

"True. And the options that are available. Aren't these graphics superb in showing exactly what the lecturer is saying? This three-way approach is well done. The oral lecture along with diagrams, photos, and written words – all there so at least one of the senses has to be reached."

Amy touched a brochure on the counter. "The handout with colored sketches of all that was shown is a great reference source later."

"And the large white margins for note-taking. I noticed lots of scribbling when he gave the dosages of medications. Amy, this is a great program the university and the hospital are making available for the public. You really do a super job here."

"Thank you. The members are so enthusiastic!" She held up the forms. "I like to read their comments."

"I've been doing some reading when I get here early," Nola said. "There are so many good reference books in your library. Up-to-date material."

"Anything particular?" Amy inquired, leaning her elbows on the counter.

"The aging process. I want to know more about the members who come to these programs. I think you're right on target here offering a wide variety of programs. The intellectual and practical matters of health, and then the fun things. The cooking demonstrations, the holiday dance, exercise classes, the day trips, and the longer out-of-town jaunts. Really, it appears as if what you're presenting will give older people lots of opportunities to round out or balance their lives."

"Yes. It's a buffet of programs. You can sample some of all or just select what you're interested in or whatever may be lacking elsewhere."

Nola stated, "I was surprised to read that the number of interests and a wide circle of people in your life are more important than the longevity of your family. So these functions you have here really have great value. Plus the members don't have to spend much money. The transportation costs, which they could easily tie in with some small task at the mall such as a stop at the drugstore, post office, shopping or a walk for exercise."

"Well, keep me informed about any good hints you glean from these expert sources," Amy said. "Now, I need to call a few people about upcoming programs." As she switched off overhead lights and headed toward the double-glassed doors, she commented. "We do have a nice bunch of folks, don't we? They are well adjusted and continue to want to learn."

Nola opened the door. "They are. Their enthusiasm adds to the general tenor of the world, doesn't it? Very few are natured like Bessie Kester." Nola waited to close the door after Amy walked out. Instantly, she saw the younger woman's face contort in sadness. Nola bit her bottom lip, fully aware she should have never verbalized that thought.

She placed a hand on Amy's arm. "A mistake. I'm sorry."

Amy nodded and walked to her office. Nola stopped at the desk and held up some pencils that needed sharpening. Phyllis took the box and the loose pencils and said she would do them later.

Nola headed for the coffee area. A tall, well-dressed man stood at the counter, his attention focused on the black thermos pitchers.

Her footsteps were quiet on the carpet. As she stepped on the tile flooring, her heels clicked. The man looked over his shoulder.

"Reading the choices," he commented.

"Is it two decafs and one regular?" she asked.

"One decaf, one half decaf and half regular. And a third reads hazelnut," he replied making a half-turn toward her.

Nola lifted her eyebrows, pleased. "Something new."

He stepped back. "After you."

"No, sir. You were first."

Reading her nametag, he said, "Then may I fill a cup for you, Nola?"

"Thank you. Half and half." She noticed his nicely shaped hands, well-cared-for nails, the oxford shirt, and navy blue jacket as he pumped the thermos top. After he handed the cup over, he drew hazelnut for himself.

She picked up a napkin. He tasted the flavored coffee, announced "It's different and good," and looked around the room. "I've heard about this center. An outreach of the hospital, isn't it?"

"Yes. And the university."

"You're a volunteer?" He glanced again at her nametag.

"Yes. For a year now."

"I'd like to hear about this center." He surveyed the room.

"Would you like to sit at a table? If you have a few minutes, I'll share what I know." She picked up some brochures from the reception desk and indicated the table near the library shelves.

"The clothier I've known for years has opened a shop in the mall." He settled into a chair opposite her.

Nola sipped the hot coffee and wondered why a healthy-looking nice-looking man, probably in midsixties, would be spending leisure time in the center. By all appearances, he could afford coffee elsewhere.

"Here is a calendar of events for this month and a newsletter that includes the purpose of the center. Education is tops." She pushed the papers slightly over.

Putting his coffee down, he pulled an eyeglass case from an inside jacket pocket, adjusted the reading glasses, and scanned the newsletter and upcoming events. Finished, he looked up. "Very impressive. You should have considerable interest in your program."

"I do. We do."

"Tell me about volunteering. I'm not looking for an outlet, yet. I'm recently retired." He spoke with a mix of seriousness and humor.

She half-laughed. "I understand. I fit into that category, too."

His surging energy and interest showed in his posture, his eyes, and his reaching forward for his cup. He continued attentively, while Nola shared the initial interview with the director of volunteers, the training session, tour of some hospital sections, and the listing of volunteer opportunities.

She was impressed that he seemed so interested. As she finished, she pointed to another paper on the table. "That's an enrollment form for Healthy Living, if you're interested in becoming a member."

He scooped it up, quickly skimmed it front and back. With wry amusement, he read aloud the dollar amount. "So few dollars?"

"True. A one-time fee. This is to take the latest medical news to the people. Literally, take it to them, where they go."

"A fine, forward-looking idea."

"Would you need a second form?" she asked.

Staring at her, he knew what she was implying – one for your wife. He couldn't lie. There is a wife. She was too well bred to ask "Why are you here alone drinking coffee with a woman." He added to his assessment – a very attractive woman, probably still in her forties. And his curiosity peaked: Why is she volunteering? No wedding band?

"Another form, please." He reread a page of the newsletter. Without looking up, he said, "I doubt my wife will be interested. She stays busy." Then he looked up with a peculiar smile, though broad, not one of joy, more like feigned amusement that besought "have pity on me" response. "She likes the house to herself on tidying-up days."

"A convenient time to run errands," she commented. Checking her watch, she said, "I have an appointment. If you decide to sign up, you may leave the form at the desk or mail it."

She rose and he did too. "Thank you for the information and sharing a coffee break."

Nola nodded then crossed to the trash bin and deposited her cup and napkin. She saw he had remained standing at the table. She retraced her steps. "May I make a suggestion?" "You may." "Take time to consider your options. Windermere offers a variety of opportunities for retirees. We're still young in spirit and mentally flexible enough to investigate new interests."

Walking away, she realized she had given impromptu advice as she had done to her students at times.

Later that afternoon at home, she recalled the incident and questions surfaced. Why was a recently retired man of means at loose ends? Though he had a legitimate errand, he gave the impression that he was not welcomed at home. The idea saddened her. She allowed her mind to wander.

A man works and provides a house for his family only to realize later, when his work is done, the welcome mat is reversed: greeting the departing footsteps.

Not just the man today, there were images of those attending events, some with wives, some alone. Were the latter in the category of being shooed from homes? She hoped not. She preferred to think the men were following one of their own interests while the wives were theirs that home life was happy and agreeable for both. Some male volunteers at the center were reliable and steady, though slow-paced with basically easy but necessary duties including coffee making, restocking supplies, re-shelving library materials, occasionally assisting with audio-visual equipment, answering general questions, and leading inquirers to the reception desk.

Someone once told her that no one really knows what goes on inside a home. She instantly picked up the message, translated, and filed it in her mind: Be careful in judging a relationship between two people, especially in labeling the absent person as a negative entity.

She shook her head to dislodge these thoughts and images to consider her own agenda: the list made with her mother, plans for Bruce's next visit, and household tasks. She looked forward to welcoming Bruce not only here for the weekend but also in their future homes. And, God willing, we'll have many years together.

Chapter 16

"Link, give me twenty dollars. For the kids. Some things for school," his wife Tori said.

"Can't do it," he replied adamantly.

She retorted, "They've outgrown their clothes and shoes. They need new notebooks." She shifted her large body forward and reached for a handful of potato chips on the kitchen table.

He jerked his head side to side.

Between bites, she pursued, "Have you deposited the unemployment check? Did you get cash for running the house?"

"It's in the bank. No account will be paid in full, only the minimum amount."

"How many more months will we get the checks?"

"Not many." He pulled some money from his pocket and slapped it on the table.

"What about the hospital? Did you go back there?" She picked up the money.

"I did. Nothing. New postings will go up in a few weeks. Now quit bothering me." He fidgeted with his fork pushing the beans around the plate. "I'm sick of beans."

"Mercy, I never thought we'd come to this. Broke all the time." She choked and began to cry. "If my mama could see me now, she'd . . ."

"Say that it looks as if you eat plenty!" He scraped his chair back and stood up. "You go look for a job, see how scarce they are."

"But you've got skills. You can use the computer and do lots of office jobs. Nobody wants anyone like me. I'm a homemaker." She dabbed her eyes with a paper napkin then squinted as the salt irritated them.

"The kids have been in school for years. Go to work. Try the hospital. It doesn't discriminate. There are many there big as you. Take an entry-level job. Work your way up. Work off the fat!"

"I'll never be skinny like you. When we were married, I was a size 10. Children and . . ."

Link half turned his back, grabbed his cap by the visor from a wall peg, and slapped it against the wall before pulling it on his thinning hair. He looked down at her; her untidy appearance brought a sneer to his face. He blurted, "First, go apply at the extra-large-size shop for women for a sales job or the stockroom. That'll get you a discount."

His eyes raked over her with contempt. Hers registered disbelief.

"Pop!" A chorus from the hallway preceded two upper-elementary-age children. A plump girl with bangs and straight-around haircut in a blue blouse and short denim skirt entered. Immediately behind her appeared a lean fellow in jeans and striped tee shirt. Soon as she cleared the doorway, he sidled past.

"Pop, I'm older. I have my school list here." He shot his hand toward Link.

"But I want some new clothes. Look how out of style these are!" She stopped and pointed from her neck to her feet.

Link pressed his fingers to his cap and palms over his ears and gritted his teeth. "I don't have any money now. I had to pay the bills. Ask your mama if she has any left from her house money." He yanked the door open and slammed it behind him.

Starting his old-model sedan, he fumed. "This is not how I thought life would be. I've got to get work. The hospital is the biggest employer in town now. They'll find a place for me. They will! I didn't get fired from the last two positions. One downsized and the other was merged. Unemployment twice! So many forms and applications to fill out for work and to prove to the government you're making an effort." He banged a hand on the steering wheel and hissed, "Which is worse, the government or the economy?"

Nola waited by Phyllis to finish a phone conversation so that she could get the final list of reservations for the afternoon event. She saw Matt enter the center.

Simultaneously, they greeted each other.

"Did you grow this African violet? It's gorgeous, so many blossoms." She leaned over to inspect it closely. "Very healthy."

"I did. This is for Joyce," he said and handed it to her as she came to the desk.

She read the name on the envelope. "For me?" She pulled a card out. "From my husband. How perfect. He knew I wanted one. Thank you, Matt."

Nola said, "When spring comes, I'll be out to select some herbs and roses at your nursery. We'll touch base next week about flowers for the wedding."

"Right," he agreed and left the center.

Link exited the mall computer supply shop. The forced smiled he had shown while talking with the manager about employment possibilities reverted to a turned-down position, the same as his application. He pulled his cap back on, his black mood returned. Rehashing the brief interview, he stumbled on blindly in his own world.

At a corner he collided with Matt, and Link had to right himself quickly or take a tumble on the granite floor. Matt reached forward but Link flung his arm out, resisted help, and backed away.

"Sorry, sir," Matt stopped and said with concern.

Irritated and embarrassed, Link glanced about. Seeing no one else pausing or staring, he gruffly said, "Yeah. Watch where you walk."

Matt bent his head slightly and leaned forward. His expression was searching. He wondered where he had seen the man. Somewhere he took flowers?

Link glared only an instant at the younger, stronger man then hoisted his shoulders and walked down the hall toward the health center.

Matt stood watching him and his jerky way of walking. He wished he could have seen the man's face better, but the cap sat low on his forehead. Unpleasant guy, Matt labeled him, but it'll come to me. Like flowers, I forget a name once in a while – roses have so many names – but sooner or later, they come to me.

Several women were walking into the health center as Link approached. He stopped beside the display window, read the poster, and knew this was not a lecture for men. Cautiously, he stepped to the center's wide entrance and paused. Amid the crowd, he spotted the volunteer checking in participants. The same one he had seen last time he was here. Standing the other side of the desk and giving out membership forms was the receptionist whom he had run-ins with. Twice, she had said he wasn't registered for a seminar, once she was reluctant to give him a second pencil when he said he'd dropped his. She frowned at him when he appeared to be exiting the center with one of their library books, and he dropped it on a table near the exit before leaving.

He thought it was stupid, not to let people check out books! She's always watching for me to commit some crime. I'd downsize her in a snap of the fingers. And she didn't like that talkative Kester woman either. I noticed how she grimaced as soon as the woman turned her back when she was getting free coffee or had asked a stupid question at the desk.

He was staring at Phyllis and she turned toward the entrance and riveted a sharp look at him.

Women! Link shuddered. Who needs them! He glared an instance before hastily crossing the hall toward an outside exit and lowering his cap to his eyebrows.

Nola was surprised at the number of women who wanted to attend this seminar and at the range of ages. Several appeared barely eligible, fifty being the required age for the programs Amy planned; others had the posture, wrinkles, demeanor of women in their sixties and seventies. Why, she wondered, did the older ones want to know about menopause? She considered them several years past that stage of life.

When Amy had called asking for help this afternoon, she confessed that there was a full enrollment and several names on the waiting list. "Nola, we have had so many requests for a program on this topic. I have an unexpected meeting during lunch with the marketing director, and I may not be back in time for handling the registrations or to start the program."

"I'll be glad to help. Who will introduce the speaker?"

"Joyce. Thanks so much. I appreciate it."

At the center, Nola read fifty preregistered names and fifteen add-ons. Quickly, she opened the auditorium door and counted the seats – fifty. How am I going to get all these women in? She placed legal pads and sweaters on two chairs, reserving them for Amy and herself.

Nola sought Joyce. "Are there any extra chairs in the center? We have a long waiting list."

"Only those in the conference room. Could you ask the women at the desk to get them? I need to finish setting up for the speaker. Do you know her?"

"No, but I'll be alert for a woman coming in with a briefcase and or other academic paraphernalia." Nola returned to her table on the other side of the door.

Two women approached cautiously. One spoke. "Do you have room for the two of us? We forgot to phone in our registrations."

"I can add your names to the waiting list. It will depend upon how many who are preregistered show up." The women looked at each other as if trying to make a decision. Their hesitation caused Nola to say, "But we will seat you if at all possible."

Relief showed on their faces; they nodded to each other. One gave her name and watched Nola write the name before stepping back. The other lady spelled her last name quietly. "Thank you, young lady."

Nola darted a look. The older woman showed an agreeable expression. Nola smiled. Now, do I look young because I probably am ten to twenty years her junior? Or could it be that being loved and having a proposal have erased some lines from my face?

She didn't have time to form any answers for she spotted an attractive, professional-looking woman about forty years of age striding into the center. She held an expandable file tucked under one arm and a large briefcase in the other hand. Her eyes focused toward the auditorium.

Nola stepped forward and asked if woman was the speaker for the seminar.

"Yes. I'm Marsha Willard."

"Hello. I'm Nola Gilbert. Amy had a called meeting," Nola opened the door and walked into the auditorium with the speaker and closed the door. "She will be here before the seminar is over. Joyce can assist you with any arrangements."

"Thank you." Marsha walked to the long table against the back wall and placed her file and briefcase on top. She withdrew sets of papers from slots in the file and placed them separately beside her case.

Nola closed the door and resumed her duties. She called out in her controlled carrying voice, "Is there anyone who preregistered and hasn't checked in?" She held her clipboard forward. Three women, who were seated, rose and came to the table.

Five minutes before the hour, the doors were opened and the women proceeded into the auditorium. As soon as the preregistered members found seats, Nola counted fourteen unfilled. Fifteen women waited. Fourteen filed in. The one left appeared so disappointed that Phyllis said, "I can spare my chair."

"I wouldn't want you to have to work standing, but I appreciate your offer." The lady refused.

Phyllis picked up the chair. "No problem. I can use the time to file some papers in the office. And I have to stand for that."

After the chair was placed beside the ones reserved for Nola and Amy, the grateful woman sat down. Joyce was giving the academic credentials of Dr. Willard as Nola closed the doors and lowered the blinds. Nola squeezed past the woman and left an empty seat between them. Nola reached for the handouts and the pencil before she sat down. She slipped the clipboard beneath her chair then skimmed the written materials.

One page showed sketches of women at puberty, young adult, middle-aged, and upward stages. A second had side views of the spine at youth, middle age, and seventies. Another page was titled: What is Menopause? When does it end?

Topics were in bold print and information was bulleted underneath.

Nola ran a finger down the topics: Onset, Symptoms, Treatments, Attitudes, New Interests and Pursuits, Lifestyle, Sex.

She wondered why she hadn't been more curious about this stage. Lurking in her mind was the idea that menopause was the cessation of periods. Since she hadn't reached that stage, she delayed delving into medical books for information. Several of her friends had already gone through what they called "that time of life." Some had hot flashes; others had emotional highs and lows. A few complained and a like number rejoiced that those days of "the curse" were ending. She had listened to their vocalizing and responded with words that seemed appropriate for the various moods her friends were experiencing. Reading the material now, she realized menopause was a stage that women neither looked forward to nor planned for. It was inevitable and required no preparation. They intuited that the "word" signaled an ending of the fertile stage and fearfully heralded a waning of femininity and attractiveness.

That thought provoked a clutching of muscles in Nola's chest. Her throat constricted and her limbs tensed. What am I thinking about? Falling in love when my time is almost over? Getting married? Having a lover? Oh, being a lover? How long will I have? Will I be a shrew in a few months? A year? Soak the bed with hot flashes? Heaven forbid, I embarrass Bruce if I bead perspiration on my face or fog my reading glasses when we're out.

How quickly will I age? Look old? Wrinkled, drawn, stooped? I can't look at these women in the room now. When did they begin to age physically? The first signs . . . let me remember my relatives. Their eyes had drooping lids or puffiness underneath then their jowls and neck sagged. She shut out other images.

Not turning her head but shifting her eyes to the right and ahead of her, she checked that no one was staring her way. All the other people in the room were attending to the drawings and diagrams on the large screen and apparently listening to the gynecologist. Nola considered she may be missing some information that was not on the handout and tried to read the sentences; however, the overhead sheet was changed and left a gap in her following the direction of the presentation.

She had a flashback of some of her pokey or lazy students not following the lecture. When they asked her to put the transparency back on, she remembered saying, "Everyone seems to have notes already; stay after class and you can copy from the overhead sheet." There wasn't likely to be an option of catching up here.

How well she knew that so much material, especially new material, was easier to assimilate when a knowledgeable teacher stood in front of you and developed it sequentially or in order of importance. Transparencies on a large screen permitted students to follow the red dot of a laser on a diagram without showing the shadow of the instructor. Key words and text loomed large and easily readable, thus viewers did not have to ask a person in the next seat, what did she say? How do you spell that? All a student had to do was concentrate, listen, look, and copy rapidly. She hadn't been doing that.

A faint sound of the door opening and closing registered with Nola. Before she could turn around, she spied Amy passing the woman on the end of the row and sitting down in the next chair. Nola whispered, "A full house. We seated everyone."

"Good," Amy responded and gave her attention to the speaker.

Dr. Willard paused before changing transparencies and a woman near the front raised her hand. She was recognized with a "yes?"

"Is it normal for a woman to be still having periods at age fifty?"

"Yes. The average age of menopause is fifty-two." Gasps escaped many in the audience. Dr. Willard continued. "Some women may miss a period or two then resume periods. Especially during their forties, women may notice a change in the flow or a missed period and think they are beginning menopause. Often that is not the case."

The woman who asked the question spoke again. "Are you saying that it is possible for a woman to become pregnant at fifty?"

"It is. Menopause is often stated as being between ages forty-five and fifty-five."

She paused and waited for the women to exchange puzzled expressions and jot figures on the handouts. "In fact until twelve months after the last period, I suggest to my patients the use of some form of contraception."

"What type of contraceptive do you recommend?" asked a woman who appeared to be in her early fifties.

Dr. Willard replied, "It depends on the patient. What she's comfortable with. There are several choices."

Another woman asked, "What are some of those?"

"There are the hormone replacement therapies in pill form that have been around for many years. And several natural hormones are available in topical creams. Other options are hormonal patches, inserts, and injections. These are about 99 percent effective. There are caps and devices for insertion."

Stunned by the doctor's information and recommendation, Nola stared ahead. Slowly lowering her gaze and penciling a few words, she cleared her throat before focusing on the next overhead sheet. Nola sensed that Amy had become tense. And it was the first time she had felt discomfort in the younger woman's presence. It was not for anything said or done by the other but a mutual reaction from some information. Nola did not try to imagine which statement had brought about a change in Amy.

However, Nola knew she herself was shaken by the fact that although she had yet to go through the dreaded physical symptoms that were attributed to menopausal females, paramount was the realization that she could become pregnant. Long ago – perhaps ten years – she had accepted that she probably would never bear a child. What in heavens name would she, would Bruce, think if that happened?

Realizing there was much that she didn't know about this stage, Nola hoped some other questions would come from the group. For once she wished there were another Bessie Kester to keep the questions and answers going. After an inquiry that had a lengthy reply, Dr. Willard directed attention to the final page of the handout.

"The bibliography has been updated recently and these sources should be available at the library or in bookstores. If not, the publisher is noted and you can contact the company." She closed the seminar with the suggestion that for those with concerns to contact their gynecologist.

Amy stepped into the center aisle and upon reaching the podium thanked Dr. Willard for coming. The transparency was removed from the overhead projector screen and the auditorium lights were brightened. A few women edged their way to speak to the doctor. Nola scooted to open the doors and collect the evaluation sheets and pencils.

Arriving home, Nola headed straight for the telephone. She dialed her primary care physician. When the receptionist answered, Nola asked for a recommendation for a gynecologist. Next, she requested the receptionist to make an appointment for the doctor's earliest opening. "It's not a physical emergency, but I do want to talk with her as soon as possible."

Nola was put on hold while a call was placed. She was pleased that a woman doctor had been recommended, anticipating the topic would be personal and close-textured. Today's lecture alerted her that she had limited knowledge about this upcoming time of her life. Surely, with the entire medical and research advances of recent decades, information abounded on ways to handle problems or mere nuisances. Within minutes, the receptionist was back on the line. "Is Monday at two o'clock convenient with you?" "Yes, and thank you so much. Yes, I know the office building."

Next, Nola phoned the main public library and asked about three of the books listed on the handouts. Two were in and she reserved those. Straightaway, she drove downtown and picked up the copies, planning to lose no time in becoming further educated.

Following hours of copious reading, she changed her sandals for walking shoes. After locking the door and stepping onto her walkway, she saw a neighbor wave and head her way. Immediately, Nola decided to drive to a public stroll way a few miles west of her street. She smiled, waved in response to the friendly woman and opened her car door, turned on the ignition and shifted to reverse. Fortunately, the neighbor had to wait on her curb for two passing cars, and Nola backed out and drove on.

Nola chastised herself briefly for being impolite but recognized her need for pondering material in the books was preeminent. As she parked in the stroll way lot, a quick glance revealed few walkers: the hour was early for the sun was still high and bright.

With information from the books, she was more aware of the negative view that society as a whole had of older women and how those experiencing menopause, more or less, accepted the "old" label. Attitudes were absorbed, such as mood swings are normal, and downgrading of oneself often followed. But that did not have to be the case, the authors who were also practicing clinicians postulated. Both writers documented years of experience with their women patients who had gone through this time of change without physical or mental suffering.

In fact, many used the increased energy they felt in pursuing projects or for other purposes that added positively to their lives. The doctors recorded that sexual activity did not have to cease and that many women found their pleasure heightened.

But as in every stage of healthy living that took some good habits. Nola was familiar with good diets, physical exercise, and a cheerful outlook. What she didn't know was particular exercises of internal organs. The books listed some, but the gynecologist should have additional ones. As Nola walked at a steady pace, she decided to call the gym and sign up for an exercise class or find out about fitness machines.

Returning to her car, she remembered the last seminar when she saw Bessie Kester. The woman had been annoying to the audience with her numerous questions. When Nola opened her car door, she suddenly felt uncomfortable and looked back, then hastily slid onto the driver's seat, and thrust the key forward and turned on the engine. She locked the door, switched on the air conditioner, and closed the window she had left open an inch because she had parked in a sunny spot.

Driving out of the lot, she wondered if Bessie had had any warning that she was ill, or, perish the thought, that someone was about to cause her harm. Remorsefully, she regretted that she had not been kind to her, at least had smiled upon greeting her at check-in that day. What causes a woman to ward off people? Has she been hurt or is she overburdened? Does her husband, in Bessie's case, harangue so frequently that she has forgotten how to be socially friendly?

Once, Nola recalled mentioning to a coworker a woman who appeared lonely and wanted to know if anyone has ever tried to help her. The coworker's answer had been a surprise. "Yes, to no avail. She is lonely. Before you try to get close to her, consider how much time and effort you are willing to give." Nola remembered having given a questioning look, for the coworker added. "The task will consume much patience and energy."

Could it be that the health center staff had already been that route? Well, Nola prayed that someday a method would evolve to guide us in extending the right hand of assistance and fellowship toward healing such women.

Chapter 17

Bruce watched Nola closely. She was unusually quiet. Her kiss upon greeting had been light and brief then she had taken his hand and walked him to the den. Somehow, he sensed this was not to initiate a cozy session on the couch. So, he was surprised when she led him there and bid him be seated.

However, she sat down leaving a couple of feet of space between them. He waited. She folded her hands in her lap, stared at them. Next she glanced at him, making eye contact and as swiftly lowered her gaze and folded her arms with her hands clasping her upper arms. After a couple of deep breaths, she turned at an angle toward him.

"I thought saying anything to you would be easy. I'm sorry I don't intend to dramatize what I'm going to say. But, well, I'm so unaccustomed to talking about very personal subjects." She looked at him. He had a patient expression. She realized that trait was one that was so dear in him. He didn't push her to hurry, had never shown exasperation. Instinctively, she reached out a hand, but quickly withdrew it, placing it once more on her arm.

"No. I'll want to say some things first. I visited a gynecologist this week. There's nothing wrong," she assured him. He nodded, but his eyes cast a shadow of a question.

"I had been to a seminar at the center last week. The topic was menopause. I was there to greet because Amy had a meeting," she explained. "Bruce, this is difficult so I'll just say the facts straight out. I haven't begun that stage yet. I had expected it would have come or some signs of it by this time. But it hasn't. And I've not worried about it. Something the lecturer said shocked me. She was answering a question for someone in the audience and said that it was possible to become pregnant at age fifty."

She stopped and made eye contact and waited for him to speak.

Quietly, he asked, "And . . . ?"

"She said the average age of menopause is fifty-two. So I don't know how much longer it will go on for me. Periods that is."

Again she stopped. Again, he said, "And . . . ?"

"My dear Bruce, you are the most patient man, and I know the wisest guy in the world. Bottom line, the gyn said she recommends some form of contraceptive for a full year after the last period." She sat back against the sofa cushion and closed her eyes. She dropped her hands in her lap.

"But she found everything all right with you physically."

"Yes. I'd had an exam with my regular doctor several months ago, but I did have another with her."

"And you talked about contraceptives?"

"Yes."

He moved close to her and turned her to face him. "What are your thoughts?"

With tears in her eyes, she muttered, "I never considered that I could conceive a child. Not at forty-nine. Almost fifty. Never gave a thought to protection."

"Are you thinking this will change how I feel about you?"

"Will it?"

"Not in any way. Nola, there is one concern. I don't want to hurt you, physically."

"Oh, Bruce, you won't."

He had a puzzled expression. "I shall try not to."

"I've learned some things in the past week. Leave it to me to be ready."

As she relaxed, he pulled her into his arms and the warmth of their love was renewed. When she put her head back on the cushions, she said, "Amy came into the seminar in time to hear that fact about late pregnancy possibilities. We haven't discussed it and I probably won't bring it up. We are so close, but I can't think of any way we can toss this topic about except in a joking way." She looked at Bruce. "But it's not a joking issue to me now. I have to adjust my mind to the possibility. I certainly won't breathe a word of this to my mom or dad." She grimaced and then grinned.

Bruce laughed lightly. "My dear Nola, you just made a joke about . . ."

Placing a hand over his lips quickly, she smiled. "Please, say I didn't do that!"

They sat side by side, near hands with fingers entwined. Each pondered his dreams and future. Finally, Bruce broke the silence.

"Can we keep this news in the back of our minds and do what is necessary at the time? I'm happy with you – talking, loving, and seeing a future with you always beside me. Possibilities that could spoil our marriage are remote."

"Yes, way in the back. It's not a thorn, just a speck – a little fact. I love you all the more than I did yesterday because the possibility hasn't upset you. Oh, another fact: women do not have to be crabby or shrewish during menopause. All the energy that hypes women's bodies during the cycles can be channeled into other activities in this change-of-life time." She announced empathetically.

Uncharacteristically, Bruce slapped his thigh and bellowed. "Well, that shall be a time to welcome. Nola, the energetic woman of my life, shall be inexhaustible. I shall kiss at our wedding your seminar leader or the gyn – whoever slanted light on that phase." He sat up, a gleam in his eye. "Now, I am going to claim the current share of energy that you have stored for a few days."

Before the weather turned too cold to enjoy the patio, Nola and Bruce invited Amy and Lou and Robert and Susan to dinner at Nola's. Choosing a menu that was appropriate for the season and easy to serve, Nola suggested barbecue and Bruce agreed.

Nola ordered barbecue, slaw, Brunswick stew, french fires and rolls from a popular restaurant, and a chess pie and lemon tarts from a local bakery. She prepared iced tea and made coffee.

The weather was pleasant and the young couples felt at ease. The foods were familiar and the serving was informal. Relaxation and conversation came easily. The women offered to take care of the minimal cleanup, and the men stood up and stretched.

Inside, Nola walked to the front of the house and switched on a pair of table lamps in the living room and closed the front door. She paused at the hall table and glanced at herself in the mirror. Noticing her lipstick had vanished while eating the meal, she went to her bathroom to add some color.

Susan and Amy finished the tidying-up in the kitchen. "This is a lovely house, isn't it? So much room for one person," exclaimed Susan.

"It is both of those. I hear it was a very good buy and her father wanted it for her." Amy folded a drying towel and hung it on a rack.

"I wonder if she ever gets frightened all by herself?"

"She hasn't said so. Up until last year, she was at school all day and probably busy at night grading papers and attending all the concerts that she enjoys."

Susan commented. "True. I used to hear teachers talk about hours of paper grading." She looked around the kitchen. "This really is a great house. I'm glad she and Dad Bruce are going to be living here at least half the time."

"So am I."

"He appears to be very happy. He's always been young looking and handsome, but he is more so now." Susan said.

Amy forced a smile. "I think so, too. But it has been a whirlwind courtship, hasn't it?"

"I love it! It would make great literature." Susan sighed. "Amy, I hope we can be so romantic when we're their age."

"Has Robert softened about the engagement?"

"A little. But I'm sure he'll come around – accept the marriage – as soon as the ceremony is over. Well, in due time."

"Nola is a really neat person. And Dad loves her," said Amy.

"I liked her immediately," said Susan. "Everybody deserves a companion. We need to march first in someone's parade."

"Right," Amy commented decisively. "And Robert is trying to be agreeable."

Sensing someone approaching, Amy shook her head slightly.

"Thank you for finishing up," Nola said as she walked into the kitchen, a sweater around her shoulders. "Shall we join the men on the deck? The night can turn chilly quickly. Are your sweaters outside?"

The girls said yes, gave a quick survey that all was in order then followed her into the hall and out the rear door.

Inside light streamed through the glass door and unshaded windows onto the patio. Torch lamps glowed around the edges; and from a center table, a wide glass globe magnified a candle flame. The warmth of the fall day was giving way to the cool of evening via a slight northwesterly wind and disappearance of the last rays of the sun.

The men were comparing the condition of greens on area golf courses after a dry late summer and early autumn. They broke off their conversation as the women rejoined them in the chairs they had vacated after the supper outside.

Susan teased, "Well, have you replayed all the games? And your teams are all winners now?"

The men answered in words of "we have" and "you bet."

The atmosphere was amicable, and an ensuing pause allowed their senses to take pleasure in scent of tallow candles, wafting of fragrant geraniums, reddish gold glow of flames, breezes whisking pass their neck and face, changing shadow patterns.

Robert asked, "So are there any more pre-Thanksgiving plans?"

Bruce turned to Nola who was sitting beside him on the glider. "I'll let the wedding planner take the question."

"Mom's handling the decorating details of the church chapel and the reception though she kindly runs the selections by me. A floral designer and a caterer are overseeing both occasions. Susan pointed us to a great source for invitations, announcements, and programs. Amy is taking care of rooms for everyone from Bruce's family who will be staying overnight. Let's see, what am I doing? Nothing much except shopping endlessly." She laughed.

Robert probed. "What about the honeymoon?"

Nola nudged Bruce. "That's his department."

"And that's top secret!" Bruce replied.

"Come on, Dad. We have no tricks up our sleeve," continued Robert.

"There are a few weeks between now and then. Your mind may conjure some." Bruce answered.

"Well, here's a question that we'd like to know the answer to," Robert tried again. "Why the week before Thanksgiving or November?"

Bruce looked at Nola and she merely looked at him fondly. She answered with a coy reluctance. "Well, I would like to say that I was married in my forties. My birthday is in December."

The young couples exchanged glances then smiles merged into grins and each chuckled. "That's priceless, Nola," said Lou. "Great going," added Susan. Amy stated, "That's a good age."

Lou stared at Bruce. "Your turn, Bruce, do you have a reason for the date?"

"Well, now that you persist, but I warn you the answer won't ring well in Amy's ears." He waited a moment. "Age is also part of my answer. In January I'll be fifty-five and I sure want to be married and very busy getting settled in here. And Nola and I will be in Raleigh some days most every week. Thus, my lovely, capable, persuasive daughter will not be signing me up for her over-fifty health programs."

"Dad, I wouldn't do that to you!"

"No?" he asked light-heartily.

Amy frowned as if she had been unjustly chided. The others watched as the light and shadows flicked across her face. "Dad, you are eligible. If you move here, you know you will want to attend some of our great seminars. Just ask Nola how good . . ."

Everyone laughed in amusement.

"What did I tell you guys? Lou, has she been taking salesmanship from you?"

"But Dad. Tell him, Nola," Amy pleaded.

"Well, Amy," Nola began, "I'm not eligible and I wouldn't want him going alone. Not with all those single women and widows around the center and the mall."

Amy perked up. "Oh, Nola, but you will be. We have an exception about the age. A member's spouse can join even if she or he is younger!"

Nola extended her hands palm out toward Amy. "Thank you, my dear friend, but I'll remain a volunteer when I'm in town."

Bruce took her hand and tucked her arm under his. "I owe you one," he whispered.

Susan stood up and said she and Robert needed to get on the road.

Tomorrow held a full schedule. Nola noticed how pretty she was in the candlelight. She recalled the first time she saw Susan and sensed there was something special about her, an inner glow, and healthy aspect in body and spirit.

As the two couples departed, Nola and Bruce stood on the porch watching until they were out of sight. Now that the engagement had been announced, neither felt conspicuous holding hands or standing close. Nevertheless, they waited until they were inside for a good-night kiss.

"The question about the November date was unexpected," Bruce said. "What if those young folks knew it's a test of restraint?"

"Well, the countdown is closer to when you won't have to walk out of here with the locking of doors and turning off of lights. Nor I in Raleigh."

Chapter 18

The mid-November morning was raw; cold air swept in from the northwest, a surprise during the unusually warm fall weather to date. Link Stein hunched his shoulders against the wind and hustled from an on-street parking space to save the parking deck fee at the hospital.

He felt presentable for his task ahead in an old conservative sport jacket, white shirt and tie, and dry-cleaned tan slacks – a luxury service even at a discount cleaner. He stepped inside an entry hall with a bank of elevators in the hospital administrative area.

Joining a half-dozen people, Link entered the next open elevator and punched the button for the fourth floor. The doors closed, opened twice for passengers to get off. At the third opening, Link exited.

He knew where Human Resources was located. Scowling, he stopped anyway, forcing a searching-for-office numbers over the doorways. No anxious look, no begging attitude: that won't get me a job, not even a favorable response from the girl Friday at the desk. He smoothed his shirt around the waist, checked that his tie and jacket were straight. He glanced at the picture on the wall, using the glass to form a neutral expression. No smile emerged. He generated an SOS to his feet: step briskly.

They quickened and he entered Human Resources reception room. He made sure the door closed before facing the bulletin board a few feet over on the back wall. That's where current openings for positions were posted. The lists were by categories: office entry level – file clerks, typists, secretaries, mailroom, switchboard; electronic – technicians, computer specialists; research laboratories.

Link stopped reading, knowing labs needed bottle washers and cleanup workers at minimum wages. He backed up to scan the computer list. Worst luck! All new listings required a four-year degree and work experience. The single part-time opening wanted a two-year degree and two years' work experience on a program he'd used. He'd trade his car for a recommendation for that one. He gritted his teeth to stifle an ironic laugh. His car had about a thousand-four-hundred-dollar value. His only transportation! To boot, who would recommend him for a job? Sure not the volunteer director after that damn incident with the Kester woman!

He placed a hand on the frame around the glass door over the bulletin board. The postings were protected! As Link debated copying any positions, a man came in, skimmed the board, and tried to pull the door open. Frustrated, the man cursed in a low voice. He turned to Link. "They must think somebody's going to rip off the best prospects." He glanced at his watch, cursed again, and huffed out the door.

Yeah, Link said to the closing door. They sure would and beat everybody interested.

The girl Friday made some noises at the counter. Link looked over his shoulder, made a tight spin, and walked over.

"Can I help you?" she asked.

Link couldn't imagine who hired these girls with no memories. He'd talked with her in person twice. "Yes, Mary," he put on an arrogant attitude he'd witnessed often. "I was in the building and wanted to check if my application was in your active file." Seeing her blank expression, her mouth opening, he added, "I was in two weeks ago."

"Your name?"

Slowly and empathetically, he replied, "Link Stein."

She flipped through a stack of folders on the workspace below the high counter between them. Link leaned forward; she halted and looked up until he stepped back.

Finished, she said, "No. Have you been called?"

He shook his head. "The line may have been busy."

"Did you want to update your information? Apply for one of the current listings?" She looked toward the bulletin board.

"Let me have my file." Mary raised her shoulders. Link resumed, "The last application."

She pulled a paper from a shelf of forms. "Fill in this."

Link took the blank form. "All of it?"

"Yes, with the position to be considered. And date it."

"Isn't this a waste of time? And paper?"

"Human Resources prefers to keep applications updated."

"Are the new lists up on Mondays?"

"Yes. Positions that require immediate filling are added as they come in. On the lower right under Urgent Need."

Link took the form, turned, stopped, and pivoted. "I need a pen."

Mary scoured the worktop, found one, and handed it over. "This is my last one. Please, return it when you're through."

Irritated, Link thrust his chin outward, snatched the pen, and strode to the back of the room. The only entry under Urgent he wanted was courier. Its tag end stated in bold print with dependable car – state year and model. Scratch that! Link declared.

One item caught his eye. Needed attendant for parking tollbooth – quick with handling money – Monday through Friday 3 to 11 p.m. Half-hour breaks 6 - 6:30 and 9:30 - 10:00. Start minimum wages.

Torn between the level of the position now and a computer one he qualified for but they didn't have open, he dropped onto the nearest chair, his back to Mary. He stared at the application, hopeless and distraught. The black typed lines were stark against the empty white spaces.

The bottom line questions for references were a cord around his neck. He had no one to count on for a good word about him. A deep sigh clogged his throat. The words his mind conjured couldn't escape: Tori could get a decent word or two from the school's placement office and a girl friend in a post office branch. Why not, he churned the thought.

Handling change was her way of life. Nothing physical. Her size wouldn't count against her. The kids? Exchange a few hours sitting with someone's preschoolers for watching out for Kari and Ronnie after school.

He focused on the paper while grabbing a magazine. He flopped both on his lap. Then his hand printed neatly the information. He was so intent on the process that the door opened and closed and Matt McDowell was halfway down the room before Link looked up and around.

He liked the neat well-fitted denim jacket that came only to the waist. The color was strong and matched the tight blue jeans. The man was muscular and moved with confidence. As he approached the counter, Mary said, "Hello, Matt. What do we have here?"

Matt stepped to the middle of the counter. Link could see his tanned face and broad smile. He was holding a basket of flowers. Link grimaced and saw a waste: here was a virile young man, strong, cheerful, and nothing but an errand boy.

"A delivery for your boss." Matt placed the arrangement on the counter.

"How lovely. She'll be surprised. It's for her birthday." Mary leaned forward and sniffed the flowers. "Did you grow these?"

"I did. Glad you like them." Matt noted the time on his delivery list and checked where the next few orders were to go.

Finished with the form, Link stood up and walked to the counter. He handed it to Mary.

She skimmed it. "This is not for you?"

"For my wife. I filled it out for her."

"She'll have to sign it."

"I put my initials above her name."

"It has to be in her handwriting," she looked puzzled at Link.

"If you will make a copy, I'll have her sign it and mail it back today."

Mary copied it. She handed the original to Link.

Matt folded his list. As he put it in his pocket, he looked at Link and frowned as if trying to recall something. Link caught his expression and realized that this was the man he had collided with in the mall outside Healthy Living Center.

Quickly, he took a couple of steps but stopped when Mary spoke loudly. "Wait! I need my pen!" He reached back and laid the pen on the counter. He hurried toward the door and never heard her curt thank you.

As the door closed, Matt stared at Mary. "Do you know who that was?"

"Yes, I do. A job seeker." She looked at the copy she'd made of the application. "His initials are L. S. His wife's last name is Stein. Oh, he's listed as next of kin. Link Stein."

"I think I've seen the guy before. Somewhere here. You say he's looking for a job?"

"Yes. He's been in several times recently. I should have remembered him, but I didn't when he came in today. He was miffed that I didn't know him. I don't say this about many of the applicants who come in here. But he's one I'd like to forget. Kind of creepy. Looked neater today. Must have been hoping for an interview."

"Sure he's not a volunteer? I believe I saw him in the hospital with a volunteer badge on when I delivered flowers there. Maybe a year or so ago." Matt gave a confused face that quickly switched to his typical good humor countenance.

"I wouldn't doubt you're right, Matt. You have an excellent memory," she agreed.

"Thanks. Yours is sharp, too. I'm going to call Phyllis at the health center and ask her about Link Stein. He may go there for seminars. I had a little bump in with him right outside the center not too long ago. Well, have a good day."

"Same to you." She took the basket into her boss's office.

When he reached his truck, Matt pulled out his cell phone, punched some numbers, and climbed into the driver's seat.

Phyllis handed an enrollment form and a pen to the lady who asked for them and said, "You may take it to one of the tables to fill out." As the lady thanked her and walked across the room, Phyllis swiveled her chair to face Joyce.

"This pain I have in my stomach, do you think it could be an ulcer?"

Before answering, Joyce regarded Phyllis closely. "That's a possibility. Or diverticulitis. Have you ruled out a virus?"

"Pretty much. Nobody at home has it or you or Amy? If I thought I had something contagious, I wouldn't come to work. These older adults don't have as strong immunity as young people. That is what you said, didn't you?"

"True. But Amy's not perky herself. She hasn't eaten well this week. And she drinks lots of carbonated sodas. Has she complained to you?"

Phyllis said, "Not to me. But she really doesn't have as much pep. Course she could be caught up in the wedding doings. Ooh. I feel kind of weak again." She bent over slightly and put her palms on her abdomen.

Joyce said, "Phyllis, go see your primary care doctor. It's better to know. The secretary will work you in today or tomorrow. Call now. Go on, pick up the phone. I can handle the traffic here. And do tell the doctor about your stress. That your husband could well be in the next layoff."

Her hand on the phone, Phyllis replied. "Oh, don't remind me. I try not to think of it."

"Well, it's time to think about it. Don't borrow trouble. I know the old saying, but having some plans if it happens could give you some strength. Fortify yourself and your man will be the stronger for it, too."

"Oh, Joyce. I have to keep my job. I can't be sick," she moaned.

"Then find out what's wrong. It may be nothing but nerves or fear. You may not want to take any medications to calm you, but don't shut that option out. I haven't heard of any cuts being considered here. Lord knows, we need every hand and every healthy body. Pick up that phone. And remember, Phyllis, we have the computer workshop that's right on us. We have to go to that to know how to update our files. If you don't know how to assess the records that you are responsible for, then you may be looking for a job." Joyce made the point clear without rancor.

Phyllis lifted the phone and dialed. She mouthed a thank-you to the nurse. After she hung up, she wrote a note and showed it to Joyce: first appt 2 p.m. today. Joyce gave an okay sign with her fingers and thumb.

The phone rang. Phyllis picked up first.

Matt McDowell said, "Phyllis, I just saw a man in Human Resources. I thought I remembered him when he bumped into me near the doorway from the hall to your center."

"Who's that, Matt?"

"It's come to me that he is Link Stein. Is he one of your members?"

"Let me check the membership list for you." She entered a code, the list popped up, and she scrolled to the *S*'s. You said Stein, spelled s-t-e-i-n?"

"I guess so, but you might try some variations. Mary said he's been in a lot asking about postings."

"Matt, I don't see any member by that name. None close with a first name Link. Is there a problem?"

"I guess not. I like to know names. You know how I am about my plants, flowers, and customers. It's a habit. Thanks for checking." Matt started to click off but added, "He's a strange guy. Looked neat today, but I swear he's wearing different type of clothes most of the time with a cap of some sort. Well, have a good day."

She said the same. Hoping as she hung up that it would be better if the doctor tells her what's wrong. Link Stein would be a hard name to forget. She hoped whatever was causing her pain would be an easy name to pronounce and say and not a disease or, worst, a strange new virus from a foreign country without a cure.

The evening brought a drop in temperature and the bitter cold penetrated Link's jacket, his sweater, sport shirt, and his undershirt. He snugged the toboggan over his ears and jammed his hands into his jacket pockets. He'd lost his gloves somewhere. A plastic grocery bag dangled from his wrist.

Frostbite is the last indignity, he proclaimed, but there was nobody on the street to hear. I'm not asking for a handout: I want a job. My hands can type messages equal to any college graduate's. Companies fork over sinful salaries to those geeks. Nothing is left in the till for us with tech school diplomas earned fair and square. We didn't play our way through the two years.

He jerked his hands from his pockets and cupped them over his face, exhaling warm air for the six more long blocks to trek home. He blasted his decision to spend gas money for bread and Vienna sausages for his supper. But he had had enough of beans and complaints from his wife and begging from the kids.

Hands back in his pockets, his face felt the cold. He took a deep breath only to suffer a chill in his mouth and throat.

How did we ever come to this point? He saw images of Tori and himself walking this street years ago when both were high school seniors. He'd taken her to a movie. She'd dressed up real pretty and made up her face and sprayed on some sweet-smelling perfume and talked real pleasantly. When they enrolled in the community technical college, he helped her with some of the subjects that she found difficult. One thing led to another and he proposed.

Both found jobs right after getting their diplomas. Their combined salaries encouraged them to rent a two-bedroom apartment with plans to have a home office and computer in the second room. But that never materialized. There were too many other things to buy. She became dissatisfied with her situation and began to dig into the fattening foods – comfort foods, she told him and showed him an article about the topic. She stopped work and said she'd look for a better job. She took away a general recommendation in writing that her work had been satisfactory. That's better than I got.

What I got a month later was the news we were going to become parents. Her happiness lasted until the second child was two years old and funds got tighter and tighter. She got fatter and fatter and slovenly in her personal habits and housework.

How did all this happen? I worked every extra day and shift needed at the company. And they downsized me! Who got to stay? Guys willing to move and who could afford the expense to do so. Or those who took on the load I had carried. I wasn't offered that option. That was wrong; I was already doing a job and a half. Now I have nothing left to sell – no one to borrow money from.

He stopped in front of his apartment building. The lights were out in his windows. Climbing the steps to his second-floor apartment with the grocery bag bumping against his legs, he greedily anticipated heating his sausage and eating the whole can and all the toasted bread he wanted. His craving to be satisfied consumed his soul-sick mind.

Chapter 19

Amy came out of the bathroom wiping perspiration from her forehead. She eased into a chair and held a cold, wet cloth against her cheeks.

"Amy, I'm leaving . . .," Lou called as he strode down the hall. Poking his head around the doorway, he stood upright then quickly reached her chair. He dropped to his knees. "Honey, are you all right?"

Weakly, she nodded. "In a minute." She swallowed, took a deep breath, and closed her eyes. "It's just as miserable as everyone said it was."

"Anything I can do?" he asked concerned.

"No." She opened her eyes. "The nausea is leaving. Thank goodness. This stage doesn't last long. I heard that, too."

"Do you think you can go to the center?"

She nodded weakly.

"Let me take you. I plan to be in the office today. If you need me, I can be there quickly."

"You're a good caretaker. I'm not ready to go now. But I'll go in early. Nola's coming to help me with some boxes before we open."

Assertively, he stated, "You're not to lift anything heavy. And I've heard that ultimatum for pregnant women."

She blushed. "I can hardly think of myself as such. It's so early."

"Not too early to register on that tester. And nausea is not a warning sign, right?" He sounded encouraging but also wanting agreement.

"According to the books it's frequent. For a few weeks. Lou, we won't tell anybody yet. We did agree." She could see the reluctance on his tightened lips. "Dad needs this time free of worry about me. Nola, too. It's one of our gifts to them. I have to plan how to tell the committee that hired me. These first three months are crucial." She reached for his hand. "I have only positive feelings about this pregnancy, although we have many friends who had miscarriages."

He forced a halfway cheerful expression. "You're right. We'll tell folks later. If they say you look piqued, just toss it off with we watched the late show or whatever. With ten vacation days in sight, you should get some rest even with the wedding."

She stood up. "Right. Now, go on to work. I promise to call if I need you."

Seeing she looked somewhat recovered, he left.

In her nauseous condition, she had spoken of miscarriages and wished she had controlled her words. Later, when the waves subsided and her face no longer glistened, she knew excitement about pregnancy would rebound. When symptoms weren't obvious, it was easier for her to keep secret the new life forming.

Link Stein circled the mall slowly twice. He counted cars near the main entrance. The number was average for early-morning strollers. Shortly, most of those would return to their cars, their exercise for the day finished. Lazy folks, he grunted. The second group would show up fifteen minutes before the shops opened. Lazier, he snorted. Walk first, shop second, and go home to rest. What do they know about men like me who'll have to work all my life?

Approaching the east side of the buildings, he took no pleasure seeing the lot empty. The few cars he saw were in the spaces across the main road; those belonged to employees who had the earliest shifts. Usually, the first arrivals were the assistant managers and office personnel. He had checked the going-and-coming traffic for a week. Nothing was unusual today.

Smoothly, no slamming on breaks or squealing of tires, Link drove his car into the first empty rear slot, alongside a large RUV. It was a row with single parking spaces. How smart I am to have planned all this: a direct dash from the mall door, my car aimed toward an exit. I'll be out of here with what I came for in minutes. Last check of the target entry!

Getting out of his car to see beyond the RUV, he scouted the loading docks and the truck pull-in areas. One delivery truck was backed up to the dock he was interested in. As Link walked up the empty parking lot, he spotted two men in blue work clothes near the truck. As he drew closer, the men passed large boxes onto the dock.

Not wanting to draw attention, he changed his surveillance right to left of the walls and the entrances. The few large gray steel doors were unmarked. Shoppers could not detect where the doors opened inside the mall. No exit signs were visible. From his search inside the mall, he knew that the ways in were not located along the public accesses. Somehow, deliveries to the health center had to be nearby and most likely none were through shoppers' entries. They had to be taken in between the dock and the main entrance – that left the solid steel door.

His riding around at various hours had paid off: he watched drivers of delivery vans pull up and walk inside the loading area and pick up a handset and speak. Next, drivers unloaded boxes and placed them near the steel door. Then, they would open the door and secure it with a chain against an inside wall. After the boxes were transferred, the men released the holding chain and the door came shut. Each time, the men would test that the door was locked.

One morning, Link had rubbed his hands at his great stroke of luck: spotting Amy Umstead getting out of her car which she had parked near the mall entrance. She pulled the handle on the large glass door only to find it did not open. Thus, she walked left to the steel door, stopped and plunged her hand into her carry bag. He had watched for her arrival the past few weeks. She came in early the day of deliveries. And he'd bet anybody that she checked the invoices. She was the boss. Anything not up to snuff, she'd catch the devil. What I'd have given to be there when she learned that old woman was found in the parking lot.

Now as Link neared the walkway that ran from this loading area to the next one, secured from sight at the far end of the building, he saw the delivery guy take a clipboard from the dock attendant up near the elevated platform. Quickly, without being sighted, Link stepped to the side of the large trash container left of the loading entry. The driver shut and latched the rear door of the truck and climbed into the cab. Link drew back before the driver pulled out and turned left. Link felt luck was holding on his side. There was no way the driver could have seen him out a rear mirror.

Too soon, smugness disappeared from his face. He recognized Amy's car pulling into the lot and stopping close to the building a mere two rows beyond the dock. She was early. The knot in his stomach alerted him to trouble. Where was the maintenance van? It was always at this dock at eight thirty. Another car pulled up beside Amy's.

Trouble came double the same as luck. Squinting, he cursed and the words stuck in his throat compounding his internal tightness. It was that volunteer Nola Gilbert. The two women had made his last months miserable. The fear of their recognizing him as being at the lecture the day that interfering Bessie died had forced him to slink about the mall. Switching hats, jackets, and even his shoes – strained his wardrobe, but disguises became essential. And he'd turned thief for the dark gray uniform he had on now, had seen it on the backseat of an old car, doors unlocked. Link's decision had been instantaneous. Little messages darted in his mind . . . maintenance staff wore gray pants and shirt . . . a perfect disguise . . . no questions . . . carry something in, simply to throw away . . . a cloth, a cleaning cloth . . . yeah. When he shed the uniform, his khakis and green sweater over a plaid shirt wouldn't draw attention.

Pressing back against the cold metal trash container, Link hiked his pants up and tightened his belt over the two layers of clothes. His waistline had shrunk until the tong of the belt poked though the last hole and the long end had to be double-backed under the keeper. The lean body was close to being emaciated: he had no appetite and the little food he ate did not sit well in his stomach as if his muscles warred with the contents. Yeah, he groaned, that's what I'd like to find out from those nurses or doctors when they talk at the center. About battles going on inside me. But I can't ask questions or describe symptoms that could focus attention on me.

These matters flashed through his mind as he pulled his collar up to keep the chill from his skinny neck. He fumed: too late to ask his fat wife to move a button over. How can she be so obese? It can't be she gains from eating the food I shove back across the table. She ought to come hear all the experts harangue about cutting down on calories, fried chips, and all the foods she shovels down.

If he could laugh about his children, it would be seeing his girl bloated like her mama and his boy skinny as himself. Laughter was no companion. His disposition was soured with continual unemployment. He had forced his vision away from his offspring. Sight of their threadbare clothes wove across their pleas for money to buy the essentials that education required, the styles their peers proclaimed must-have, and the whimsies that the media dangled constantly to assure happiness. He could see in his life a fabric too flimsy for use, and he had no means to strengthen the fiber or alter the pattern.

Unless, he landed a job with the medical center. One chance, that's all I need. I can do the job.

He heard the women greet each other.

"Hi. You're so good to come." "I'm glad to be of help." "We'll have to go through the rear door. I like your culottes. Is that a one-piece style?" "Thank you. It is. I'm already for the bending and lifting. And layered for the chilly day."

When their footsteps and voices were no longer heard, Link cautiously craned his neck and looked around the trash container. Amy was pulling a set of keys from her bag. Inserting one, she turned back toward Nola.

"*Brr*, it's a cold morning. This door is very heavy. If you'll hold it a minute after I get it unlocked, I can scoot through and you follow quickly. It can shut in a hurry."

"Okay," Nola said and clutched her shoulder bag close against her side.

Link jerked a white cloth from his jacket pocket, pulled the bill of the cleaning cap well over his forehead and the flaps over his ears. He hunched his shoulders, bent his legs ready to dash through the door as soon as Amy removed the key. The door unlocked, the key withdrawn, she swiftly stepped inside and Link sprinted past Nola.

Surprised, she called out. "Wait a minute!" She had let go the door and swiveled to catch it but it closed with a resounding swoosh.

"Maintenance," Link muttered in a deep voice. "Late," he added and sped up, the white cloth waving at his side. He turned the corner well ahead of them.

"Amy, does the maintenance staff use this entrance?"

"I didn't think so. I don't come this way unless I have to. It's a spooky place to me." She shivered and slowed for Nola.

"Dark, isn't it? Why aren't there any lights in here?"

"There are two in the ceiling. Maybe they are burned out. I'll call maintenance."

"That rude man ahead?"

"No. The office. Our boxes should be up front near the door to the center. That way, we don't have far to carry them." She attempted to laugh in spite of the chill. "And if we need something from them before unpacking is finished, they are nearby."

Nola had stopped walking and turned slightly to glance back. The skin on her neck felt prickly like an invisible alert. Seeing nothing but gray walls, ceilings, and floors, she turned again toward Amy. She put a hand on Amy's arm.

"Do you have to unlock the door?" she asked.

"Yes, both doors have to be opened with a key. Why?" she asked while tightening her hold of the keys.

"I haven't heard the door ahead open, that's all." Now, Nola thrust her feet as quietly as possible on the echoing tiles, thankful she had worn soft-soled walkers.

As they followed the angle of the hall, they saw numerous boxes stacked on the left. At first, they didn't see the maintenance guy. Then, Amy elbowed Nola and nodded toward the left. Nola followed the direction of the nod and spotted the guy between the boxes. He raised slightly, picked up a box, but remained in a crouched position.

Amy drew up to her fullest height, threw back her shoulders, and spoke with authority but without meanness. "We'll get to those later." She reached the door and put in her key. "Nola, we'll go inside first."

She pulled the heavy door into the hall very slowly. When it was about two feet open, Link edged away from the stacks.

"Carrying one in," he muttered walking toward the open door. Amy slid the keys into her pocket then held the door open.

Link darted in front of Nola. Instantly, he pivoted and thrust the box from his hands in her path. He spun around, shoved Amy toward the doorway, threw an arm around her neck, pushed her back, and kicked her feet forward.

Amy screamed. Link pressed his arm tighter against her throat and thrust her across the threshold. Nola opened her mouth to cry for help, instead took a deep breath and vaulted the box. She reached the door and grabbed the knob trying desperately to pull it toward her. Link, with one arm holding Amy in a tight grip close to him, reached his free hand back and grasped the inside handle.

Nola strained her arm muscles and the whole right side of her body in an attempt to wedge into the rapidly narrowing space between the steel door and steel jamb; she struggled for breath and summoned all reserved strength. The space, and with it light, narrowed. In a mighty effort, she heaved her left side forward. Her sleeve and culottes pants flipped through the last few open inches.

Simultaneously, she witnessed the last sliver of space disappear and felt the pressure of the door against her leg. Miraculously, she pulled her body back before it could be crushed between the rigid steel of door and jamb.

With a pounding heart, she let out a deep breath. She pulled her left hand toward her chest; it only moved an inch. Looking down at her sleeve, she realized it was caught in the door. She pulled at the densely woven fabric, but it didn't give. Then she yanked her arm with the same restrictive results. When she tried to lean backward, she felt the futility of her strength against inert metal. Desperately assessing her situation, she looked down her left side and saw that the fabric of the culottes was tight against her thigh and leg.

"Pull!" she commanded both arm and leg. "One, two, three!" She counted and summoned her muscles to respond in unison. A second time she exerted energy to move her body away from the door. But she could not free herself.

The one-piece clothing that had delighted her in the shop was now a major factor in her torment. The long sleeves and pants cut with sufficient material for comfortable movement caught her now in an ironic situation – limited motion.

Stop struggling, she chided herself. Think. For three seconds, she closed her eyes and prayed "Dear God, help me." Calmed somewhat, she dropped her eyes and studied the clothing. It zipped up the front from the neck to a few inches below the waist. She would be able to manage the zipper tab with her right hand. Visualizing the process, she couldn't shake her right hand and arm free of the blouse nor pull her leg or foot high enough to ease either free, not with the left side being tightly held by the door. She was bound by the one-piece clothing.

Blocked mentally in this approach, she leaned against the door. Coldness of the steel caused Nola to consider the consequences of being half-dressed in this isolated hall for an hour or more. The under layer of scoop neck tee shirt and cotton-spandex panty hose would not be sufficient to ward off a chill. Keep thinking, she urged her mind and pressed her forehead against the firm, cold metal to confirm the knowledge that she could not change its composition or placement.

Isolation and helpless feelings of aloneness seeped into her thoughts causing her muscles to contract, her organs to tighten protectively. Blood left the skin and felt limited in flow and captive in the softer tissue. Nola wanted to shiver and shrivel to become like the narrow metal key Amy had inserted into the outside door. Once like the key she could open the door to the world.

Stop this hallucination, Nola commanded her wishful thoughts. Amy, I must think of Amy. Why did that man rush into the hall with us? Maintenance man? Something isn't right with that excuse. Would a staff person who cleans offer to take one box in? And when he was told to leave it, why did he continue to hold it? Except to throw in my path? He couldn't have known that I was coming and how would he know Amy was coming early?

Maybe we weren't his targets. So what is he doing here? No, I mustn't follow this track. She shook her head. Think, darn you! Think about Amy. Concentrate on her! She's alone in the center with some man who has abducted her. Why? She didn't act as if she knew him, didn't try to indicate to me that she did. She didn't call his name. Yet, there was something familiar about the man. His thinness, his hunching between the boxes, and his furtiveness. Who have I seen like that? No name came to her.

Amy, what can I do? How can I help to rescue you? There has to be some way.

She's in more danger than I am. With that awareness, Nola pulled away from the door as much as possible and forced her body to stand erect. She wanted to be away from tangible support, wanted to center herself to find a solution. Relaxation was needed to increase the flow of blood to warm her skin. Slowly, she stopped shivering and ignored the cold.

Gaining control of her thoughts, she pushed fear aside, allowed it only shadow room beside her. *If I was in the center and an emergency arose, I would ask for help. A nurse was always on duty, seldom was the reception area or the auditorium empty. But, if no one was there at a critical moment, I'd do what everyone does, call 911.*

My cell phone, she cried exultantly. Reaching down her right side, she experienced the first glimmer of hope since the steel door closed and snared her. Her shoulder bag had stayed in place during her jumping the box and struggle with the door.

Easy, she cautioned: *if you drop it, you won't be able to reach down for it.* Her hand groped for the flap then she slid her fingers slowly underneath to release the snap. That done, she delved inside the bag and fumbled for the small black phone. That done, she carefully pulled it out.

As she flipped the cover and stared at the number pad, she stared at the numeral 6 – the speed dial for Bruce. *Bruce? Yes, Bruce. I'll call him. What time is it? No more than ten minutes since we came in. Where would he be now? Driving to work? You haven't time to waste, Nola. Punch it! Now!* While the series of numbers beeped, a plan scripted across the blackness of her closed eyes. Her patience diminished with incredible speed, but she forced her mind's eye to see the writing and repeated each word, though barely audible she relied on the sense of hearing to duplicate the message, a backup to the visual imagery.

The pleasant expectancy that always heightened her senses when she dialed his number and waited for his voice was now intensified with frantic energy. The phone was not answered after the first ring. "Come on, Bruce!" She pled. After the second ring with no response, she moaned, "Please, Bruce, answer."

At the third trial of the phone number, while she waited, she inched her head toward the door and pressed her now feverish forehead against the cold steel. "Please pick up. My dearest Bruce, I need you. Amy needs you."

She mumbled one more ring then I'll have to hang up. Dial 911. "Oh, God, help me keep my wits about me. Take care of Amy, my friend – Bruce's daughter. And God, in a few days my daughter too. If . . ."

Chapter 20

Fresh brewed coffee wafted from the break room to Lou's office and down the halls. Its strong aroma beckoned the office personnel. The sales reps in coat and tie left briefcases on desktops and filed toward the break room while secretaries quickly stashed purses in their desks and changed from heels to cushioned soled, supportive shoes. Before joining the coffee crowd, the women opened calendars or displayed papers indicating work was in progress.

Initial morning summaries of last night's events, be they positive or negative, were bantered companionably around the coffee maker and the tables. It was a ritual that concluded the final wake-up step for the working day. One of the secretaries drained the pot into her thermal cup.

"Oh, no, you thirsty woman!" a rep cried in mock torment. The others laughed.

Lou's secretary Margie, who had been leaning against a counter, offered to make another pot. Sighs of relief went up. The other women returned to their desks.

"Margie, is the coffee perking yet? Look who's coming to join us." A rep called out.

Lou entered the room. The group was surprised by his early-morning visit; usually he took his first coffee midmorning. "Hi, Lou. Did your coffee maker go on the blink?" "Is my watch right, guys?" "Sorry, the last cup just walked out."

"Good morning, boss. How's Amy?" Margie yanked a Styrofoam cup from the packaging, lifted the pot, and poured out a cup that she handed to Lou.

"No fair there, Margie. You don't let us swipe the first cup." A rep spoke jovially.

"Hush, Charlie. If I weren't looking, you'd have done the same," she said as she tapped him on the shoulder. She walked to the door then turned around. "Did you say how Amy was?"

"Not too perky today," Lou answered and stirred his coffee.

"Hope it's not a bug. A little early for that," she added.

"Probably not . . . a virus." He glanced toward her.

"Tell her I hope she's better tomorrow." Margie tried to read something in his expression, couldn't, and left the room.

Lou stood by the counter and asked to no particular person. "What's up?"

They answered in generalities: not much, nothing new, same old sports rehash. Lou volunteered no information when someone inquired about his evening. Lou had the look of a man who wanted to say something but decided to clinch his jaw instead. Almost in unison, the men recognized his tension, rose, and headed to their offices.

Lou tasted his coffee. Bitter he labeled it. He added a spoon of sugar. The news he really wanted to shout at them was far sweeter than the little granules he dumped and stirred in dark fluid. But he realized Amy was right that it was too early to share their news. But soon, a few weeks and he'd tell everyone he knew that in summer there would be three in the family.

How had he answered Margie when she asked about Amy? Not too perky. Well, that was the truth. He felt so sorry for her in mornings now. It was hard to leave her after the nausea and retching. But like she said, this wouldn't last long. Well, perk yourself up, old man: wow, I never used that term about myself. Gosh, that's what I'll be to the little fellow.

What a relief though that Amy was calmed down before I left the house. And she'll be fine at the center. There's always somebody nearby with medical knowledge.

Over in Groton, an agonizing Susan stood facing the full-length mirror. The gold dress had short sleeves and a flattering fold over the bodice and shoulders. Fortunately, the well-known designer cut the fabric generously thus now providing room for her swollen breasts. The skirt also was full though it fell straight at the side. Nola had selected a style that was becoming to both Amy's and Susan's body shapes. She swung sideways and gazed over a shoulder at her profile. Dismayed at the sight, she swished to the rear view and held up a hand mirror. She had hooked the single top eye but had not been able even with much squirming and tugging to pull the zipper up very far. A gap of an inch or more at the waistline of the bridesmaid gown caused Susan to gasp.

How can I get by at the wedding? she lamented. Everyone will think I've gotten fat or that I'm pregnant. And Robert and I agreed that it's not the best time to make our announcement. What if they already suspect? No, they wouldn't. My tunic tops have been great camouflage. And I've never had morning sickness.

Suddenly, she felt something move inside and touched her abdomen with her free hand. She stood still until a second movement then dropped the hand mirror on the carpet and spread the other hand over the moiré-pleated skirt. A big smile spread over her face. She turned to look directly into the mirror. Now the pregnancy is real. I felt the little one kick me. I can't wait to tell Robert. She moved toward the phone but stopped midway across the room.

No. This moment is too long-awaited an event for a telephone call. All this suspense, along with the excitement of the wedding, is a strain. Surely, it will not hurt me or the baby. I'll plan some special way to tell him when he comes home. Her shoulders hunched up as she hugged her arms across her abdomen. The family will be so surprised when we tell them in a couple of weeks. Especially Amy. She's been low the past few weeks. So preoccupied with work – and that dreadful death of one of her members. If the mystery of that can be determined, she might perk up.

Now back to my dress problem. Solution time! It will simply have to be let out in the seams. For a few hours, I can torture my growing belly in a body shaper and hold my bouquet at the waist. Lifting the long skirt, she hobbled to the bedside table, drew from the drawer the phone directory, and flipped the yellow pages to alterations.

In the University Medical Center computer training room, a software specialist was explaining the updates on a personnel data program. The volunteer file program of the medical center was keyed into for illustration. Next entered was the center's redesigned program that allowed a quicker connection between member names and their phone numbers and seminars and events. Preregistration lists could be run quickly and checked later for those who attended or failed to show. When an event had to be cancelled for whatever reason – snow, illness of speaker, and such, the members could be contacted quickly.

Time had become increasingly important. The staff was capable but pressed with a full slate of duties. The membership list had duplication of addresses and phone numbers for members of the same family joining on different dates. Husbands might have signed up first and been enthused enough that spouses joined. In some cases, something similar happened with sisters, or mothers and daughters. It was expeditious for mailing monthly calendars and brochures as well as making phone contact, to have addresses and phones numbers consolidated. Postage was expensive.

Now that the software was to be installed and the specialist who had worked on it available, all staff that worked with the computer program were brought together this morning for a demonstration and a hands-on session at individual computers.

Phyllis and Joyce had been listening to the explanations and following the diagrams on a large overhead screen. When they were given a ten-minute break, they were ready for coffee.

"Gosh, this is early to be absorbing these changes," Phyllis yawned and quickly covered her mouth. "I didn't get enough sleep last night."

Joyce stood up and stretched. "Nor did I. I had to make a lot of arrangements at home. You want to take the first restroom break? And I'll go for coffee or tea. How's your stomach?"

"Much more settled, but I'll have tea. Thanks for making me call the doctor." Phyllis agreed. Both left the room.

Other trainees straggled out of the room to do likewise. A few made phone calls or stepped outside for a quick smoke.

While Joyce and Phyllis were enjoying their beverages, Phyllis commented that it felt strange not to be in the center this morning.

"The center should have closed this morning. Amy and Nola will have their hands full with no one to help them," Joyce commented. "Let's hope all the phones don't start ringing at once."

"Or the walkers come by for a chat, a blood pressure check, or water."

"Or coffee. No volunteer signed up for this morning?"

"Right. Maybe Amy will delay opening the door. She was going in to check the last shipment, wasn't she?" Phyllis asked as she tossed her empty cup in the trash basket.

"Yes. She's anxious to check in the special order of pencils, notepads, cups, and all the items imprinted with the center's name. Wants to see they are right. It'll be great to have something to give the people."

Phyllis said, "Good PR and advertising."

"Yeah, and more names for us to add to the computer. And more work . . . I mean that we'll have to work to do. This is a good job. Don't you think the people who come in are mostly very pleasant?" Joyce asked as she stretched again.

"They are. Only a few are tedious and defensive if we don't have an answer they want. Or the data we have on the computer about them is not correct."

"Well, what we're learning today will help clear that up. The facts will be all there. Unless somebody comes along and touches the wrong key and out goes the information," Phyllis stated.

Joyce grimaced. "Glory be, Phyllis, don't even think that. Amy and I are the only ones who can enter certain files on our program. She came in last week for a demo of the updates and said it was simple. She didn't mention a security problem."

"Good, but computer hacks can break into most any program if they have a reason and spend time trying." The instructor returned and hand signaled everyone to return to his or her computers. Joyce whispered to Phyllis, "And if we aren't careful, we could key into other programs."

After the heavy door slammed behind Link, he stepped back and pressed against the rear wall of a short hall that led into the auditorium. Amy continued pawing at the air in front of her and thrusting her feet outward, struggling to break from her abductor.

Tersely, Link put his mouth close to her ear. "Didn't you learn anything listening to all those lectures? Don't put your neck in a vise. The pressure could cut off the air. You can choke yourself to death." He paused. "Um. But I wouldn't be to blame, now would I?"

She tried to grab his arms. He tightened his hold on her neck. Her face contorted with pain forcing her to drop her hands. Her legs became limp. The pressure of his body against her repulsed her and her eyes squinted till they ached. Desperate, she desired for tears to wash her eyes and saliva to moisten her dried mouth. She longed to cry for help and relief to come.

As she lowered her drawn-up shoulders, he whispered. "That's better. See I can tell you what those doctors couldn't get you to understand." Still clinching her about the neck, he angled forward and peered toward the auditorium. The room was empty and dark.

"Now, we're going to walk toward that door. Don't try to break this armlock if you want to keep this neck holding your head up. Okay, easy, now. Move your right foot, then your left. Together we'll get there."

One step at a time, Amy led the way across the gray carpet that she had tread with such anticipation in her role at Healthy Living, never believing that she would retrace those steps in fear of her life. I can't breathe anymore, she told her body. I can't. The pain, the fear! Why, why is he doing this? I can't even speak to ask him! God, have I hurt the man? I can't remember . . . can't remember. As they stepped like staccato notes in the aisle between the rows of chairs, her fuzzy vision saw gray-haired people seated, faced forward. Why are they there? Can't they see me? No, I'm disoriented. But they do come and sit here. Why? Amy, to learn. To be educated. Keeping their brains alert. Link stopped. Having thrust a foot forward, she was instantly unbalanced. Feeling her bounce against his chest, he eased his arm a bit. She released a deep sigh then dropped her head downward.

He stretched full height and looked toward the double glass door. The blinds were pulled up and the reception room visible. No lights were on. Narrowing his eyes and jutting his head over Amy's shoulder, he saw the door that opened to the mall was closed.

"Walk! Don't make a sound. Take short steps." He dictated with clinched teeth. Like a giant inchworm, they moved forward. Amy sensed she had a short reprieve. Think, she commanded her mind. Not slow, in inched measures. Be speedy but like a horse with a steady gait. Don't relax your body, but don't struggle. Like your first pony, this man is scared or he wouldn't be skittish, ready to bolt and to take you along in his wild abandonment. He's circling the fences. He'll wear himself out – imprinting the ground like the pony with his hooves. He wanted the barn. This man is after some security. You need to know what that is. She reminded herself to be quiet, vigilant. Reserve your strength. He'll let you know. Keep your head. If he falls and rolls over, you'll get crushed. Steady, Amy, try to get control. Any way you can. Words, questions, caring. God, please let me care, push down any hostility. I pray, take care of me, take of . . . us.

Bruce removed the cell phone from the briefcase then tossed the case onto the backseat of his car. After sliding into the driver's seat, he dialed his office to tell his secretary that he was going to Durham for a nine thirty appointment.

He checked visibility on all the mirrors and placed the phone on the console to his right side. Before backing from his parking space, he checked the dashboard clock and the temperature. His timing was good and the temperature was seasonably chilly.

He turned on the radio, preset for a local station that frequently cited traffic tie-ups throughout the heavily congested areas in and surrounding Raleigh. This stretch of roads called for drivers' alertness. When his phone beeped, he was passing a car and didn't pick up instantly. As he moved ahead then back into a center lane, he reached for the phone. Customarily while driving, he answered only if he recognized the caller and considered he needed to pick up.

Nola's cell phone number showed on the screen. Already a series of three beeps had sounded, so he hastily pressed talk. "Hi."

"Bruce, thank God, you've answered. I was about to hang up." Nola's voice sounded relieved but tense.

"I'll always pick up for you," he said.

"We need help. Now!"

"What's the problem?"

She rushed her words. "We need 911."

"Why . . ."

She interrupted. "Just listen. I'll be brief. Call 911 or get someone to. Amy has been abducted. We were coming in the back door to the center and a man rushed in. Amy unlocked the door. He ran by me. Grabbed her. Pushed her out and shut the door. I'm trapped in here."

"Are you all right?"

"Yes. Tell whoever opens the door – do not fling it open. My clothing has me caught. Get help for Amy now. Call mall security." Her words sounded frantic and she doubted they were coherent. She added, "Understand?"

"Yes. A stranger has Amy inside the mall," he stated.

"The health center. Bruce, I love you," she said emotionally. "I'm clicking off." She pressed the end button. He'll know whom to contact first, she said with conviction then held her hand with the phone over her heart.

His experience did not include dealing with abductions. Needing a minute to get the sequence of calls right, he put on his blinker and merged into the right lane then off the highway shoulder, a wide paved strip clearly visible to moving vehicles.

Nola had said 911 or somebody. That would be 911 in Windermere not in Raleigh – Durham area. Lou. He would call Lou's office. He dialed the number.

Margie answered after the second ring. "Louis Umstead's office. This is Margie."

"Margie. This is Bruce Braddock. I need to talk with Louis. It's urgent."

"He's in a meeting, Mr. Braddock."

"This is an emergency," Bruce stated bluntly.

"Hold on. I'll buzz him."

Before she could put him on hold, he commanded, "Go get him now!"

"Yes, sir." She recognized the imperative tone.

After Margie punched hold, Bruce pressed the highway patrol number. For years, he had read the sign with the number to call for help and it popped up in his memory instantly.

When a dispatcher answered, Bruce said he needed information to handle an emergency. "First, what are the road conditions on I-40 west from the Cary entrance ramp to the Saunders Mall exit in Windermere? Second, I just had a call that my daughter has been abducted in the mall. Not from. I don't know where she is . . . let me put this on three-way call. My son-in-law's phone is beeping."

Bruce clicked buttons. "Lou? Good. Listen carefully. Time is important. I have the highway patrol on this line, too. I got a call two minutes ago from Nola. She and Amy entered a rear door into a hallway that leads to the health center in the mall. A man ran in behind them. Amy unlocked and opened the door to the center. The man ran past Nola, grabbed Amy, and pushed her into the center. Nola is trapped in the hall. Listen! Do not thrust the door open violently! Nola is caught right there. That's all she said. Lou, call 911 and mall security. Hang up this line. I'll get back with you."

Bruce heard the click. "Okay, did you get all that?" he asked the patrol dispatcher.

"I did. Who is Nola?"

"Nola Gilbert. My fiancée. My daughter Amy is the director of the health center. Nola is her volunteer."

"Could Nola identify the abductor?"

Bruce was annoyed. Questions delayed his getting back on the highway. "Officer, I pulled off the road to call. I'm going to merge back on." He started the engine, signaled his entry at a gap in traffic. "Now, what's the traffic like ahead?"

"No problems reported. What's your phone number? I can update you if there's a change."

Bruce rattled the numbers. "Thank you. If you have a patrolman out here making an emergency call this way, an escort would be welcomed."

"Hear you."

Bruce pressed end on the phone pad but leaned his foot on the accelerator lifting it when the speedometer reached seventy-five. He could feel sweat beading on his forehead and his hands clammy on the wheel. Who could want to harm Amy? No answer. She was a kind, gentle, caring person. Strong and resourceful enough to direct a program for the medical center but never overly aggressive or belligerent, she was not one who made enemies. And she's small. She'd be no match physically for a strong man. But she can think in tight situations. Think, Amy. Think. Don't do anything rash. Be cautious like you were around the big farm animals.

Bruce cautioned himself not to floor the accelerator. Keep your eyes focused on the road. Be alert for chances to pass any hesitating drivers.

"We think you will find this updated software will save you time. If you have a question, key into the help tab." The instructor switched off the overhead and removed the transparency. After inserting it in his folder, he stood with an attitude, "That's all." Quickly, Joyce and Phyllis gathered their materials and left the room.

Joyce said, "Wait a minute. Let me put my coat on."

Phyllis carried hers over her arm. "We're out early. I need to stop by the volunteer office. Do you have time to go with me?"

"Sure."

As they walked along corridors, several white-coated personnel approached briskly from the opposite direction. On another floor, outpatients and hospital workers in green pants and short-sleeve tops entered the flow of traffic. After a couple of turns to other corridors, Phyllis pointed to a sign protruding over a door: Volunteer Office. They entered a small waiting room, which had a low counter with stacks of bulletins, a box of scrap paper for notes, an assortment of office supplies, and a computer. A new employee was concentrating on the computer screen. After striking several keys rapidly, she looked up. Not recognizing them, she read their name badges then asked cheerfully if she could help them.

From a carry bag, Phyllis pulled out a sheath of papers. "These are the volunteer logs for last month." She handed them over. "And may I have a copy of the latest newsletter mailed to volunteers? A few volunteers have asked me about an item mentioned in it. It would be helpful to have one to refer to."

"Thank you for the logs. Let me get a newsletter for you." She pushed her swivel chair back, stood, and walked to a supply closet.

The outer door opened and closed and a woman who appeared about fifty years old walked to the counter. She wore a soft yellow smock with Hospital Volunteer embroidered on the upper left side. When Joyce turned around, the woman smiled. "Joyce, how good to see you again."

Joyce said, "How are you, Sarah? It's nice to see you're still volunteering."

"Oh, yes. Not in the research projects, though."

"I can tell by the jacket you're with the hospital. Do you like this better?"

Phyllis turned and Joyce introduced them.

After brief hellos, Sarah answered. "Yes, I do. We don't have the meddlesome volunteers where I'm assigned. We deliver flowers to the patients and change water in any vases that need it."

The woman had such a happy countenance and pleasant voice that Phyllis showed a puzzled expression at the comments.

As if understanding Phyllis's concern, the volunteer put out a hand toward Phyllis and Joyce. "Oh, I didn't mean to speak out of turn. Most volunteers, just like the marvelous staff here in the hospital and in the research projects, are really helpful and very agreeable to work with. We had one incident that made us uncomfortable." She looked at Joyce. "You remember a couple of years ago?"

"Vaguely."

"Bessie Kester. Have they found out what caused her death?" she asked with a note of compassion. "It was such a shock to us. Her dying in the locked car."

"Heat stroke. I had forgotten she was involved in that matter. Weren't you volunteering on that same project." "Yes." "Tell me again what happened."

Sarah peered around the room. When the door opened and two soft-smocked women entered chatting, Sarah nodded toward the chairs. "Let's go over there." Phyllis and Joyce walked toward the furthermost grouping of seats.

Before joining them, Sarah greeted the other volunteers. "Hello, ladies."

"Hi, Sarah. We're getting lunch passes. Can you join us?"

"Some other time, thanks."

The receptionist returned, walked over to Joyce, and handed her the newsletter. She spoke to Sarah then to the other volunteers who were leaving. Her assistance not needed, she returned to the computer.

Sarah turned her back to the counter and spoke softly to Joyce and Phyllis. "The problem was complicated. I'll try to remember exactly how the events occurred. Bessie was an aggravating person. Talked too much, overbearing, and always watching what everybody else was doing. She was a volunteer and had no authority. We never knew why but Link Stein, another volunteer, really annoyed her."

At the mention of Link Stein, Phyllis and Joyce immediately eyed each other for a couple of seconds. Sarah continued. "One day, Link was in the file room standing beside a row of notebooks containing records of volunteers involved in a research project. Bessie came to the door. When she saw him, she stepped back and watched him reading some pages. She saw him reshelf the notebook. When he turned to leave the room, she stood midcenter of the doorway. He jumped back, startled. Next he bolted forward, and she barely escaped being hit as he squeezed out the door.

"Well, she reported the matter to the head nurse – your supervisor, I think, Joyce." Joyce nodded. Sarah reflected a moment. "When Link was confronted, he claimed he'd not been in the room that morning. It was his word against hers. And that didn't improve her animosity. She kept a sharp lookout for him. The two seldom had the same hours after that. He was also a volunteer that participated in another research project, so he was in the area a couple times when she was. But that's not where the trouble really came to a head."

Joyce asked keenly interested. "When was that?"

"About a year ago. There was a birthday party for a staff member and all the staff was in the lunchroom. The supervisor went back to get some matches to light the candles for the cake. She passed by the file room and saw Link looking at a notebook. She knew his assignment that day was to collate and staple five pages of forms, a task done in a workroom. She returned to the lunchroom and asked if anyone had asked Link to file papers in notebooks. No, the staff told her.

"Well, she beckoned one of the nurses to follow her. She confronted Link and asked for the notebook. He tried to reshelf it. She is so commanding that when she asked a second time, he shoved it in her hands. When he said he was filing some papers for Mrs. Lucas, she told him his assignment had been in the workroom. If you've finished that task, you may leave now."

"Did he leave?" Joyce asked.

"Very disgruntled. As I best remember, he had been on the list for one more day that week. Before then, the supervisor talked with the project director. He came down to that research area while Link was there, and he listened to Link, the supervisor, and the other nurse who had witnessed the incident."

Joyce interjected. "Were you there when this took place?"

Sarah shook her head. "No, I had already requested a transfer. Much as I liked the staff and the clerical side of the project, I didn't want to work around Bessie and Link. After all, volunteering is a pleasant service. This last bit is what I heard from a volunteer there at the time though not in the conference. Link was asked to hand over his volunteer badge and not to come into the research area again. Well, I need to scoot. I came down to stamp my parking ticket."

Joyce put out a hand and touched Sarah's arm. "Thank you for sharing this. One more question. Do you know whose record Link was looking at that first day when Bessie saw him?"

She answered. "It was Bessie's. She was also a participant in a research project. Makes you wonder what he saw, doesn't it?"

Phyllis spoke up. "Sarah, do you know if Bessie was still in the project?"

"I heard she withdrew the day she caught Link in the file room. And she stopped volunteering soon afterwards. I wish I could stay, but I have an appointment downtown."

Sarah stamped her ticket at the counter and waved to them as she left the room. Joyce was quiet, frowning as if working on a mental puzzle. Phyllis sat and waited. She realized they might have heard some vital information.

Joyce looked at Phyllis. "Link was caught reading some information, confidential information, in Bessie's records. Sarah said Bessie had watched him replace the book. If she knew those notebooks were for the project she participated in and checked that that particular book included her records, she'd be spiteful. Maybe retaliate? Right?"

"Sounds right to me. And if she knew the nurse believed her but had no proof, she would feel violated at having her records read by someone she already disliked and angry at his not being penalized," Phyllis surmised.

"And when Link was dismissed, he would feel she had caused the staff to be suspicious and on the lookout for his doing that again," Joyce responded.

"Joyce, this is scary. That gives him a reason to . . .," she stared at Joyce, "to get back at her."

"I know. We can't even say the word harm her. I've seen death, accident victims, so much pain, but I can't imagine killing someone to get even." Joyce was pensive. "There has to be something else. Maybe something current."

Phyllis fluted her brows as she sought some direction. "Didn't Sarah say he had to turn in his badge? Would they be kept or thrown away? Could it be here?"

Both of them jumped up and dashed to the counter. Joyce blurted, "Do you keep badges of volunteers who used to be here? Those that were turned in when they left?"

The receptionist jerked her head up. "Why?"

"Do you? It may be very important." Joyce pled.

"Yes, for a few years. In case they decide to volunteer again. Saves time..."

"What about badges for volunteers who have been asked to leave... and to turn the badges in?" Joyce emphasized.

"That's very rare. I haven't dealt with that situation. Is it really important?"

Phyllis answered first. "It could be. His picture would be on it?"

"And we need to identify a former volunteer. Please, is there someone we can ask?" Joyce begged.

"The director might know. I'll buzz her." She punched a number on the intercom. "Could you speak to a nurse from the health center at the mall? She's in the office. It sounds urgent." She put the receiver down and told Joyce to go in.

Joyce nodded to Phyllis to come with her. "You were the one who thought about the badges. And we may need to search through a pile."

After explaining the reasons for wanting information about Link Stein and to see a photo of him, the director offered to let them look through the badges. She pulled a box from a cabinet for them to search through.

Suddenly, Phyllis had a thought. "Would you keep records on the computer of volunteers? That would give us more information such as his height and weight, color of hair and eyes. We know he's about five feet nine, thin, probably medium brown hair. We don't know his skills. He just did very basic clerical work for the research project."

"Yes, we do." She picked up the phone and asked the receptionist to come in. When she did, the director asked her to bring up the volunteer files. "What was the name and do you know when he was here?" she directed the questions to Joyce.

"Link Stein... s-t-e-i-n. We heard he left a project a year or so ago. Was asked to leave. Sometime prior to that Bessie Kester had caught him reading her records. But that couldn't be proved." Joyce paused before adding, "You've heard about Bessie's death. There is some suspicion about the cause. And the police have asked us about Link. There has been no motive uncovered."

The director absorbed this information. "I can see why you are interested in his photograph." In a serious tone, she told the receptionist to key in a search all for data related to Link Stein.

Chapter 21

Link Stein pushed his arm a few inches from Amy's neck and slid it down in a thirty-degree angle right side of their forward-moving bodies. But his left hand clinched her upper arm in a viselike grip that wouldn't be easily detected from the doors.

"Don't try to run. Head toward your office. Slow and steady."

As he talked, Amy moved forward but darted her sight toward the closed front doors. The hall was empty. She lamented, why can't one of the early walkers pass by or any one to spot us. She returned her focus on the glassed doors that led to another small hall around which were clustered the offices of the director and manager, a supply room, a restroom, and a laboratory of sorts for clinicians. In the few seconds it would take to reach the hall, she forced her mind to try to empathize with her captor. Neither his intentions nor his reasons for being in the center could be tapped into.

Entering the hexagonal hall, he ordered her to open her door and gruffly added, "Easy."

She slowly put her hand on the knob turned it and opened the door. Pushing her forward, he grabbed her wrist and bent her arm backward and pressed it against her waist.

"Ouch!" she screamed.

His left hand jerked up and clamped her mouth shut. "No sounds! Do that again and I'll twist it way up your back!"

She moved her head up and down and stanched the tears welling in her eyes. He pressed closer and pushed his legs against her so that they took the few steps to her desk against the wall. "Sit in that chair." She summoned all her control so as not to scream again or recoil in utter disgust at his physical contact.

He dropped his hand from her mouth to her upper left arm and squeezed until she dropped onto her swivel chair. He leaned over, switched on the computer.

"I know about computers. Don't try any funny business. Click on the printer. And key into the artwork software."

Immediately, Amy entered messages to her brain: nerves don't tense up; arm and finger muscles be steady. She moved the mouse onto the symbol to bring up the artwork. After it was displayed, she clicked open.

"Now, say yes to banner. That's it. The word *banner*. Okay. Write the word *Closed*." He watched as the letters appeared on the screen. His foot hit a chair caster. The blow moved the chair on its clear, plastic carpet protector. Lurching forward, he grabbed the backrest, to stop the rolling.

Turning his head as if he expected some alarm to be set off, he scowled. "Turn the printer on. While it's preparing itself, scroll down to the largest print."

"It won't fit on the single sheets," Amy said.

"We'll tape the pieces together. First, change setting to landscape. Now hit OK. This will take a while for the heavy black letters." Link clutched his abdomen and hunched his shoulders.

Amy glanced sideways and saw pain wrinkle his face. Empathizing, she commanded her reaction. "Are you all right? Your stomach . . ."

"Hungry," he barked.

She scanned her desktop where usually there was a box of crackers or a can of snacks. Spotting a tall box, she said, "Crackers are good for hunger pangs." She lifted her hand toward the box.

"Stop. Put your hand in your lap." He turned his head from side to side as if the mechanical movements of the printer annoyed him. Leaning far over the desk but keeping a tight hold on the chair back, he clutched the box and dragged it toward him. With one hand he flipped the top flaps, then dug his hand inside and brought out several crackers. He munched greedily. Then he swallowed hard.

"Dry." He cleared his throat. Squeakily, he asked, "Coke. Is there any Coke around here?"

"On the floor in the corner," she pointed under her desk. She ducked her head to search for one.

"Sit up! Don't unplug the printer. Or is there an alarm?" Rapidly, he pivoted and scanned the ceilings and the electronic equipment. Seeing nothing like an alarm box, he sat in a chair close to the corner and pulled her chair over. Slightly bending and keeping an eye on her, he spotted a liter Coke bottle. He angled his foot underneath the shelving and brought the bottle forward.

He handed the plastic bottle to her. "Don't shake it! Aim toward the trash basket and turn the top slowly. You don't want to spray it in my eyes!"

She stared at him a moment and considered that option. His hatred was so obvious; she answered with quiet control. "No, sir. I wouldn't want you to be hurt." She twisted the cap slowly. "I'm sorry your stomach hurts. And crackers and Coke are what we keep in case someone needs nourishment immediately."

The liquid was warm and did not fizzle over the bottleneck. "May I reach over to the right of the computer for some paper cups?" Her polite natural voice sounded as if a stranger was talking. How could she address this man who had treated her so roughly? Amy, ask later! Now keep calm as you can.

He followed where she pointed and seeing nothing sharp or heavy, he nodded. "Thank you, sir. I need something to drink, too. My throat . . ." she decided it unwise to draw his attention to her neck or to show her pain.

She turned to face him and carefully poured Coke into a cup and handed it to him.

"Wait until I finish." He gulped the contents quickly and held the empty cup and nodded for a refill.

She poured the cup full and gave it to him, then slowly took the extra cup, filled it, and set the bottle on the desk. The warm liquid fizzled in her mouth before she swallowed. As soon as she tilted the cup again, the printer ceased its repetitive noise.

Link listened then stood and shot around her chair. "It's done." He pulled the page from the printer tray, yanked clear tape from the desk dispenser. "Here, take two long strips. Be quick."

Amy understood what he planned to do and did his bidding. Holding her hands away from her and keeping the tape from twisting, she waited for him to open the office door. Again, he pressed close to her as they walked through the hexagonal hallway and into the reception room

"Act natural. Head toward the mall door. Keep your eyes down. If anybody walks by, don't look up."

She nodded and focused on the narrow strips of tape floating from her fingers, caught between a finger and thumb. Could the tape puzzle its destiny? Could it feel a state of unreality having been spun from its security of connection into this vast airiness? Where was its next resting place? The purpose was to hold, to secure objects. Amy felt an urge to quiet the tape – this is my center to direct: I know what's going on: I will see you serve your purpose by pressing you over the paper and against the glass of the door.

Her positiveness in the imaginary conversation penetrated the fuzziness in her head and renewed her energy. The instant she reached the door, Link jabbed the banner against a glass pane and whispered harshly, "Tape it on!" One handed, he released the cord of the translucent blind on the other door and it fell easily. When Amy applied the second piece of tape, he pulled that door blind down.

Without a word, he spun her to face the reception room, and then ordered her to move naturally as before back to her office. She saw objects moving up and down, felt dizzy as she tried to walk, and heard Link's voice ringing in her ears.

"Move! You want your arm twisted back again?" He increased the force of his grip on an upper arm and pushed the back of her knees with his.

Amy closed her eyes and prayed she could cross the room using motor memory. With every short step, she said silently: don't faint, don't faint. Nausea was forming in her stomach. There can't be any food in me. The Coke. It's churning upward. If I can only swallow, I can breathe slowly, deeply.

"Watch it," he ordered for she had bumped into the edge of the reception desk.

She opened her eyes and forced herself to select an object on the hexagonal wall now in view. The fire extinguisher. I'll look at that. Is there a fire alarm lever somewhere? Firemen know what to do. They rescue people. Ouch, she groaned low. He's hurting my arm. I will fall on the floor if he squeezes any harder. But his hand is holding me up. She lost the fire extinguisher focal point as he twisted her to the right and into her office.

"Let me sit down. I feel sick."

He shoved her into the chair. "Sit there," he said rolling her chair to the right and pulling the other chair in front of her computer. "Stay there, don't push back or move." He stared at her with a fierce frown.

She nodded that she understood. "May I put my head on the desk? I'm . . ."

"No." He faced the computer that he had left on and keyed into the program files.

Bruce was speeding on the interstate when his phone beeped. He snatched the handset. "Yes?"

"Bruce, it's Lou. I've contacted 911 and the mall security. I'm on my way to the mall. This is a sorry time to tell you this. Amy's pregnant."

"God, Lou. This is a shock."

"She's only a few weeks. She was sick, vomiting this morning. I tried to get her to stay home. If he hurts her . . ."

"Lou, think she's all right. Keep your phone with you. I'm going to call Nola. Find out what else she can tell me and ring you back."

"Right."

He punched in Nola's number. She answered instantly. "Bruce, tell me what's going on?"

"Lou is on his way to the mall. Any change in your condition?"

"No. I'm still caught in the door."

He asked tensely, "Was the man rough with Amy?"

"Yes! He grabbed her and armlocked her around the neck. Pushed her knees to make her go ahead. I thought she was going to crumple right there. They both got through the doorway then he pulled it shut. Why Amy?"

"We don't know. You've never seen the man before?"

"Maybe. I'm trying so hard to recall where and when. There's something familiar."

"Lou just told that me Amy's a few weeks pregnant."

Nola gasped. "Oh, dear God, what a nightmare this must be for her. Bruce, what good news this would be some other day. Well, it's still good but . . ."

"It's added concern for her safety. Heaven and hell together."

"Yes. She'll need some medical reassurance when help reaches her."

"Good thinking."

"She probably hasn't seen an OB this early. Joyce, the center nurse, won't be in till much later."

"This maniac must know a lot about the facility and the health setup. Who could it be?"

Trying not to complicate the situation, she racked her brain to be of help and be brief. Time was essential. "Lou can call their doctor. Bruce, believe that security or the police will get to them before he can take her out of the mall."

"Thanks, I love you. Hang in there and that's not a joke. Another call." He clicked off then on for the highway patrol dispatcher.

"Bruce Braddock here."

"The dispatcher here. A patrolman is on an emergency run going your way. What's your license number?"

Bruce said the letters and numbers clearly, one at a time. The dispatcher repeated them and heard them confirmed.

"Are you driving a reliable vehicle that can keep up with a patrol car?"

"The latest Mercedes-Benz Cabriolet CLK 320. Blue convertible, top up. Raring to be tested."

"I asked didn't I?" The response was jovial. "Exactly where are you on the interstate? Read me the first exit sign number or mileage marker to some city."

Bruce gave the general area he was in. A minute later he spotted an exit sign, read the number aloud.

"I got that. The patrol car is a few miles back. He'll turn on his blue light when he has your car in sight. There were Braddocks in Acorn . . ."

"My family."

"The accent comes back in a crisis. Did you learn to drive on the dirt roads over there?"

"I did."

"You'll keep up."

In the rearview mirror, Bruce saw a patrol car approaching on an outside lane; the blue light began flashing. "He's right behind me. Thanks for assistance."

The dispatcher cautioned, "Good men are on duty at the mall. Concentrate on the road ahead."

Bruce nodded at the patrolman who paced beside him long enough for recognition before he accelerated. The Mercedes veered into the far-left lane behind the patrol car. Bruce felt the energy surge of an athlete primed to take the ball down the court. Focused and goal oriented, his nerves controlled to serve his intentions as he sped down the concrete lanes. But this wasn't a game. This was life. The life of his daughter and his almost-wife. And, by God's grace, his grandchild.

Nola pressed against the cold steel door, weary with tugging to free her clothing from door and frame. She admonished her lack of speed that had prevented her holding the door and escaping before it closed. What was happening to Amy? Where were they now? She put the side of her face on the cold metal surface. Wake up! You're not problem solving!

Picture the center. See the reception room. Close your eyes. Search your memory. What do you do there that's important? For Amy, I greet the people at the seminars. Okay. Go on. I check the names off when they come up to say they are preregistered. Then, start a waiting list for those who aren't. Is there any seminar where there was something unusual? Some procedure out of the ordinary? A day when something important happened. A day that you can link to something else.

Nola opened her eyes wide, jerked her face away from the door, and lifted her shoulders upright. What did I just say – a word? Link. That's it! Link Stein. He came up to me before the Heart Healthy Habits seminar. I wrote his name down. He was the last person to be seated – two rows in front of me and Amy. I'm sure that was his name. Link Stein. But it had been erased from the list. I told Amy I was sure there was another name. That was the day Bessie Kester died.

There must be a connection. He's not on our membership roll. The way he hunched over as he walked and dropped something and searched under his chair. He crept out early, bent, I thought so he wouldn't block the overhead projector slide being shown on the front screen. That's the way the man in the maintenance uniform stooped between the boxes. He has the same small frame and tense motions of Link Stein at the seminar. He's shifty and sly. I need to do something. He's dangerous.

I need to tell Lou. No, I don't have his cell phone number. 911. They can call the name to the security or whoever is out there by this time. Steadying her hands, she punched the numbers. Quick and frightened, she alerted the dispatcher. "This is Nola Gilbert. Tell whoever is responding to the call of the woman abducted and taken into the health center at Saunders Mall that I believe the male abductor is Link Stein. He was at the seminar in the center the day Bessie Kester died. I am all right. Please, open the door slowly here for I am trapped immediately behind it."

She signed off sighing with relief at remembering Link's name. But she felt intense anguish that wrenched her mind, heart, and her whole being. She would have begged for relief had anyone been there to heed her plea. She was alone. Bruce was speeding down the highway relaying reports of their physical distress. Lou was where? I don't know how he's involved at this moment.

I've never been helpless. Always there were options. This is aloneness. This is the cold sensation of being trapped. This is near immobility. This is the onset of fear. Fear for Amy's life and the one she is carrying. And for my life if Link gets trapped and his only chance out is through this door. Amy first. I must think of her first. Her danger isn't *if,* it's real and now.

Lou maneuvered his Jeep across town via the interstate thankful that morning commuter traffic peaked a quarter hour earlier. He pulled off at Saunders Mall exit, waited impatiently at the red light on the traffic signal. Come on green, he growled; his teeth clenched.

As soon as the light changed, he checked that the oncoming Mall Boulevard cars had stopped: no late driver was speeding under the yellow light. The road clear, he raced the Jeep into the right lane, aware the next turn into the mall was immediately after a complex of converging roads and lanes. Stop and yield signs controlled those drivers.

He aimed the Jeep up a lane that ended near the only entrance open early. A few cars were parked nearby. Suddenly, he spotted men and women running from the large triple sets of doors. Lou adeptly swerved right out of their departure routes. He leaned over the steering wheel and scanned the cars near the front of the building: four white police cars, two security vehicles, and a fire truck.

"Great guns!" he declared and swung his vehicle far right and back onto the circling road. He wanted to hold his breath until he had the rear side in his view, but he could hear deep jets of air escape from his throat. His mouth became moist then dry.

Scoping the parking areas either side of the road, he rushed along. On the left where the early employees parked, the short rows were filled. To the right was what he wanted to see: there were more police and security cars. And, with a lump in his throat, he recognized Amy's car and close by, Nola's.

Policemen and security huddled in groups near their cars and on either side of the entrance door. Lou accelerated past them and screeched to a halt near Amy's car. He jumped out. The policemen closest turned, saw him, and instantly made their way in his direction.

Lou flung his hands up. "I'm Lou Umstead." He pointed his thumbs at himself. "My wife's in there!"

"This cursed computer! The files I need won't come up. What's this? Documents in use?" A heel of a hand at his head, Link glared at the screen. "By whom?"

Frustrated, Link tried to access the document again. He appeared frightened that whoever was searching the hospital volunteer files might pull up his data. No, he snorted, convincing himself that there were thousands of names listed. He muttered, "Some clerk adding new recruits' names. Why now?"

He swiveled his head right and watched Amy with narrowed eyes. Could she have done something to send word out? Nothing had been moved on the desk beside her. No phone was nearby. Eyeing the clock, he shot a fist upward.

Amy flinched, drew back in her chair, then clutched her stomach and doubled up.

Bringing his arm down swiftly, he aimed toward her head. Without seeing his anger, she dropped her head to her knees.

"You weakling. You stride out there," he flung an arm back of him toward the door, "like you own the world. Head high, so proud of yourself." He spit in the wastebasket between them. "Ten minutes. That's all we've got before those doors open."

Link bound from his chair, opened the door, and peered into the hall. Reeling around to keep Amy in view, he ordered her not to move. He stepped into the hall and stared toward the front door. Suddenly, he drew back against the wall, hiding but keeping the door in surveillance. A walker stopped and tried to open the door. He stepped back to read the sign. He raised a hand in what appeared to be a wait-a-minute signal to someone on his left. Again, the man leaned forward and cupped his hands over his forehead to peer in the narrow space between the blind and doorframe. He shook his head and walked toward the mall shops.

Chapter 22

Security chief Ralph Pierce watched the photo on the paper as it eked from the printer. Quick as the full sheet landed in the tray, he jerked it out. The face wasn't one he recognized.

He placed it on the copier and pressed 40. The copies spit out; Pierce lifted only the first; the others needed minutes to dry.

"Hector!"

Hector stopped pacing. "Yes, sir."

"Run these to the officers outside." Pierce handed over a stack. "Stay away from entrance doors to Healthy Living Center. Don't stop to talk. Speed is necessary." Pierce beckoned to Lemuel. "Hand these to officers inside the mall. You know the floor plan. Don't go down the hall to the center. If there're uniforms or personnel you know are official, signal one to come for handout. We must avoid scaring the abductor. Got it?"

With a precise nod, Lemuel took the flyers and hastened on his mission.

Bright-eyed and jittery, Hector dashed back into the security office. "Chief! I know this man. Seen him at the center. And at Human Resources. Looking at openings on the bulletin board. He's a suspicious-looking guy." Before Pierce spoke, Hector was out of the room.

Pierce grimaced, relieved Hector was unarmed. He started down the list of names to be updated on emergency information. He remained alert for beeps from officers of all units involved. Security office staff manned other phone lines jotting notes or talking to Pierce between his calls. This was a first-time abduction of a store employee at the mall, and the atmosphere was tense.

Amy doubled over, clutched the seat of the chair. "Please, let me put my head down."

Link scorned her weakness. "I ache in the middle myself. I bet you never miss a meal. Well, I have and so has my family."

Suddenly, Amy reached over and pulled the wastebasket to her chair. Link thrust out his hand. Amy lowered her head and wretched into the basket. He recoiled.

"Ugh, there's nothing but foam. No food. Are you making yourself vomit?"

She spewed again. Perspiration dripped from her forehead. Weakly, she shook her head.

"You think you've got it bad. But you don't. I've seen you coming here in your late-model car. You're always in new clothes. Smiling, talking to those people out there," he flung his hand in the direction of the reception room. "Do your children have to beg you for money for school supplies, clothes, the things their school friends have?"

Struggling with spasms of nausea, she managed to say, "I won't have those problems if I lose this one."

Link stared at her. "What do mean?"

She swayed back and forth clutching her abdomen. "I'm going to have a baby. It doesn't show yet."

Link sank back in his chair. His face paled with shock. She's pregnant, he anguished. God, what kind of luck are you handing me? I've got to get us out of here quick. I can't wait for the computer to clear. Is she really too weak to walk? Angry, he stealthily moved to the front door and looked out the narrow space. He saw two men talking in the hall near the outside entrance both in shirtsleeves like clerks wear every day. Were they positioned to open the door at a precise time to let customers in?

Link backed away from the doors and stood close to the inside wall. He peered again and saw two other men turning away shrugging their shoulders. Under his breath, he cursed the mall strollers. He needed to get out now. Worse luck! He beat a fist into the palm of his hand as a pair of security cops approached, unarmed. Are they there to guard the door? Will they let people in or out? What a crock!

He looked back toward the office area suddenly aware Amy had time to make a call. No one peering in the door to see him, he sped to the office.

At the service entrance Pierce unlocked the steel door. He held it open and four police officers entered using standard procedures of caution and alertness. As Pierce hooked the door against the interior wall, Lou came up rapidly.

"They're in?" he asked.

"Yes." Lou took two steps as if to enter the hallway. Pierce put out his arm. "Wait! Let the officers handle this."

Lou stepped back, tense and anxious. He clenched his hands, tightened his lips, and narrowed his eyes. The minutes dragged by. Pierce remained controlled and listened for any sounds of approach. Then faint footsteps echoed down the hallway. Pierce turned in defensive posture and moved an arm across the doorway warning Lou to stay put.

The first person they saw rounding the corner was a blue-uniformed officer. Next, came Nola supported with his outstretched arm. Lou hastened forward. Again, he was stopped by Pierce's stiff arm blocking the passage. Lou obeyed but didn't back off.

Nola opened her mouth to shout. A second police officer cautioned her. Lou saw his lips move, but the words were not audible. Nola nodded and moved forward quickly. Her left sleeve had been cut and the sides flapped beneath the officer's grasp. The sides of her culottes, inches below her waist, were jagged from the hasty cutting, exposing her long strong legs.

Instantly, Lou pulled off his jacket and folded it around Nola's shoulders as the officers released her and sped back down the hall.

Pierce stood so that he could survey the hall and speak to Nola now in front of him. "How are you?"

She nodded. "Okay, now. Are they going to rescue Amy?" Her voice deepened with concern.

"Soon." He pulled a printout from his pocket and showed it to Nola. "Do you recognize this man?"

She squinted, leaned closer, and blinked her eyes. "Yes. That's the man who grabbed Amy. I saw his face only a few seconds in there," she turned her head to the hall. "But his manner, walk, size make me believe he's Link Stein. I have seen him at the health center."

Pierce asked, "Do you know any reason he would abduct her?"

"Absolutely none." She looked at Lou. "Have you told the men she's pregnant?"

"They know." Tension filled his throat.

"Lou, I'm so sorry about all this. We have to believe she's okay. She's strong and resourceful." Tears welled in her eyes, and, after she saw him nod, she dropped her head to his shoulder. She felt she was taking refuge against a body as rigid as the steel door she had just been freed from.

Lou held her firmly. "Thank God, you're out." Looking at Pierce, he asked, "Can I take her to the car? It's cold. I have a blanket. We need to ward off shock."

"Yes, do. I'll contact the police. They'll send an officer with you. And Mr. Umstead, we will get your wife out." His confident tone and manner gave hope to Lou and Nola.

Pierce spoke into the pager. "Nola Gilbert is out. Lou Umstead is with her. Keep her under watch. Can you space an officer? Good. He'll want to be at the door when – any developments inside? Yeah, it could be a long morning." He clicked off.

Link and Amy looked at the clock. Link hissed, "Time for the mall doors to open!"

"Not yet. I keep my clock ahead."

Link spun to the door, "Why isn't the man opening it?"

Amy forced her words. "The clock's fast so I won't be late . . . for meetings."

"I've got to get out of here," he grumbled and roughly grabbed Amy's arm.

"Link, please go on." He didn't move. She changed tactics. "Try the computer again."

He wavered a second, then dragged her to her desk. He leaned forward, moved the mouse, and tried to enter the volunteer files again. Program in Use warning was displayed. Link made a fist and crashed it on the keyboard.

Amy, trying to pull away, toppled the chair. Link caught her hands, brought her upright then gripped her shoulders. "Enough time wasted here. Come on." He pushed her to the door.

Someone was pulling the handle on the center's door from the hall. It didn't open. Link retreated, keeping Amy as a shield in front of him until they were back in her office and out of sight.

Amy begged, "Go on by yourself. Once in the hall, there are many other exits from this building. Link, I won't report you."

He didn't respond.

She remembered how her kind words and self-confidence helped her pony when he was skittish, didn't know what to do in a threatened situation: a thunderstorm, a new horse in ring, a snake across his path. She swallowed her fear, allowed her persuasive skills to surface, and her natural outreaching spirit to prevail.

"Link, before you go, will you tell me about Bessie? What happened in the parking lot?"

"I saw her come out of the mall and walk to her car. She opened her handbag, dropped a little white plastic bag in it, and pulled out some keys. She was putting a key in the door when I called out to her. She unlocked it and opened it wide. I put my hand on her shoulder. She looked back and recognized me then spun around and said right in my face to leave her alone.

"Leave her alone? I wanted her to stay out of my business, and I gave her fair warning not to badmouth me." He slowly turned his head and looked at Amy. "What did she do? She pushed me, swung her handbag at me. It was heavy; it hit my chest. I grabbed it with both my hands.

"She jumped into her car and locked the doors. Her face was mad. She searched for something around the seats and on the floor, then it seemed she was putting her hands in her skirt pockets. She glared out the window at me like I was some bit of dirt."

Amy asked with pathos. "What did you do then, Link?"

"Nothing. I stood there. Her face was furious. She bent and was searching the floor again. When she sat back up straight, she wiped her forehead with her hand. Then she waved her hand at me to go away."

"Did she seem ill?" Amy pressed with compassion.

Link shook his head. "I don't know. She squinted at me then leaned her head on the steering wheel. I gave up and left."

"That's all?" Any waited for an answer. He made no reply. "You still had her handbag?" Link shrugged. "The car keys were in the car door?" He remained silent.

"They were found in her handbag." Amy spoke softly.

"She could have got out," Link offered.

"If she hadn't passed out."

"I didn't know that."

"Did you wait to see?" Link had no response. Amy prodded carefully, "Did you open the door to check?"

"No. She could have had extra keys under the seat."

Amy said, "None were found."

"She was a mean, hard-bitten woman, sticking her nose in my business!"

"But she died, Link!"

He faced her and his voice rang of hopelessness. "She killed my chances at a livelihood."

Amy looked at his eyes. "You didn't kill her, Link. You didn't know she was dying. But don't take me away. Don't harm me or the baby. The police will let you go."

Instantly, his face contorted, his voice and manner roughened. "Shut up that stupid talk. We're going to walk out of here. Don't call attention to yourself. Don't make a sound."

He led her into the hall and the reception room. "My car is straight across the parking lot. You walk willingly beside me. Or for your sake, you better pretend to."

As they walked beside the reception desk, Link caught the glimmer of a metallic letter opener in the pencil canister. He reached and withdrew it. In a quarter turn, he faced Amy and held the long blade between them, the point under her chin. With a swift stroke of his hand, controlled, an inch from her jaw, he whispered harshly. "The point is sharp. You don't want it against your pampered skin."

He stepped back beside her with a hand firmly on her upper arm and the letter opener in his other hand.

Amy judged this was her last chance to help herself and Link. She had to make this final effort. Without fear, she stopped short a few feet from the doors to the mall hallway and stepped in front of Link. He squeezed her arm tighter. She did not flinch.

"Link, think about your family. You care about them. You want them to have what's necessary – a home and food; and you also want them to have things other children have. You are willing and capable to work. You're not asking for charity. You want a job. I'll help you find one."

Link listened and wanted to believe her, but he couldn't trust anyone. A gnawing voice in his head was short-circuiting the sentences. There were gaps between food and children and work and charity and job. He lifted his arm to rub his temple and the blade glittered and he quickly dropped his hand, shook his head, and pulled his shoulders back in efforts to be controlled and in charge.

"Shut up!"

Before he could move forward, Amy held her ground. No pawing, no hesitation. "I will only slow you down getting out of here and across the driveway and the parking lot. What you're doing to me, causing physical stress, could make me lose the baby. Right now, Link, no one can say you caused Bessie Kester's death. But think about two deaths! Your family will suffer. They will have no husband, no father. They will be disgraced if you kill us."

His hand flew to his head. It ached. He rubbed with the heel, the letter opener wobbling up and down. The voice messages disrupted his thoughts. Nothing made sense. He felt trapped. He had to keep hold of Amy. She was talking and he couldn't find words to shut her up. His eyes weren't focusing. His stomach was churning. He sensed Amy was pulling away emotionally or mentally or both. She stood still. Was she taking the lead? He felt his power over her slipping.

She spoke in soft, comforting tones. "Leave me here. I won't call or shout. The hall is empty. Go now."

He shook his head side to side. The ache was intense. He released her arm and pressed his hand to his head again.

Quietly, she said, "Link, give me the letter opener." Slowly, she reached toward it as he began to lower his hand in wavering motions. As the blade descended to Link's waist, she extended her hand and carefully clasped the blade. He let it go.

Now he had two hands to rub his temples.

Through his pain, Link heard Amy speaking to him as a human being worthy of respectful words: Link, thank you for letting me have the letter opener. You can leave knowing you haven't harmed me or the new life I'm carrying. Life will be better for you. Tears wet his eyes and fell on his cheeks. He tried to see her clearly but the vision was blurred. The voice was soothing. The last words he heard were you have your life.

He could leave now. He opened a door to the center and staggered out. Store fronts and floors were distorted. He wiped his hands across his eyes. The exit doors were a few feet away. Outside, vehicles were moving blurs in the traffic lanes.

A tapping sound echoed from the far end of the hall. Link twisted to locate the source. Policemen were running toward him. He was too late. Instinct turned him toward the outside doors. Distraught with pain and fear, he pushed them out on the run. He rubbed his eyes with his hands. The eyelids stung. He held up a gray-sleeved arm shielding his eyes from the morning glare. Then, he saw uniformed officers to the right and the left of the entry. They were closing in.

"Stop!" The shout reverberated endlessly against the buildings and the hard surfaces of the walk and parking lots.

Link heard the exit door swing outward and oncoming footsteps charging behind him. He ran forward his arms out, his hands up, his fingers spread, no weapons. Blindly, he dashed off the walkway into the traffic lane. He never saw the delivery trucks coming right or left.

The nearer driver screeched his brakes but couldn't stop in time to avoid hitting Link.

The officers converged around the front of the truck. Link died on impact.

Chapter 23

My volunteer badge was still intact though askew on the blouse of the one-piece outfit I had put on early this morning. I briefly thought of pinning the sides of the culottes together. Instead I straightened the badge. I could point to my name and connection at Saunders Mall, if another officer or person involved in this summing up the abduction situation or restoring order to the mall inquired.

After EMTs checked her, Lou had brought Amy to her car. I relinquished his jacket and the blanket. He gently wrapped her in both. She refused to go to their doctor or a counselor yet. Lou assured her that the doctor would see them as soon as she arrived. I sat in the backseat listening as she recounted the time in the health center with Link. Every few sentences, she choked up and blew her nose on Lou's handkerchief.

I don't know whether I saw the blue Mercedes or heard the abrupt braking first, but I knew Bruce was with us. I never longed to see anyone so much in my life as I did him.

He was out of his car in a heartbeat. He lifted a hand, waved to a group of policemen who were watching him. "My family! Thanks to all of you." He saw a large truck, an ambulance, police cars, and numerous people and assumed the body might still be on the lot. There were blockades at entrances to this lot, but he had been allowed to pass through.

I rolled my window down and thrust out my hand. Bruce grabbed it and restored my feeling of security. He opened the front passenger door, bent to look at Amy. I released his hand. As she turned to him, he gathered her tenderly in his arms. The expressions on their faces needed no words. Both cried. After a tight hug, Bruce lessened his hold and slowly pulled back.

"Are you all right?"

"Yes. Lou told you about the pregnancy?"

"He did. My dear girl, you've survived incredible stress. What a strong woman you are. What a story you'll have to tell that little one some years hence." He glanced at Lou. "Has she seen a doctor or are you on your way?"

"On our way. Thanks, Bruce, for everything. The call – all of it," Lou said.

Bruce acknowledged that with a firm head-down nod, opened the back door, and climbed in beside me. "I've never been so glad to see any two people safe in my life. Nola, your clothes, are you cold?" He was taking off his coat as he talked.

"Lou," he asked, "do you have an emergency kit? Or a small stapler, scotch tape, paper clips..."

"I think he's asking is there anything is the car to join the cut sleeve and culottes?" I explained.

"There's adhesive tape in the first-aid kit, will that help?" offered Amy.

I laughed quietly. "We can give it a try."

"I do have a small hand stapler," Lou said and reached over to open the glove compartment.

Bruce took it and began stapling the cut edges together. "I know you're anxious to see medical attention. We'll be out soon."

Amy put a hand on Lou's arm. "Not yet. There's something I have to do first." She turned and opened her door.

"No," he exclaimed bewildered. "You mean inside the mall?" She didn't answer as she moved cautiously across the seat. "To your office? What do you need? I can..."

"To get back on the pony." She looked at Lou, then back at Bruce for understanding.

Bruce nodded. Amy got out. The door remained ajar.

Bruce said, "Lou, it's her way to conquer her fear, to resume control of her life."

I listened to the men while watching Amy slowly walk to the building. A realization hit me. I had to go, too. Before the men were aware that I had opened the door, I was on the pavement. I looked at Bruce. "I need to lay this to rest." I exchanged eye contact with Lou before I headed toward the building.

Instantly, Lou got out of the car. As he rushed beside Bruce, he pointed to the truck and rescue squad vehicle. "They shouldn't go in that way." Both men started toward the women.

Amy saw the vehicles and numerous officers clustered between her and the mall entrance. She had come out that way. As an attendant stood up, she saw a man's legs for a second before the gap closed.

Saying "Amy" once, I quickened my steps and she paused. Her hand withdrew a set of keys from a pocket. She clutched them and focused on the maintenance entrance. We headed that way without speaking.

She inserted a key in the entry lock slowly. I hastened to hold the door as she withdrew the key and walked inside. I followed and let it close; we heard the lock click home. The ceiling lights were on. I put my hands on her shoulders. We both inhaled the still air and exhaled slowly. She placed a hand on mine, lifted her head, then removed her hand and we walked to the end of the hall and turned the corner.

The boxes were where we last saw them – was that only a few hours ago? It seemed time beyond measure: an episode in a bygone life. Later, there would be details to clear up and messages to be relayed. Now we were treading on ghosts of that episode. They would not haunt us later.

Entering Healthy Living Center, we went first into the reception room. I stood aside while Amy retraced her steps from the entry to the hexagonal hall. When she walked into the hall, I moved to those doors and again waited. Twice she stepped in and out of the hall into her office. The second time, she remained a few minutes.

She came back with a wastebasket, unlocked the restroom, and closed the door. She reappeared without the basket. She looked at the door to the mall hallway and stood long enough to regain her composure then signaled she was ready to return via the steel door and maintenance hall where this life-threatening experience had started.

I agreed and voluntarily followed my director to free ourselves for the future we anticipated of enriched and united lives.

BVG